FRED ADAMS JR.
PULP WRITER

AIRSHIP 27 PRODUCTIONS

Fred Adams Jr. Pulp Writer
© 2019 Fred Adams Jr.

Published by Airship 27 Productions
www.airship27.com
www.airship27hangar.com

Cover and interior illustrations © 2019 Rob Davis

Editor: Ron Fortier
Associate Editor: Rob Davis
Marketing and Promotions Manager: Michael Vance
Production and design by Rob Davis

ISBN-13: 978-1-946183-58-3
ISBN-10: 1-946183-58-X

Printed in the United States of America

10 9 8 7 6 5 4 3 2 1

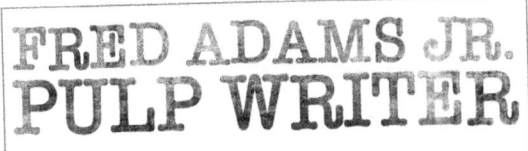

TABLE OF CONTENTS

WHAT MAKES A PULP WRITER?

N ow that's a question I never would have asked myself fifteen years ago. Back then my connection with the world of pulp fiction was negligible. Other than having read paperback reprints of the Shadow, Doc Savage and Conan the Barbarian, and knowing that comics, which I've been writing for almost fifty years, were born from the pulps, my interest was pretty much non-existent. Then eleven years ago, without going into that detailed history, artist Rob Davis and I created Airship 27 Productions, a publishing venture devoted to producing novels and anthologies featuring classic pulp characters that had long ago fallen into public domain.

Little did we know at that time that we were a part of a new burgeoning literary movement that would be labeled "New Pulp." In the decade since then, I've read and edited hundreds of amazing short stories and several dozen novels by some of today's finest action-adventure writers. Currently the Airship 27 catalog is almost two hundred titles strong. It still blows my mind when I think about it.

Of all those writers who bravely signed on with us, none has ever amazed me more than Mr. Fred Adams Jr. Airship 27 had been around at least five years when Fred first walked up to our tables at the Windy City Pulp and Paper Convention; an annual event that takes place in Chicago every Spring. He introduced himself as a writer and listened to my spiel about New Pulp and what it was we did. Fred is of average height, with thinning gray hair and a short matching beard. He's got a round nose and eyes that light up whenever he talks about his latest new story idea. I'm no Sherlock Holmes. My first impressions were that he was your average blue collar worker who was well read with a friendly personality. We hit it off immediately and before ending that very first conversation, Fred had my business card and promised me to send me samples of his work.

Within a week of that meeting, short stories started popping up in my e-mails. Fred dove into pulp fiction like a dolphin through a storm wave. Soon he was writing Secret Agent X stories, Sherlock Holmes mysteries and others I've since forgotten. The thing is every one of his submissions was a gem. When you've been editing hundreds of writers for over eleven years, you soon develop a decent skill in picking out what's okay, what's good and the rarest of the rare, what is brilliant. Everything Fred sent me was simply wonderful and of professional caliber. Which in itself was perplexing and made me realize I really didn't know all that much about this guy.

When he pitched me a novel he'd written about the murder of a rock roll star, I was receptive but hesitant. Most classic pulp was written in the third person and we'd fashioned Airship 27 in the same mold. But this book, "Dead Man's Melody," had been penned in first person. The tale was narrated by a musician/song composer named Sam Dunne. Having been won over by Fred's shorts, we accepted the novel. Reading it was as yet another revelation. Fred's knowledge of music and that world of entertainment were clearly gleaned from personal experience. It only added to the book's authenticity. It was all too obvious Fred Adams Jr. was writing about something he knew intimately.

So, aside from being a talented writer, the guy was also a musician. Just another piece of the puzzle. Then before we could get "Dead Man's Melody" in print, Fred sent me another manuscript. This one was about a 1970s Green Beret home from Vietnam who is turned into a werewolf by a New Jersey mob to be their assassin. Fred explained that "Hitwolf" would be the first in a series he planned on writing. Whoa. "Hitwolf" was about as pure pulp as you can get. Then only a few months later along came "Six-Gun Terror" a weird western about two Civil War veterans working as cowboys on a Texas ranch who get involved with supernatural monsters. Oh, and Fred off-the-cuff mentioned that was going to be a series as well.

All right, now I was totally bamboozled. Who the hell was this guy and how was he pumping out all this crazy, beautiful fiction so damn fast? I remember telling my partner, Rob, at the time, that this Fred Adams guy was a writing machine. Eventually, we would hook up again at Windy City and the Columbus held PulpFest over the next few years. It was through these new encounters, that Fred gradually revealed his history and left me pretty much in awe of the man. Fred was anything but a blue collar Joe, in fact he'd been a college professor, with a Phd in English and had taught writing and other related courses before retiring just about the time we met.

In fact, while on one panel I was moderating, Fred told the audience that he had wanted to write for many, many years but had been unable to because his career demanded he spend his time teaching others how to do it. Thus when that obligation was lifted from him, he opened the floodgates and began writing...and writing...and writing.

And you, dear reader, like me, are now the beneficiary of all that pent up creativity. In the pages that follow you will not only meet Sam Dunne, the werewolf commandos, and the Civil War cowboys, but a WW II veteran named C.O. Jones who can sense magic in others. Ike Mars, a private eye who can alter the shape of his face and the Smith Bros, Chinese Siamese twins living in San Francisco during the turn of the 20th century. All of these are the stars of on-going series now being published by Airship 27 Productions. And we couldn't be happier.

Fred Adams Jr.'s fiction is a throwback to the days of classic pulp. All of it is filled with wondrous characters, horrendous monsters and tough-as-nails heroes. As Sam Spade once said, "It is the stuff that dreams are made of." I say it is the cloth that only pulp writers can weave and Fred is above all else, a pulp writer.

Ron Fortier
Managing Editor
Airship 27 Productions
Fort Collins, CO
2/6/2019

HITWOLF - John Slate, a Viet-Nam era black ops agent and his team have been sold out by the CIA. Returning stateside, he adopts a construction worker identity to hide in plain sight until he can avenge himself and his men. A bar fight calls attention to his considerable skills, and he is kidnapped by a mobster who has Slate infected with lycanthropy to use him as an enforcer. Slate escapes, and his enemies find that he is just as dangerous in human form when he reassembles his team to strike back at the gangsters. Along the way, he runs afoul of a sorcerer known only as the Whisperer who wants Slate for his own ends. As the series progresses, Slate turns the members of his team and they become an ultimate mercenary force in an unsteady alliance with the Government. In "Extraction," the Hitwolf team is assigned to rescue an undercover agent captured by a banana republic warlord.

HITWOLF : EXTRACTION

Tom MacDonald slowed his Crown Vic to a stop as the light turned from amber to red. A blue Impala convertible full of teens pulled up beside him, top down in the autumn chill The Doors blared from its eight-track tape deck:

> *Five to one, baby, one in five*
> *No one here gets out alive*

True enough, Mac thought, and those punks beside me are dumb enough to think they'll live forever. Another year, and half of them will be drafted and come home from Nam in a box if they don't run to Canada in the meantime.

The kid driving the Impala revved the engine and looked sidewise at Mac, a challenge.

Kid's even dumber than he looks, thought Mac. Anybody with any street smarts would notice the little hubcaps on a plain Crown Vic and see Cop Car, and if their music wasn't so loud, they'd hear the twin four-barrels on the Interceptor engine sucking down hi-test and know their dreamboat wouldn't have a chance in hell against it in a quarter-mile.

The light turned green and the kid roared off with a squeal of tires. One of the assholes in the back seat gave Mac the finger. "Hate to say it, kid, but you're the one who's getting screwed."

Mac turned the corner and headed into the old-money gentility of Georgetown. The Company provided him with a nice townhouse on a tree-lined street that was a minor fortress; bulletproof glass in the windows, solid steel doors, and an alarm system that wouldn't let an ant crawl across the threshold unannounced. It was home for the moment, but at any time it could become a safe house for someone the Company wanted to protect.

He reached to the visor and pushed the button on the garage door control. The door swung upward. White walls reflected the Vic's headlights. The garage was empty, no place for an enemy to hide himself or anything else. Mac pulled the car inside and closed the door behind him. He climbed out of the Vic and walked around the trunk to the door leading into the house. He pushed numbered buttons on the box mounted on the door frame, shutting off the burglar alarm. Once inside, he reentered the code and climbed the steps to the main floor.

He took off his jacket and tie and draped them over a chair. His shoulder rig and pistol went next. He crossed to the kitchen and took a glass from the cupboard. Ice from the tray in the refrigerator, and three fingers of Cutty Sark, and he slumped into a recliner.

"Hello, Mac."

The voice from behind his chair froze Mac's blood. Don't move, he thought. Don't give him an excuse. "Hello, John."

"Got your message."

"How did you get in here?"

"It's what you pay me to do isn't it?"

"I'm going to stand." No sudden moves.

"No, you're fine where you are."

John Slate walked around the chair and stood in front of MacDonald. He had a beard now; it and his hair were dyed a convincing shade of red. His nondescript workingman's clothes would make him disappear into any crowd. "So, how's our friend Carlton Briggs?"

"The Boss sends his regards." Briggs, Mac's superior pulled the strings on secret ops around the world, and Mac was his handler for the CIA's most secret asset.

"I'll bet. So what's Briggs need this time?"

A bead of cold sweat ran down Mac's forehead. Good, he thought, get him talking assignment and keep his mind off other things. "San Columbo.

A little island country between Cuba and Guatemala. Intel says the Soviets want to use it as a missile base."

"And?"

"So far, Phillipe Farrago, the President is shaking his head. We bought him a long time ago and we keep him propped up."

"But?"

"Generalissimo Antonio Mendoza is plotting a coup. To succeed, he needs money, and he's now found a way to get it. One of our operatives, Charles Beaumont, has been seized by Mendoza, who wants to sell him to the KGB. Beaumont's tough, but he's human. He could give up info that would compromise a half dozen of our ops in the Western Hemisphere."

"So?"

"We want Beaumont back. Without him to sell, Mendoza won't be able to finance his coup, and we maintain the *status quo*."

"I know Briggs. There's always more. What else?"

"Kill Mendoza so something like this doesn't happen again."

"Shouldn't be a problem. What recon have you got?"

"In my pocket. Microfilm with maps, a diagram of Mendoza's compound, photos of Beaumont. All you need."

"Hand it over."

Mac reached into his trouser pocket and held out a small cylinder in his palm. Slate took it from him and turned it in his fingers.

"I'll have a plane ready for you at 0700 hours tomorrow."

"No, thanks, Mac. For all I know Briggs would get us in the air and blow it up. I'll make my own arrangements." He started for the door but stopped and turned back to MacDonald. "You know, Mac, someday, Briggs will replace my team with something he likes better; he's tried once already." Slate's tone was as frightening as his sudden appearance because he spoke to Mac as if he were talking about a Redskins game or the weather. "You'll go when we do because once we're gone, he'll have no use for you, either. Enjoy all this," Slate made a sweeping gesture with his hand, "while you can."

Slate smiled, showing teeth through his beard that so far weren't fangs. "Did you look at the almanac lately?"

Mac shook his head.

"The full moon rises in less than an hour. I'd better be going, unless of course you'd like me to stick around."

Mac said nothing.

"That's what I thought. Don't get up. I'll show myself out." Slate strode out of the room and in a moment, Mac heard the front door click shut. The alarm was silent.

Mac let out a long-held breath. Dealing with Slate was scary because he still blamed Mac along with Briggs and others for leaving him and his team dangling in Laos. They were never supposed to come back from a black op that officially never happened in a place American troops weren't supposed to be. Though officially dead, they survived, and one by one slipped in stateside. Then something happened, something Mac still found hard to believe.

Slate was shanghaied by mobsters working for Michael Monzo who had Slate bitten by an honest-to-goodness werewolf with the plan to use him as an enforcer. Slate escaped, reunited with his men, and turned them into werewolves and they became the most vicious black ops team Mac had ever seen. The veiled message Slate was sending with his parting shot: someday, the Hitwolf team would outgrow their need of him, maybe sooner than Briggs would.

• • •

The cabin cruiser bobbed in the gentle waves off the shore of San Colombo. It was a smuggler's boat confiscated by the Coast Guard, a pair of powerful in-board Mercury engines and armor plate around the cabin. Singer had dropped anchor two miles off a beach close to the armed compound of Generalissimo Mendoza. An extraction, the Company's diplomatic name for abduction. Taking a captured agent from a walled camp with twenty or thirty armed men was a tough one, but business as usual for the Hitwolf team.

Singer was the only member of John Slate's original team to not be turned as a werewolf. As John put it, somebody has to drive the van. but Singer was just as happy staying totally human. He was never really comfortable around the men in their werewolf state, but he'd come to accept it as part of the job. And of course, there was Maura.

Maura Jameson, Ph.D. Professor, Anthropologist, world traveler, and expert on lycanthropy. Maura had uncovered the secrets behind the amulet called the *farkas ostor*, the "wolf whip" that allowed her to control the pack and to ease the pain that came with the transition. With it, she had aided the three werewolves, John, Swede, and Haines to come to grips physically and psychologically with their lycanthropy. And now, they were the CIA's deepest secret, known only to Tom MacDonald, their liaison, and to Carlton Briggs, Mac's boss.

"Nice place to visit." Maura sat beside him and took off her blouse revealing a red bikini top. Her athletic build wasn't exactly *Playboy* material, but Singer thought that she looked damned good in a bathing suit.

"I'm not even sure about that," Singer said, "based on the reports I read about political upheaval; armed patrols on the streets in the capital, midnight arrests of dissenters, and such."

"They all work the same way, don't they? Dictators, I mean. When they get power, it's all about payback."

"That and holding onto that power. I don't know how they sleep at night."

The sun was dipping toward the horizon, and painting the clouds with a spectacular pastel palette.

"Moonrise at 9:07."

Singer nodded. "Can't wait. I hate this sitting around more than anything."

Maura nodded. "I get it. You miss being part of the action, don't you?"

"Yeah, I guess I do. But even though I'm more glorified support than anything else these days, I'm still part of the team."

"Would you want to turn?"

"I don't know. The thought still scares me."

"Well, right now it's not necessary, and what you do is important."

"'They also serve who stand and wait,' huh?"

"Right."

Swede climbed the steps from the galley with a six-pack of Budweiser under his arm. The big, beefy blond pulled a can from the wrapper and threw it to Singer then another to Maura. He opened a can of his own and chugged it down in one pull. He pulled another from the cardboard and pulled the tab, flicking it with his finger over the side.

"You gonna drink the other four by yourself?" Haines came around the cabin. Scars from a dozen encounters shone white against the tan of his shirtless chest. "Gimme one."

"Better stop at one," Maura said. "I'm not sure I could handle a drunken werewolf."

"Where's John?"

"Below decks studying the aerials."

"How current are they?" Maura asked.

"Two weeks." Haines replied. "We go in at the beach and it's a mile plus through the jungle to Mendoza's compound. Getting there is easy. Getting out, maybe not so easy."

"The plan looks pretty solid," Swede said.

"Yeah, but the plan always looks good 'til the first shot's fired." Haines looked toward the shore. "People ain't cogs and gears."

"We always manage," Swede said.

"So far." Haines raised his can. "To the mission."

• • •

Maura stepped onto the deck. The moon would rise in two minutes and the transformation would begin. "I can't imagine the pain it puts you through," she had said once to Slate, "your joints realigning, fangs pushing through your gums, your skin stretching and ripping."

"It is intense," Slate told her, "but like all things, you adjust. I'm glad you have the amulet, though. It makes the change a lot easier."

She unwrapped the *farkas ostor*. The amulet was heavy, cast from silver, and consisted of snakelike vines twisted into a rough hexagon. The vines were inscribed with runic symbols, and in its center the amulet held a glowing purple gemstone that pulsed when the moon's rays fell on it.

"Ready?"

Slate, Swede, and Haines sat nude in the stern. "Ready," Slate said for the group. Singer turned his back. Watching the change still gave him the willies.

The moon rose over the island, and the stone in the amulet glowed. The men began to twitch and snort. Their faces distorted , jaws elongated, and bulging muscles split their skin only to heal almost immediately.

Maura held the *farkas ostor* high and recited the incantation. The men lay back against the gunwale, their agitation calmed, and drifted into a quiet sleep as the transformation took place. When it was complete, Maura recited another phrase, and the team awoke, not as men, but as fanged, hairy monsters. Slate gave a thumbs up and the sign was returned by Haines and Swede. The three dove over the side and set off swimming toward the beach two miles away.

Maura slipped the amulet into the pocket of her cut off jeans. She'd need it again when the moon set.

• • •

Raphael wiped sweat from his brow with two fingers and flicked beads of water into the dust. He leaned his carbine against the compound's twelve-foot adobe wall and fished in the pocket of his khaki uniform blouse for his cigarettes. He shook one from the pack and put it between his lips, swatting at a mosquito with his other hand as he did. The full moon seemed to call them all from the jungle swamps.

The match flared, and he cupped his hand around it. A touch of the flame, and the cigarette's tip glowed orange. Raphael dribbled smoke from the corners of his mouth. The local cigarettes were lousy, but the mosquitoes seemed to dislike the smoke even more than he.

He slung his rifle over his shoulder and set out to walk the perimeter of the compound. General Mendoza had a special guest this night, and all of the men were on watch. Raphael had seen the guest at the jungle outpost when the General's car arrived a half hour before between a pair of Jeeps armed with swivel machine guns in the back. The guest didn't look like much, a little man, almost frail, with a shaved head and rimless glasses. He wore a dark suit, starched white shirt, and necktie despite the dripping tropical heat. In his hand he carried a leather briefcase, and Raphael had caught a glimpse of the shining links of a handcuff joining the case to his wrist.

The little man was flanked by two bodyguards, one as big as a refrigerator, and the other, the one Raphael considered the more dangerous of the two, a whip lean man with military hair. They too wore suits and ties and sweat oozed from their faces as soon as they left the air-conditioned Mercedes-Benz. The guest had been escorted from the car into the mansion by no less than four armed men wearing the dark green uniform of Mendoza's elite guard. How foolish, Raphael thought. He looks as if I could pick him up and break him over my knee. Someday, he thought, I will wear the green uniform and be inside, not walking around and around this wall and swatting at these damned mosquitoes.

As if it read his mind, another of the blood-sucking devils whined at his ear. As he passed a doorway, he raised his hand to swat it away, but before he could, a hand shot from the shadows and plucked it out of the air. Raphael jumped back, startled and found himself staring into a pair of eyes that glowed like the tip of his cigarette.

He would have cried out, but a hand clamped around his throat and dug its claws into the back of his neck. He looked down and saw the hand was covered in coarse dark fur. The hand lifted him until his feet dangled. Raphael kicked and pried at the hand with both of his own but could not relax its grip. The figure turned to press Raphael's back against the wall, and when it did, it moved into the dim light.

The guard found himself staring into the raw face of terror; a fur-covered face with a slanted brow and an underslung jaw studded with fangs. Raphael's eyes bulged as the terror raised a furred fist and brought it down, driving the crown of the guard's skull into his brain.

John Slate dropped the guard to the ground and took the carbine from his shoulder. He threw the rifle and sent it spinning into the jungle. One down.

On the other side of the compound, Swede and Haines would be scaling the wall. If the intel that Singer got from the Agency was correct, Charles Beaumont would be held inside the big house in a secure room at the building's heart. Getting in would be difficult, getting out would be worse. Taking Beaumont with them alive would be all but impossible, and that was only the beginning of the operation.

Slate tested the door. It was substantial; slabs like railroad ties banded with iron strapping, likely barred from the inside. The trees and brush had been cut a good ten feet from the entire perimeter wall to prevent invaders from dropping into the compound from above. Of course, that was effective only with ordinary soldiers.

He crossed the bare strip with a blur of speed and found a tall palm that leaned toward the wall. Slate dug his claws into the trunk of the tree and noiselessly scrambled up its height. In seconds he was hidden in the shadows of its fronds. The treetop gave him a good view of most of the courtyard. Nothing had changed since the spy plane took photos of the place nearly a year before. The big house dominated the center of the compound with outbuildings and a small barracks behind. Like a medieval fief, thought Slate. In the courtyard he saw soldiers in khaki with sidearms and rifles propped against trucks and Jeeps parked on the hard-packed earth. Eight men that he could see.

Slate could also see the top of the wall where barbed wire lay in loops and coils. He would have to choose his landing carefully, not so much to avoid the sting of the barbs as to avoid the scrape and rattle of the wire on the masonry. He dug his claws into the tree, braced himself, and launched into space. His feet landed on either side of a loop of wire, and he jackknifed over the edge of the wall to land on the canvas tarp over the bed of a truck parked just inside. He rolled off the tarp and onto the ground then under the truck before any of the soldiers could notice.

He peered from his covert to the bell that hung from a pole near the

He braced himself, and launched into space.

gate. He was ready. When Haines and Swede were in position, they would ring the bell, and the party would begin.

• • •

In his study General Mendoza took a cigar from the carved box on his desk. The General was lean and hard in his uniform, a soldier who had fought his way up the winding staircase of the military and the political through grit, savvy, and feral cunning to stand a simple coup away from control of San Columbo. The little island nation was no paradise, but as Milton's Satan once observed, it is better to rule in hell than to serve in heaven.

"Would you like one, Colonel Gagarin?" Mendoza said, showing a row of broken teeth in a crooked smile, "Wonderful tobacco from our friends in Cuba."

"Thank you, no." Mikhail Gagarin sat in an armchair facing the General's desk. His men flanked the chair, standing at attention, unlike Mendoza's churlish, undisciplined guards, who slouched against the wall behind the General. If those were my men, Gagarin thought, I would have them whipped to their last breath.

"Perhaps a drink?" Mendoza gestured to a serving cart in the corner of the room amply stocked with bottles and a filigreed silver bucket heaped with inviting ice.

"Thank you, no." Gagarin repeated in perfect formal Spanish.

Mendoza frowned. Does this prissy little insect think he is too good to drink with me, to smoke with me? Who does he think he is, sitting there with his fingers steepled and leg crossed, showing me the bottom of his shoe, as if that were my place — under his foot.

"Perhaps we could perform our exchange." Gagarin stared cold-eyed at Mendoza with thinly veiled contempt.

"Yes, of course. I have no doubt you are eager to return to your embassy. Your KGB no doubt has much to keep you busy." He laughed at his own joke and turned to one of the soldiers behind him, one wearing the stripes of rank on his sleeve. "Bring the prisoner."

• • •

Charles Beaumont sat on the edge of his cot in the windowless room. A cot and a bucket, he thought. Not exactly a jug of wine, a loaf of bread, and thou beside me in the wilderness, but I've had worse accommodations. His hands were tied in front of him, palm to palm; it made him look pious, as if he were praying for his life. Two of Mendoza's green-shirt elite sat in chairs flanking the door, hands on their pistols.

Beaumont's pale blue pipe cord suit was sullied with patches of dirt and spatters of blood not his own. The CIA operative was captured, but it took seven of Mendoza's men to do the job. Two were dead, and one would crawl for the rest of his days. They should have killed me, Beaumont thought, but they didn't. That tells me they had orders to take me alive at any cost.

It had been almost eight years since JFK had gone toe to toe with Kruschev over missiles in Cuba and the CIA stopped hunting Nazis south of the equator and started hunting Commies. Beaumont was still trying to figure out what blew his cover as a sugar importer, something to watch out for next time. Next time? Who am I kidding? He looked down at his bare feet. They took his shoes, his belt, and his watch, which now graced the arm of one of his guards. Too bad; the belt had a length of piano wire, the shoes a stiletto in the hollowed left heel, and a small explosive charge hid behind the face of the bulky Rolex. That the guard was wearing his watch told him that greed not caution led to their seizure.

What they missed was the cyanide tipped needle sewn inside the lapel of his jacket. If I can get close to Mendoza, Beaumont thought, he'll pay for my life with his own.

A knock at the door and some quiet words. The green guards stood. "En tus pies, cabron." Each of the guards took an arm just above the elbow and marched Beaumont through the door into a carpeted hallway. His mind was running options when hands from behind pulled a burlap sack over his head and cinched it tight at the neck. So much for breaking and running, he thought. Let's just wait and see what happens next.

· · ·

Haines studied the face of the rough wall. Not much in the way of handholds. He motioned to his companion and signed a command. Swede gave an affirmative with a clawed thumb. Haines cupped his hands as a foot hold and boosted the werewolf to his shoulders. Swede reached over his head and carefully pulled himself onto the top of the wall, barely touching the tangle of barbed wire that ran along its surface. He lay on his belly and reached an arm over the edge. Haines caught his hand, and with Swede's help, scrambled onto the wall unnoticed by the guards below.

Swede peered over the edge into the courtyard. The light was dim, but wolf eyes made the scene as bright as noon. Eight men in a circle just five yards away. Rifles propped against a truck. Holstered sidearms. One machine gun, an old Sten on a sling under one soldier's arm. He goes first. Swede reached into his fanged mouth and pulled out the stone he'd been carrying. He drew back his arm and took aim at the bell on the post near the gate. Only one shot. Had to get it right.

• • •

Beaumont stumbled on the staircase, and one of his guards punched him in his kidney. The staircase, uncarpeted, thought Beaumont. They're taking me down to the foyer. At the foot of the stairs, the guards steered Beaumont to the left and down a corridor toward the rear of the mansion. A door opened ahead of them, and Beaumont was led into a room. Carpet underfoot. Cigar smoke. Breathing, more than a few people.

The sack was yanked from his head, and Beaumont blinked in the light of a desk lamp that was turned to shine into his face. "You see our mutual friend." Beaumont recognized the voice as Mendoza. "Now may I see the money?"

"Yes." Beaumont heard the click of a latch. He turned his head far enough to recognize an old adversary.

"Comrade Gagarin." Beaumont revised the target for his poisoned needles.

Gagarin drew a photograph from his jacket and compared it to the prisoner standing beside him. The hair was bleached blond, and the lantern jaw was clean shaven, but the thin scar up the side of the spy's nose was unmistakable. "Good evening, Beaumont." Gagarin unclasped the top of the briefcase and held it open for Beaumont to look inside and see banded stacks of hundred-dollar bills.

"Looks as if my price has gone up," Beaumont quipped. "Inflation."

Gagarin ignored the jape and took a key from his pocket to unlock the cuff from his wrist. He nodded to the bodyguard to his left, and the man took the briefcase to Mendoza's desk where he set it down.

Mendoza reached into the case and drew out a packet of bills. He tore off the band. He fanned the bills on the desk. Mendoza smiled. "He is yours, my friend. Take him."

• • •

Slate reached up and gently worked the handle on the driver's door of the truck. He slowly opened it wide enough to slip into the cab. He was in luck; the keys were in the ignition. Through the cracked windshield he saw the wide steps that led to the double doors from the veranda into the foyer. Twenty yards away, Mendoza's men were standing in a circle, smoking cigarettes and passing around a bottle of wine. In the truck's mirror Slate saw the wrought iron gate seventy feet behind him, a single rank of spear tipped bars hinged to the left to swing either direction.

This is taking too long, Slate thought. Someone will find that guard soon. Where the hell are Swede and Haines?

Slate caught a shadow in the corner of his eye, then two.

Dark, furred shapes crept in the shadows along the top of the wall until they were within a few yards of the knot of men. On the wall, the larger of the shapes hurled something that bounced off the bell with a loud peal. Showtime.

• • •

The soldiers in the courtyard all turned toward the unexpected sound of the bell, and as they did, a dark shape vaulted from the wall and landed in the center of their circle. A vicious swipe with a clawed hand ripped the throat from the soldier with the Sten. Two of the men drew automatics from their holsters and panic fired, one of them hitting the soldier to Swede's right.

The other hit Swede in the shoulder, to him no more than the sting of a wasp, a second before the werewolf grabbed another man and threw him bodily into the gunman, knocking him on his back. A soldier scrambled for his carbine, but as he frantically worked the bolt, Haines slashed at the back of his neck, claws nearly severing his head from his spine. He dug his claws into another soldier's shoulders and spun, ramming his head through the bullet proof window of the Mercedes.

Across the courtyard, Slate turned the key in the truck's ignition and the engine ground to life. He jammed the gear shift into low and popped the clutch, sending the truck hurtling across the yard toward the house. The steps were wide, but it would be close.

• • •

The bell rang, and everyone in the room turned his head at the unexpected sound but Beaumont.

He brought his bare heel down hard on the instep of the guard to his right and shouldered the man, making him stumble and let go of his arm. Beaumont brought his bound hands across his chest in a blow to the other guard that shattered his windpipe. The guard reflexively reached for his throat and as he did, Beaumont stripped the watch from his wrist and pumped the stem three times.

The larger of Gagarin's bodyguards lunged at Beaumont but his bulk made the effort clumsy. Beaumont grabbed the lapel of his suit and rammed the needle through the fabric and into the man's neck. The bodyguard fell forward and tried to get up but never made it to his feet. The lean bodyguard reached for his pistol, but one of Mendoza's men mistook his intentions and shot him in the back.

Before Gagarin could rise from his chair, Beaumont threw the watch into his lap. The Colonel reached for it but wasn't quick enough. A second later, the sharp crack of detonation sprayed blood and tattered flesh across the room. From the courtyard Beaumont heard gunshots and screaming. The guard beside the door was drawing his pistol as Mendoza screamed frantic orders to his men. Now or nothing, Beaumont thought as he lowered his head and charged.

• • •

Slate pressed the truck's accelerator to the floor and the truck shot across the courtyard and up the steps to the front door of the mansion. Two men firing automatics ran through the double doors. Glass spidered the truck's windshield as Slate drove it across the veranda and through the doors into the foyer, sweeping the gunmen aside.

In the study, Beaumont rushed the guard, who aimed his pistol at Beaumont's head but remembering the order to keep him alive, hesitated to pull the trigger. Beaumont spread his bound hands like a pair of wings, his crossed thumbs catching the muzzle between them as he pushed upward. His fingers closed around the frame of the automatic with one hand and the grips with the other. He bent the pistol backward and twisted, tearing off the screaming soldier's finger. Beaumont bent the gun backward until it aimed at the guard's forehead. A tug at the trigger, and the back of the guard's head spattered the door behind him.

Holding the automatic upside down, Beaumont swiveled and sprayed the room with gunfire, making Mendoza and his guards duck behind the desk for cover. Beaumont took the chance and grabbed the briefcase, tucking it under his arm. A crash in the foyer. One more second, and Beaumont was out the door and gone.

He dashed up the hallway and stopped short at what he saw. One of Mendoza's trucks had run through the doors and into the foyer. Behind the wheel was what Beaumont could describe only as a werewolf. A man in a mask? The hairy face pushed through the missing panel of the windshield and growled in a voice so guttural he could barely understand the words, "Get in."

Beaumont paused for a beat then heard Mendoza and his soldiers coming after him. He yanked the door open and clambered onto the seat. A glance to his left showed him it was more than a mask. His savior was a werewolf head to toe. Slate yanked the gearshift into reverse and with a shrieking of metal backed the truck through the ruins of the doorway.

Mendoza and his men came running after the truck, guns blazing. Bullets whanged off its fenders, and Beaumont fired the last three shots in his pistol, missing Mendoza but hitting one of the green-clad soldiers.

Slate fish-hooked the truck into the courtyard, its wheels thumping over dead bodies then slammed it into gear, pulling away from the mansion and toward the gate. Beaumont turned to look out the rear window of the truck and saw Mendoza and his men running after them.

As he stared, a figure leapt through the opening in the canvas and into the bed. It landed with a thump and rolled to the side as another came running behind the truck, grabbed the tail gate and clambered over it. A face appeared at the glass, and Beaumont started back at the sight of another fanged nightmare.

Slate was afraid the truck wouldn't be up to speed to break through the heavy gate, but hinged to swing inside or out, the gate had no stops on either side. The truck broke through, all but tearing the gate from its hinges then roared away from the compound, bouncing and heaving down the rutted jungle road.

Beaumont was speechless. The werewolf behind the wheel turned its head and saw that Beaumont's hands were still tied. A flick of its claw severed the bonds, and Beaumont rubbed his aching wrists.

By this point, his mind was completely blown. He turned toward the hairy driver and said, "Uh, you guys *are* from the Company . . . right?"

"Radio," Slate growled. "Turn it on."

Beaumont was stunned from all he'd seen in the last few minutes, but he managed to find the radio's power switch and flip it to the ON position. The dial glowed, and in less than a minute, static and frantic Spanish crackled through the speaker.

"What are they saying?"

"From what I can make out, Mendoza's got patrols watching for us and some closing in from different directions. He knows which direction we took and they're after us."

"Damn." Slate pointed to the temperature gauge whose needle was climbing into the red. "Bullet hit the radiator." He let off the accelerator and the truck coasted to a stop. The engine was beginning to knock, so he shut it off.

Slate and Beaumont climbed from the cab as Haines and Swede dropped from the bed onto the road. "We have to go on foot from here," Slate said. "Are you up to running?"

"Uh, yeah, if we don't have to run too far."

Slate jerked his head to Swede, who grabbed Beaumont around the waist and threw him over his shoulder in a fireman's carry. Haines wrenched open the truck's hood and tore the fuel line from the carburetor. He ripped the hot cable from the battery terminal and raked it over the solenoid, throwing sparks. The fumes caught with a thump like a muted drum and Haines jumped back, swatting at the burning hair on his forearm.

"Wait — wait! The money." Beaumont said, pointing toward the cab of the truck.

"Too late," Haines said.

"Let me down, damn it." But by the time he got the words out of his mouth, the werewolves had already set out at a dead run into the jungle. Behind them the fuel tank on the truck erupted with a roar and a flash.

In retrospect, Beaumont was glad Swede carried him. He could never have run so fast in his bare feet even on clear, level turf, and his rescuers' night vision allowed them to duck, dodge, and hurdle fallen trees, vines, roots and a hundred other things that would have broken his ankle, given him a concussion or at the least sent him sprawling in the dark.

There was no hesitation on the team's part. The path they were following was the shortest way to the beach where Singer and Maura waited offshore with the boat.

Slate stopped abruptly and raised a fist.

"What —what's —" Beaumont stammered.

"Shut up," Swede rumbled over his shoulder.

Noise. Men and dogs crashing through the thick undergrowth ahead and to the left on an intercept course with the team's trail. Slate signaled his men to cut to the right and they tore through the dense jungle. Haines hung back as Swede and Slate went on with Beaumont bouncing on the werewolf's shoulder.

Haines saw the lights bobbing. He crouched behind a tree and waited. He listened closely. Three distinct overlapping barks; three dogs. Their sound was closer than the men, which meant they had been let off their chains. So much the better.

Closer. Haines could smell their sweat on the viscous, humid air. He could hear their labored breathing and almost hear their pounding hearts. In what little moonlight filtered through the thick canopy overhead, Haines saw three mastiffs come boiling through the brush, fangs bared.

Haines leapt from cover and landed in a crouch. He raised his head to the sky and let out a piercing howl. Two of the dogs skidded to a stop, startled and perhaps frightened at an unnatural prey, but the third, the pack's alpha bounded forward and sprung, its jaws aimed at Haines' throat.

Haines twisted to the side, avoiding the lunge, and as the dog sailed past him, he raked the mastiff's belly with his claws, spilling its entrails on the ground. The other dogs, sensing the death of one of their own, charged Haines, snapping and snarling. Both dogs did as the first had done, as they had all been trained to do. They leapt for Haines' throat. A blow from Haines' fist knocked one of his attackers aside unconscious, but as he did, the second clamped its jaws on his forearm.

Lights. The soldiers were coming. Haines snarled and swung his arm with all the force he could muster to slam the dog against the bole of a nearby tree. A loud crack told Haines that the dog's back was broken, but its jaws held on. With a slash of his claws, Haines severed the dog's head and as he did, a flashlight beam fell on him.

"*Madre Dios!*" The soldier froze and the men following behind him ran into him, knocking his rifle, and the flashlight taped to its barrel to the ground.

Haines turned and ran, the dog's head still clamped on his forearm. He could follow the scent of the team, but without their dogs, the pursuers would have a difficult job. He could also smell the ocean close at hand. The map. Pursuit and the bloodlust of feral combat fogged Haines' mind. What lay in this direction? He broke into a clearing, and his question was answered. Ahead of him, in the moonlight, he saw Slate and Swede still carrying Beaumont, running full tilt toward the rim of a cliff. In two seconds, they disappeared, and in three more, Haines ran headlong to the edge and launched himself into space.

• • •

Mendoza caught up with his men to find them standing and staring at the dead dogs.

"What are you doing? After them!"

The men all looked away from the General, ashamed of their fear. Mendoza grabbed a sergeant, the team's leader by the shirt. and snarled, "What is the meaning of this? Go after them!"

The sergeant babbled rapidly, his eyes wide with terror. Mendoza slapped the sergeant across the jaw and backhanded him for good measure.

"*Lobizon!*" the sergeant cried. "*Lobizon!*"

Werewolf.

Mendoza pulled the sergeant's pistol from its holster and shot him in the head. He turned to the others. "Are you children, or are you soldiers? Fear me, not some man in a costume! Go!"

Mendoza's men ran after the fugitives, but with less enthusiasm than before.

The General hated to kill Sergeant Ramirez, but it was the only way to fend off panic. The General was afraid too of what he had seen, and its only possible explanation, but he was more afraid of the consequences of the dead Gagarin and the loss of the money. Beaumont's rescue upended all of his plans in the space of a few minutes. If he didn't catch Beaumont and his rescuers, there would be no money for weapons, supplies, and most important, for bribes.

Mendoza realized that his enemies were running toward the ocean. That meant a boat somewhere close by. He called to a soldier with a walkie-talkie pack on his shoulder. "Bring that here and open the channel." He took the handset from the soldier. He barked into it, "Villa, take some men and meet me at the boats."

There would be consequences, but they would be much less severe if he recaptured Beaumont. He turned to the soldier. "Come with me." I will look for a boat — any boat — he thought, and stop it. If the people on board resist, I'll kill them all. I want Beaumont, I want those devils who killed my men, and I want that money.

• • •

When they hit the water, Swede let go of Beaumont, who struggled to the surface. He shucked off his suit coat. Treading water, he looked around and saw two furred heads bobbing nearby in the moonlight. Did Mendoza's men kill the third? He heard a loud splash behind him and when he turned his head, the third of his rescuers broke the surface.

The leader struck out swimming and his companions followed suit. Beaumont was a strong swimmer, but he quickly fell behind the werewolves. He pushed harder to catch up, and before long he was gasping for breath and struggling in the waves. The leader swam back to him and took him in a cross-chest carry. Beaumont's head lolled, and he looked up at the stars shining in the ink-black sky.

I must be dreaming, he thought. This can't be real.

• • •

Singer and Maura stood in the confiscated smuggler's boat, watching for the team. Waves lapped the hull as the boat lay at anchor two miles offshore, poised to sprint at a moment's notice. Maura stood in the stern of the cabin cruiser while Singer waited at the helm, ready to start the engine. They had heard a distant explosion a half hour before, but so far neither saw any sign from Slate or the others. Singer raised a star scope to his eye and scanned the beach. Nothing moving. The southern view was miles of empty ocean.

He swung his view to the east and stopped suddenly at the sight of dark objects bobbing in the waves. "I see them," Singer said, "Draw anchor."

Maura ran to the winch and pressed the START button. The motor kicked in, and with a clank of chain, it began pulling up the anchor.

Singer started the engines and the boat vibrated with a deep rumble. "Hold on," he called to Maura and pulled back on the throttle. The twin propellers spun and the boat heaved forward. As it gathered speed, waves slapped the hull.

Maura looked over the stern and saw lights. "Singer! Behind us!"

Singer turned his head and saw the running lights of two boats. Spotlights came on, and he realized the chase boats had been lying in wait until they made a move. He gauged the pursuer's speed and knew he could never pick up Slate and the others before the boats closed on him.

Muzzle flashes. They were firing but the bouncing boats made the shooters' aim less than accurate.

He turned northwest to draw the chase boats away from the men in the water. Looking back, Singer saw the other boats keeping pace. He had to get enough distance between himself and Mendoza's men so that he could circle back for a quick rescue of John and the others. He shouted to Maura, "Come up and take the wheel."

Singer reached into the storage bin under the helm and pulled out a stubby rifle with a big bore, an M79 grenade launcher, what the Aussies called a Wombat Gun. He broke open the breech and loaded a forty-millimeter shell packed with razor-edged flechettes.

Maura climbed the ladder to the bridge and took the wheel.

"When I tell you," Singer said, "cut the throttle by a quarter. I want them to close on us. Forty yards should do it." He sat in the fighting chair in the stern and strapped on the harness. He had to make his shot count; the gun took too long to reload for a second try.

"Now!"

Maura cut the throttle and the cabin cruiser slowed to steady Singer's aim. The chase boats sped toward him side by side, throwing spray in their wake.

Closer, closer, seventy yards, sixty. Singer pulled the trigger and the gun went off with a blunt thud. Singer's timing was good. The canister exploded with an orange flash between the boats, spraying the men on both with wicked blades. The one to the left suddenly veered into its companion, riding over its prow and landing tits up, while the other boat, its nose driven under, went end over end. Singer lost sight of them as the moon slipped behind a cloud.

He climbed from the chair and shouted to Maura. "Head starboard thirty degrees. Let's circle around and get the guys before they send a god-damned helicopter." He peered through the scope and saw the heading would get them to the team in a minute or two.

Maura screamed and Singer turned his head to see the unlighted prow of a bigger boat bearing down amidships only thirty feet away. The boat had been lying in wait. They'd been herded into a trap.

"Jump!" he shouted, but he didn't know if Maura heard him as the attack boat splintered the smaller craft. The impact sent him spinning through the air to land hard and flat on the water, knocking the breath from his lungs.

• • •

Slate saw the crash and saw the boat break into two pieces. He ground his teeth and watched as the larger craft, an old World War II era PT boat slowed and circled the wreckage. He could see no sign of Singer or Maura.

"Hang back,' he growled at Haines. "Swede, with me."

With strong strokes, Slate set out toward the wreckage, Swede close behind him.

• • •

"Quickly," Mendoza shouted. "Search her before she sinks." The General would have used a torpedo but feared that it would destroy the money along with the boat. Ramming, like the ancient Roman galleys seemed the best option, but he didn't expect the boat to break in two. Four of his men stripped down and dove into the water. Two swam to each half of the boat.

The cloud slipped away from the moon, and in the cold light, he saw a body floating thirty feet off the starboard bow. "You," Mendoza pointed to a nameless private. "Put on a vest and bring me that man." I hope he is alive, Mendoza thought, although soon he will wish he were not.

• • •

Maura broke the surface inside the front half of the boat, gulping air. She was inside the pitch-black cabin. She spent a moment orienting herself; the cabin was tilted at a funhouse angle, and she had to feel her way around it in the dark. She found one of the built-in cabinets groping for the cache of weapons the team had loaded two days before. Was that a light below her? Her fingers closed around the handle of an automatic just as a strong hand grabbed her ankle and the soldier pulled her under the water. His other hand grabbed her belt and dragged her into a clumsy embrace in the darkness.

Bullets don't travel far, Maura thought, but guns fire underwater. Maura thumbed back the hammer. She pressed the muzzle of her pistol into her attacker's chest and pulled the trigger, hoping she didn't hit a bone. The automatic went off with a muffled pop, and the enemy's grip relaxed.

She bobbed back up into the tilted cabin, spitting brine and gasping for air. Suddenly, she realized she wasn't alone. The glare of a flashlight blinded her, and before she could fire the pistol again, a fist crashed into her jaw, and she slid unconscious below the surface.

• • •

Fifty yards away, Slate and Swede watched as Mendoza's men hauled Maura on board and a few minutes later, Singer. There was no way of knowing whether they were alive or dead. Red fury blazed in Slate's head. He signaled Swede, took a deep breath, and dove under the water.

The wolf-men surfaced at the stern of the old PT boat near the screws. Slate signaled to Swede to follow, and they began a careful circle of the hull, looking for a way to climb aboard.

Below, Mendoza sat on a stationary bench studying the captives bound hand and foot on the cabin deck. The man was short and stocky with broad shoulders and lean hips like a body builder. He sandy hair was close cropped, making his ears prominent. The woman was taller than the man and had an angular athletic build. Her long dark hair was pulled behind her head into a pony tail, and her fair skin was pink with sunburn.

Mendoza wanted to smoke, but years of experience taught that watching him light a cigar broke down resistance almost as much as putting its glowing tip on a victim's skin. Anticipation, he thought, fear of the unknown, a great lever.

His men had found no trace of Beaumont or the money on the shattered craft. Odds were good that the two were still together, and these two could lead him to both. The General had no illusions about his captives; they were professionals. The disabling of two of his boats and their crews with a single shot showed him that. Professionals were more difficult to break, but he had a little time, and he also knew that one alone could often withstand more pain than two watching each other suffer.

"Wake them."

One of the soldiers broke open a glass capsule, and the harsh scent of ammonia filled the cabin. He held it under Singer's nose, and in a few seconds, Singer's head stirred then jerked back, away from the capsule. Maura was next, and soon her green eyes popped open to stare into the General's gaze.

Mendoza smiled, his broken teeth looking grotesque in the dim light of the cabin. "Welcome to San Colombo, my friends. You are a long way from home, no doubt. My men searched what was left of your ship, but we found no passports. So, where would that home be? Hmm?"

Neither spoke.

Mendoza leaned forward to look Singer in the face. "I would say that I have all the time in the world, but I fear that my future is slipping through the neck of the hourglass and soon, it will be gone. So, I will be more direct. Where were you going to pick up Charles Beaumont?"

Slate and Swede watched as the men hauled Maura on board.

No answer.

"Who do you work for?"

No answer.

Mendoza sighed. He struck a match on the underside of the table. It flared and he held it at eye level, watching it burn. The matchstick charred and curled slightly as the flame worked its way down the wood. Singer and Maura watched the flame too, as it neared the pinch of the General's thumb and forefinger. At the last second before it reached his skin, Mendoza caught the burnt head of the match with his other hand and turned it upside down, using the last quarter inch of the match to light his cigar, as if he were sucking the last flame from it. A few puffs, and the tip glowed a bright orange.

Mendoza took a long pull on the cigar, and tipped his head back, letting the smoke float from his mouth in a gray cloud. Without warning, he leaned forward and grabbed Singer by the ear with one hand and held the end of the cigar at the corner of his eye. To his surprise, Singer did not flinch, but continued to stare at the General.

"You show no fear. That is admirable, but foolish. Do not worry, my stubborn friend. I will not blind you — in both of your eyes. I want to leave one for you to see what my men will do to your beautiful friend, and when they are through with her, what I will do." Mendoza took another puff at his cigar. "Do you know what the difference is between terror and horror? Terror you feel for yourself; horror you feel for another, and I will show you horrors that even you have never seen. Memories to take with you to hell."

"*Besarme el culo pendejo.*" Singer spat in his tormentor's face. He wanted Mendoza angry with him, not Maura.

The General frowned, took another puff on the cigar to brighten its tip and delicately touched it to Singer's eyelid. This time, Singer flinched.

On deck, Carlos, one of the soldiers, knelt by the ladder left over the side for Mendoza's men to re-board after their search of the cabin cruiser. Although the boat was anchored, he hung back from the edge of the flat deck, fearful that he might slip and tumble over the side. Carlos was counting his blessings. He had not been in the courtyard where his fellow soldiers were massacred by the invaders. He was not the sergeant the General had shot with his own pistol. He was not one of the men on the wrecked boats, and he was not one of the people taken prisoner.

He had heard the radio chatter from one of the attack boats, some of the men were still alive, some of them badly injured, but the General would not turn the boat to pull them from the water. Someone spoke of sharks, and the thought made him shudder. Just then he heard a scrape over the side. He gripped a mooring cleat and leaned forward and peered over the edge to see a dark shape clinging to the rungs.

Before he could cry out, the swipe of a clawed hand tore his jaw from his skull while its mate yanked him over the side. But Carlos did not fall to splash in the ocean. The monster on the ladder dangled him by the arm and lowered him gently to the waiting creature in the water. Dazed by shock, the only sound Carlos could muster was a low moan, quickly cut off as his head was pushed under the surface.

Swede gave a thumbs up, and Slate slipped quietly onto the boat. The moon was still low in the sky, and he and Swede were on the shadow side of the craft. Most of the crew were gathered around the anti-aircraft gun in the stern looking toward the flames of one of the chase boats. The boat's captain stood at the helm, and behind him, a soldier sat in one of the twin turrets manning a .50 caliber Browning machine gun.

Slate figured that Maura and Singer were below. They were the first priority. Second was stealing the boat for their getaway. If Mendoza was on board, so much the better.

On the bridge, the skipper swept the surface of the water with binoculars. He saw nothing to the west, and when he turned to the east, he found himself staring into a pair of huge glowing eyes. A blow from the heel of Swede's hand drove the eyepieces through the front of the captain's skull.

The crewman at the gun turret cried out as he saw the captain fall backwards and in a blur of motion, a dark furred shape leapt over the rim of the turret. Impossibly strong hands grabbed the gunner by the shoulders, yanked him out of the seat and hurled him through the air into the water.

The men in the stern turned at the splash. Swede spun the Browning on its mount, but it wouldn't rotate far enough to aim for the stern. He wrapped his arms around the gun and with a snapping of bolts and a screeching of metal, he ripped the Browning from its mount. He laid it on the rim of the turret and opened fire.

Most of the targets still stood in the stern. One or two had run when the shooting began, and a few had the presence of mind to throw themselves overboard. But most of Mendoza's men were chopped to pieces by the .50 caliber fire. As the gun roared, the bloodlust took hold, and Swede threw back his head to give an exultant howl.

Slate clambered down the gangway below decks to find a startled soldier, pistol in hand, rushing up to meet him. The soldier fired, hitting Slate just below his ribcage, the bullet passing out his lower back. He never got the chance to fire a second shot. Slate grabbed him by the throat and crotch, dug in his claws, and charged forward, using him as a shield. At the foot of the steps, Slate found himself in the galley where Mendoza was bent over Singer, whose face and chest were covered with angry red welts.

Mendoza drew his automatic from its holster and fired rapidly. Slate's human shield absorbed the bullets, and Slate hurled the dead man into the General, knocking him to the deck. Mendoza raised his pistol to fire again, but Singer kicked out with his bound feet and the gun went flying across the cabin. Mendoza struggled to push the dead man off him, but he was too slow.

Singer scissored his legs and crossed his ankles, clamping Mendoza's neck between his iron-hard calves. The General's eyes bulged as he struggled for breath, and the last thing he saw before his eyes went dark was a fanged mouth and a pair of glowing, feral eyes inches from his own.

The terrified men who did not die from the gunfire quickly abandoned the PT boat, taking their chances with drowning or the sharks. Slate took the helm. The anchor was raised, and he swung the boat toward the area where he'd left Beaumont with Haines. If we're lucky, he thought, they'll still be there.

• • •

Beaumont lay back in the water, supported by an improvised set of water wings his rescuer made by knotting the legs of Beaumont's trousers and swinging them around his head, trapping air inside. The werewolf treaded water as if it were as natural as breathing, but its head turned from side to side watching the ocean with its red eyes.

He knew better than to try conversation. Sound travels easily over water, and the least noise could give them away, so he waited and watched, every second grating on his nerves.

"Listen." The wolf-man heard it first, but in a second or two, Beaumont's ears picked up the sound of a motor. A boat was approaching, a big one with no lights.

Without warning, Haines slashed the inflated legs of Beaumont's trousers. "Get under. Only bob up for a breath," he growled in Beaumont's ear. Beaumont did as he was told.

If that was the rescue boat, Beaumont thought, we'd stay visible, not hide under the surface. A Navy SEAL had once told Beaumont that taking a breath and slipping below the surface until his next one could as much as triple a man's survival time in the water, as opposed to fighting to stay on the surface. Now, he'd find out whether it was true.

Slate slowed Mendoza's boat to a crawl, Swede stood at the prow scanning the surface, Maura beside him with binoculars. Allowing for tide and drift, Haines and Beaumont should be nearby.

Swede saw something bob to the top and disappear again then another something beside it. "John, thirty degrees off starboard two hundred yards."

Slate swung the boat and eased across the waves. He could see them now, heads bobbing out of the water and slipping under again. They were hiding from the boat, not knowing the team was running it. He called down to Swede, "Go get them."

Swede dove off the prow of the boat and swam toward the bobbing heads. He came within a few yards and saw Beaumont's head rise out of the water. In a second, Haines' head appeared and Swede whistled sharply. Haines' head turned and he whistled in response. The next time Beaumont's head broke the surface, Haines grabbed his shoulder and said, "Stay up."

• • •

On board, Beaumont was relieved to see humans. His mind was almost broken by what he'd witnessed in the last hour. Maura, the woman was attractive, and the man, whose name he learned was Singer, was functional, but his face was selectively burned, the marks of torture.

"I was worried about sharks," Haines said.

"They were busy elsewhere. Get us out of here," Slate growled to Singer, who climbed to the helm and pulled back the throttle, throwing Beaumont, whose knees were shaky at best, to the deck. He rose to a sitting position and leaned back against the gunwale.

Maura reached under her blouse and pulled the *farkas ostor* from the pocket like a kangaroo's pouch a Company surgeon had disguised as an appendectomy scar. The gemstone glowed in its center, and the wolf-men all turned toward it, as if on some unspoken command. "Come," she said. The werewolves followed her down the gangway below decks, leaving Beaumont alone.

He looked around him. There were no bodies, but blood was everywhere and scraps of flesh littered the deck. This was a story that would buy him a round of drinks in any bar in the world.

In a few minutes Maura came back on deck.

"As you might imagine, I have a few questions."

Maura smiled. "You were rescued. End of story."

"End of official story, you mean."

"Call it what you will. This never happened."

"Oh, come on, pretty, I was rescued by werewolves — a team of werewolf commandos. Those three weren't just guys in masks. They did things humans can't do."

"I do apologize," she said. "Our equipment went down with the boat. Otherwise, I'd've given you a shot that would make all this seem like a dream."

"A shot?"

"Lysergic acid diethylamide — you're familiar with LSD? But we'll have to wait 'til we get you to shore for that. Official story: you were drugged by your captors and hallucinating when you were extracted, raving about monsters."

"Oh, no." He started to rise to his feet, shaking his head. "You're not going to —" A hard right cross to his jaw dropped Beaumont to the deck.

Maura shook her hand and rubbed her knuckles. Male chauvinists seldom took her seriously, but it was just as well. When she made a move, they never saw it coming.

She climbed to the helm and put her arms around Singer's waist. "I'd kiss you, Singer, but I don't know what doesn't hurt."

"I'd kiss you too, but it'll be a week or so before my lips work again."

"Where are we headed?"

"Guantanamo to drop off Beaumont and sink this scow."

"And then?" She laid her head on Singer's shoulder.

"How does Nassau sound?"

"Like a nice place to visit."

THE END

SIX GUN TERRORS - Durken and McAfee, former scouts for William Tecumseh Sherman's March to the Sea, drift west and become foremen on the Triple-Six Ranch in Bacon Rock, Nevada. Their former commander conscripts them back into service to deal with situations that fall outside regulations, such as were-panthers in the High Sierras, Snake Worshippers who control masses of rattlesnakes, an extended family of roaming cannibal killers, and even H.P. Lovecraft's Old Ones. In "Spines" the pair encounter a bizarre creature that roams the nocturnal desert in search of prey.

SIX GUN TERRORS: SPINES

B illy climbed the telegraph pole like a squirrel up a tree. He pulled the lineman's pliers from the pocket of his overalls and cut the lines then clambered back down the pole.

"Good work, Billy," Red said. "All right, boys, let's go rob a bank."

Burke had ridden with him for years but never understood how Red Follansbee could be so calm just before a robbery. Of course, that was one reason why Red, not Burke was the leader of the most successful crew in three states. Red rode beside Burke as if he were on his way to a church social; no hurry, and none of the nerves Burke felt before every job. That was because Red always had a plan.

Red wore a dark, vested suit that contrasted Burke's scruffy saddle tramp outfit. Red's thinking was simple and smart at the same time. If they rode into Rimrock dressed all alike, they'd look like a gang. Billy Shanks wore bib overalls and a straw hat like a farmer and drove a buckboard, his horse in the traces wearing an English riding saddle hidden under its blanket. Tyler and Stratton looked like everyday ranch hands.

They split up a mile or so outside the town and rode in from different directions so they would look random. Red had shaved off the beard he wore in the wanted posters and hidden all but a trace of his trademark hair under a broad brimmed hat.

They arrived in Rimrock just before three in the afternoon, that time of day when the dry heat and a good lunch made people listless and complacent. The Mexicans had a good idea taking a *siesta* in the middle of the day, but Americans wanted everything all at once. Another reason for Red's choice of time was that by then, most of the bank's business would be finished; fewer customers to get in the way. The bank employees would be counting the day's money to put it in the safe for the night. Most important, the safe would be open.

Red went into the bank with Burke, playing the role of the wealthy cattleman looking for a safe place to keep his money, accompanied by his foreman. He carried a small leather satchel with two hundred dollars inside on top of an old suit of red flannel underwear. The bank, like the street, was quiet, two men at the tellers' windows and a white whiskered fellow in a suit at a desk behind the grille.

The main room of the bank was divided roughly in half by a waist high counter topped with a wrought iron grating that left windows for the tellers. Through an archway at the rear of the bank, Burke saw the safe, a free-standing affair eight feet tall on ornate ball and claw feet. The front of the safe was elaborately decorated with gold leaf vines and flowers and the words in fancy letters like a circus poster: First Bank of Rimrock. Burke chuckled at the name. As if this town will ever amount to enough to need a second one, he thought. Across the bottom of the door, Burke read, "Mosler Safe Company" and "Waterproof and Fireproof." Its door was ajar.

They stepped to the teller's window and the young man looked up from the pile of coins he was counting. "Yes, sir, may I help you?"

"My name is J. D. Cochran," Red said, in an authoritative voice, "This is my foreman Tom Smith, and I have a considerable sum to deposit for safekeeping." Red opened the satchel little and let the teller have a glimpse of his credentials. "But first, I'd like to speak to the man in charge."

"Certainly, sir," the teller said. "I'll see whether Mister Harriman is available." The teller left the window and walked past the man at the desk to rap on the door of an office with a brass nameplate too small to read at a distance. The teller went inside and returned in a moment to unlock the gate that led to the rear of the bank. "Would you come this way, please?"

Red said, "You can wait here, Tom," and followed the young man to the office.

Burke walked up to the other teller's window. He reached into his vest pocket and pulled out a twenty-dollar gold piece. He set it on the marble counter. "Could you give me smaller coins for this?" He grinned. "The saloon doesn't like to change big money."

The teller eyed him through a pair of rimless spectacles. "Certainly." Burke took note that the teller didn't call him "sir" like the other teller did Red. I could pick this hifalutin dandy up and throw him through the window, Burke thought. And maybe I will before all this is over.

Burke's reason for asking the teller to exchange the coin was so that then he would open the cash drawer and Burke could get a look inside. As the teller scooped some coins from a tray in the drawer, Burke saw the banknotes. Not as deep a stack as he would have liked to see, but you take what you get. The teller pushed four five-dollar pieces across the counter.

"Uh, could you give me some silver dollars for one of those fives?"

The teller gave Burke a look like he was a weevil in the flour sack and swept one of the five-dollar pieces back into the drawer. He counted out five silver dollars and slid them to Burke.

"Much obliged," Burke walked away from the window and stood in the open door. As he rolled a cigarette, he looked across the street where Billy was fussing with the traces on the buckboard. A few doors down, he saw Tyler lounging on a bench outside the general store drinking a bottle of sarsaparilla, his Winchester propped beside him in a fringed buckskin scabbard. Stratton watered his horse at a public trough nearby. A few people passed the doorway on some errand or another, and at the end of the street, the stagecoach from Brockton was rolling into town, a few minutes ahead of schedule.

Behind him, Burke heard Red's voice. "Well, this looks like the kind of place that will let me sleep at night." He and Harriman, a tall, slim man with dark hair and a thick moustache to match were coming out of the office. Both were smoking cigars and grinning like partners in crime.

"Let me show you our safe," Harriman said, "and I guarantee you'll have no worries." He led Red to the alcove. "Some banks try to hide their safes inside cabinetry or behind panels in the walls. We want our customers to see how secure their money really is."

"You have the only key?" Red said.

"No, there is one other locked up in the Sheriff's office, in case this one," he pulled out a heavy brass key on a chain from his pocket "should be lost somehow."

"You leave it open all day?"

Harriman chuckled, "Oh, no, the safe is opened in the morning just before business hours to supply the tellers with cash and locked again until closing time."

Burke flipped his cigarette through the doorway and into the street. He wished Red would get on with it. Red liked to play act as he called it, to gull the people he robbed before he pulled is gun. Sweat trickled down the side of Burke's face. Come on, Red, he thought.

Behind him, a clock chimed three strokes. The first teller started through the gate with a key in his hand. He was going to lock the door. Burke in the doorway, blocking his path.

"Excuse me," the teller said.

Burke didn't move.

"Step aside, please. You may remain inside, but I have to lock the door. It's three o'clock."

Burke was debating whether to argue or just knock the man down when he heard Harriman stammer, "I — I," and he realized the robbery had begun.

He whacked the teller across the side of the head with his pistol, and the man staggered backward. Burke waved an arm across the doorway. On the other side of the street Tyler stood, picking up the Winchester. He slid it out of the scabbard and thumbed back the hammer. Billy pulled the blanket from his horse's back and vaulted into the saddle, drawing his Colt.

Burke turned to see Harriman, hands in the air, backing toward the safe. Red set the valise down and reached inside, still holding his gun on the banker. He reached in, dug out the flannel union suit and tossed it aside. "Put the money in the bag. All of it."

Burke held his pistol under the first teller's chin and dragged him through the gate and to his cash drawer. He shoved the canvas sack he'd hidden in his trousers into the teller's hands. "You heard the man. Put the money in the bag." Over the teller's shoulder, he saw the whiskered cashier frozen, his hands flat on the desk. "Don't you move," Burke said, "or I'll kill you and him."

The first teller did as he was told, and Burke went to the second window. The second teller was filling the bag when the man at the desk yanked open a drawer, pulled out a pistol, swiveled in his chair, and fired two shots into Red's back.

Burke put a bullet through the cashier's head and as an afterthought, put one in the teller for good measure. The other teller cowered behind the counter, and Harriman stood open mouthed at the carnage. "You," Burke shouted. "Bring that satchel. Now!" Harriman grabbed the bag by the handles and brought it to the counter, his other hand in the air.

"Please, just take the money and go. Don't kill us."

Burke grabbed the bags and ran for the door.

Outside, two men with stars came running down the street at the sound of gunfire. Tyler shot one dead and put the other on the ground before putting a foot in the stirrup and throwing a leg over his horse. The townspeople were running for cover, ducking into doorways and around corners to get out of the line of fire.

Burke ran out of the bank and climbed into the saddle. He stuffed the loot into his saddlebags and spurred his horse into a quick gallop while Stratton and Tyler laid down cover fire. Billy emptied one pistol, scattering the citizens, threw it down, and drew another as he caught up with Burke near the stagecoach, putting his horse between the crowd and the money. "Where's Red?" he shouted.

"Dead," Burke snapped over his shoulder. As they passed the coach, the company guard, a grizzled old coot with one eye stepped from behind it and let fly with both barrels of his shotgun, knocking Billy out of the saddle. The buckshot hit Billy's horse in a few vital places, and after a couple of staggering steps, it fell into the street. Burke didn't look back.

Tyler and Stratton rode down an alleyway and clear of the commotion on Main Street. They quickly caught up with Burke and the three raced out of town and into the desert. A few miles away, the robbers stopped.

"What the hell happened back there?" Tyler demanded.

"One of them suits in the bank pulled a pistol out of a drawer and shot Red in the back."

"So, what do we do now?"

"What do you think we do?" Burke snapped. "We follow the plan."

"The plan?" Stratton said. "The plan just got two of us killed."

"I'm for taking shares and splitting up," Tyler said.

"Well, we ain't doing it yet," Burke told him. "What do you think? We pitch camp here and sit down and 'one for him and one for you and one for me' all afternoon? There'll be a posse after us any minute." Burke looked back the way they had come. "I'm surprised I don't see dust already."

"Burke's right," Stratton said. "Let's at least wait 'til dark."

"No, we follow the plan, go for the cache of food and water. Otherwise, none of us'll last a day in the desert, alone or together. Let's ride."

Burke spurred his horse and rode off. In a few seconds, Tyler and Stratton followed him.

• • •

Sheriff Ed Bannerman stood at the gun rack in the front room of the jail. He rubbed the unshaven side of his face and frowned. He'd been in the barber's chair getting a shave when the robbery occurred. He'd jumped out of the chair and run into the street with the apron still tied around his neck and his Colt drawn. Bad luck for him the action was headed for the other end of the street.

After a moment's deliberation, he chose a Henry lever action rifle, stuffed a handful of cartridges into his pocket, and walked out the door where Simms, his remaining deputy and eight of the local men stood in the street, itching to ride after the bank robbers.

"What are we waiting for? Those sons of bitches are getting away with our money," one of them shouted.

Bannerman shut him up with a hard look. "Let me explain the situation," he said. "These men ain't a bunch of yahoos, they're the Red Follansbee gang. They're professionals. They didn't just happen by Rimrock and say, 'Look, a bank; let's rob it.' Follansbee's famous for making plans."

"Well, he's dead now, ain't he?" another townsman said.

"He won't be making any more plans," Bannerman said, "but I'd bet my pay his men are following this one to the last whit." He looked at the men gathered around him. "You're shopkeepers, ranchers, everyday people, and you want to jump on horses and ride after a pack of stone-cold killers? What if the chase lasts two days? Three? What about food, water? They've got a plan. We need a plan too."

"You got one?"

"Yeah, I got one. There are only so many ways they can go across that desert and still find water. I know where the water holes are, and they likely do too. That's where we start, but we need to provision up for this and be ready to stay on it for a while. We need someone to ride the lines and find out where these bastards cut the telegraph wires and get them patched up so we can send a message to the Marshals for help."

"Help? There are only three of them. They're getting away while we stand here jawing about it."

"We've got to act smart, not jump like a scalded dog. Been enough people killed today. I don't want to see a half dozen of you die in the bargain. We'll get them, or the Marshals'll get them. They'll pay, but I want us all to live to see it happen.

"Micah, you take Mitchell and Clark over to your store and gather things we'll need for three days' journey. He turned to Simms, his deputy. "See that everyone going has a proper rifle and pistol. If they don't have one or the other, issue one from the hardware in the office." He turned to another of the men. "Colton, you go with Sawyer and find the break in the telegraph line so he can fix it. While he's there, he can tap into the line and send for help."

"But I want to go with you," Colton protested.

"The quicker you leave now, the more likely you'll be back before we ride out." He turned and went into the jail, ending the argument. Simms followed him in and closed the door.

"How good a chance you think we have catching those three?"

"Half and half. I'm figuring they'll move west and then cut south for the state line. I want to head southwest and try to block their escape route. We get a telegram off, we can have the Marshals and maybe even the Cavalry come at them from different directions and bottle them up."

"Sounds like it might work."

"Yeah, but it might fail too. If they have food and water and maybe fresh horses cached, we'll have the Devil's own time catching up with them. I said provisions for three days. In a day and a half, we'll send the others back and you and I'll ride on with the supplies that are left. Ought to last us a week or more if we're careful."

"What if the others don't want to turn back?"

"One day in that desert, let alone two and most of them will be happy to go home. Those that don't —" Bannerman shook his head. "I guess I'll just have to persuade them."

• • •

Burke, Tyler, and Stratton stopped five miles out of town. So far, they saw no sign of a posse. "I don't get it," Tyler said. "Why ain't they chasing us?"

"Because the Sheriff's smart and he knows the terrain. If he waits for sundown, his posse and their horses will need less water. He'll follow the trail because that's the fastest way for us to get away. Red figured Bannerman'd go water hole to water hole. We won't. That's why we're going off the path soon. We'll pick up food and water where Red and I hid them and the posse'll come up empty."

"Where's all this food and water hid?" Stratton said.

"Couple of different places."

"What if something happens to you? What do Tyler and me do?"

Burke shrugged. "You die, I guess. All the more reason to make sure I stay alive." Burke smiled. Red was wise to tell only him where the supplies and water were cached. Burke would never have turned on his old friend, but Red didn't trust the others to not shoot them both in the back for the money. "Watch for the big stand of cottonwoods on the right. There's where the ride gets tough."

A short time later, the trio arrived at the cluster of trees by the side of the trail. "Ok, boys," Burke said. "Dismount and cut some branches."

"What do we do with them?"

"Rope them to your saddle and drag them behind you for a mile or so to brush over our tracks. We'll ride single file. Tyler, you in the middle; Stratton, you ride tail. Get to it."

• • •

The posse was two hours out of Rimrock and still excited over the chase. Give them 'til this time tomorrow, Bannerman thought, and most of them will have had a belly full of heat, grit, and the unforgiving sun and be ready to turn back. The sun was low in the sky ahead of them, and the light was fading when he spotted the clump of cottonwoods ahead. Bannerman held up a hand for the party to halt.

"Simms, you ride on ahead and take a look at those trees. See what you might find." Bannerman pulled a piece of jerky from his saddlebag and gnawed off a piece.

Simms did as he was told and was back in a minute. "Looks like they passed by here. Some limbs fresh cut. Firewood?"

Bannerman shook his head. "These boys are tricky, but it's a trick I've seen before. I'm guessing they went off trail here. Let's go have a look." He and Simms dismounted and walked a few paces off the trail. Bannerman sat on his haunches and studied the ground. "If you look close, you can see ripples in the sand to either hand. Here it looks like it's been broomed."

"What do we do now?"

"Make torches. If we're lucky, they'll think they fooled us. If they stop for the night, we may catch up with them sooner than I hoped."

"And when we do?"

"I hope they're all asleep, but I wouldn't bet my life on it."

• • •

The outlaws arrived at the first cache just after sunset. The long shadows melted into darkness and made the whole landscape a deep violet. "Here," Burke said. He dismounted and walked to a patch of scrub beside a Joshua tree. He tugged at a bush, and it came away with a dry rustle of branches. Under it was a wooden slat crate. Inside the crate they found tinned food, beef and beans, and skins of water.

"How far to the next one?" Stratton asked.

"No further than need be."

"That's no answer."

"It's all the answer you're going to get."

Burke punched the tip of his knife through the top of a can of beef and pried the lid away with a metallic ripping sound. He pulled a chunk of the shredded beef from the can and put it in his mouth. The salt was enough to curl his tongue, but hunger put aside issues of taste.

The moon was rising, and in its cold light Burke could see that Tyler and Stratton had stepped away and had their heads together talking in low voices. In a minute, they came back.

"We need to talk," Stratton said.

"About what?"

"About the money?" Tyler said. "What if something goes wrong? Hell, something already went wrong. I say we split the money here and now. We ain't even counted it yet. We don't know what we have."

"Whatever it is, you'll get a bigger share without Red and Billy, so shut up."

"That's another thing," Tyler said. "Red always got a double share because he was leader. You think you're gonna take that now he's dead?"

Burke set down the tin. "I could." Stratton and Tyler sidled away from each other so he couldn't watch both of their gun hands at once.

"Well, you ain't Red." Tyler raised his hand and, in the moonlight, Burke saw the glint of a Derringer. It couldn't hit a board fence at fifty feet, but that close, Tyler's odds improved a lot. "We settle this here and now."

"How about you, Stratton? What do you say"

"I agree. let's settle this now." He drew his pistol and shot Tyler through the head.

Burke looked at the dead outlaw lying on the ground then back to Stratton? "Am I next?"

"Hell, no," Stratton said, holstering his gun. "You know where the water is, and I didn't want to spend the rest of this venture worrying which of you was going to draw on the other. I don't care if you hold the cash. Better to be rid of Tyler now."

"And of course, the shares just got bigger."

"Not just the money, there's the food and water to think about." Stratton

He pulled a chunk of the shredded beef from the can...

pulled a boot from the corpse and held it sole to sole with his own, gauging the size. Satisfied, he pulled off its mate.

"You're a practical man, Stratton."

"Kept me alive up to now."

Burke walked over to Tyler's horse and shot it between the eyes.

"What'd you do that for?"

"Like you said, more water for us."

• • •

Three miles from the trail, Bannerman found the discarded branches and the tracks in the sand from the outlaws' horses. The moon was near full and the hoof prints were little pockets of shadow against the blue-white sand. "How are the volunteers holding up?" he asked Simms.

"So far so good. I guess the thrill of the chase hasn't worn off yet."

"Let's stop long enough to get something to eat, then I want to get going again. Look at those tracks. The horses aren't running. These fellows are taking their time, maybe because they figure they lost us. I want to press that advantage."

• • •

Stratton and Burke didn't bother to bury Tyler. They loaded up their supplies and rode away about the time the moon hit its zenith. Desert nights are the inverse of desert days. The air cools down as quickly as the daylight fades, but this night, the wind blew hot across the sand.

Burke rode carefully, straining his eyes in the moonlight for any hazard. What I really need, he thought, is a pair of eyes in the back of my head. Stratton chose me over Tyler, but if he killed a partner that easy, he could do the same for me. I'll have to do some hard thinking before we get to the end of this ride.

Dawn painted the sky an angry red.

"That might mean trouble," Burke said, wetting a finger and gauging the wind.

"Might," Stratton agreed. "I don't much care for sandstorms."

"On the other hand, it might force a posse to turn back."

"There is that."

"Of course, we're like a rat in a downspout, halfway through and can't back out 'cause the cat's looking down at the top. No way to go but forward."

"What the hell," Stratton said, kneeing his horse in the ribs. "Neither of us is gonna live forever anyway." Two hours later, they saw the distant rolling cloud of the sandstorm come boiling from one end of the horizon to the other.

"Looks like a bad one."

"Time to dig in."

"Yep. I don't feel so bad now about not burying Tyler."

"Nature provides."

• • •

Burke and Stratton found a dry wash that allowed them to hunker down and gave their mounts some protection. They tied them together side to side and lashed blankets over the horses' heads to protect their eyes and to keep the sand from their nostrils. Their own faces they covered with their bandannas soaked with water from the canteens.

The approaching storm struck with a sound like a freight train and with no less force. The sun was blotted out, leaving the men in a brown twilight as the wind ebbed and flowed, scouring the already barren land with grit like coarse buckshot.

The outlaws huddled in the wash until the sand reached their knees and shoulders. Burke braced himself and stood, fighting his way out of the sand. The wind struck him like a giant hand, and if his legs weren't buried, he might have been tossed like a rag doll across the landscape. As it was, he felt as if the wind might snap him off at the knees like a twig.

Choking on the fine grit, he leaned down and shouted in Stratton's ear. "Stand up. You'll suffocate if you don't." He pulled Stratton to his feet, and the two locked arms and braced themselves as the hissing sand rose past their knees.

Then as quickly as it had begun, the wind died down and with a final hiss, the last of the sand sifted down from a sky turned carmine by the angry eye of the sun. Burke's ears rang with a dull tone from the roar of the wind. He pulled down his bandanna and blinked grit from the corners of his eyes. In the near distance, little sand devils whirled, barely visible through the curtain of dust that hung in the air.

"Damn," Stratton said. That was a bad 'un."

"Yeah," Burke said. "Let's see to the horses." That would have to wait. First, he had to free his legs. He struggled to pull upward and free his lower legs, finally lying bent kneed on his back while Stratton scooped the dry grit away with both hands. Once they were loose, they set to freeing the horses. It was noon by the time they were ready to move on again, and though the sun was less bright, it was no less hot.

Stratton looked around him. "I didn't think this place could look more bleak. How will you find our way out of here?"

"We'll watch the sun for direction and if the sky clears enough, we'll look for the pole star tonight. Or," he pulled an object from his trouser pocket, "we'll use this." He held a compass in the palm of his hand. "Red was pretty smart. He learned how to use one when he rode with the buffalo skinners, and he taught me."

"I'll sleep better tonight knowing that."

"Maybe tonight we both will."

• • •

"Well, we're done, I'm afraid." Bannerman shook his head. He and Simms had ridden ahead to look for tracks. The dust storm petered out before it got to the posse, but it obliterated any trace of the fugitives. "We could press a little further and see whether we pick up a sign, but I'm doubtful."

"The boys'll be disappointed."

Bannerman turned his glare to Simms. "Disappointed? Hell, I'm disappointed. But from what I could see of that dust storm, it would have killed half those townies. I was going to send them back, but now I'm ready to go back with them."

Simms shielded his eyes and turned a slow three-quarter circle. "Hold up. Look northwest."

Bannerman squinted into the harsh glare. Dark specks spiraled in the distant sky. "Vultures."

"Looks like."

"Somebody's bad luck may be our good luck. Ride back and get the posse."

Sims rode off, leaving Bannerman to stare at the slowly wheeling birds. Dear Lord, he thought, please let it be all three.

Bannerman got part of his wish. The posse found Tyler's barefoot corpse lying face up with an ugly vulture perched on his chest worrying at his upper lip with its hooked beak. Others were tearing at the dead horse as more flapped to a landing to join in the macabre banquet.

"Ugh," one of the townsmen said. Bannerman heard the click of the man's pistol.

"Don't you shoot that bird," Bannerman growled. "We find this man's partners, you might wish you still had that bullet. Besides, these birds probably have more right to be here than we do." He stepped out of the stirrup and walked up to the corpse waving his hat at the vulture and shouting "Hyah, git."

The indignant vulture hopped backward off Tyler's chest and cast a malevolent stare at Bannerman with an eye like an onyx bead nestled in raw flesh. For a moment, it hesitated, as if contemplating a fight to defend its meal from the newcomer, then it flapped its wings and retreated to the company of its fellows. It cast a last look at Bannerman over its wing as if to say, "Someday, *amigo*, you'll come onto my preserve one time too many, and then we will see who wins."

"That's one of the gang. I recognize the snakeskin hatband," Simms said, squatting beside the body. "He's been shot in the head,"

"So much for honor among thieves." Bannerman turned to the posse. "All right, fellows. That's one. Now, a couple of you come help me dig a grave."

"We ain't taking him back?"

"On what? You gonna wake up his horse? Maybe you'd like to walk back so we can throw him over your saddle. I ain't leaving anyone for these miserable birds."

Once Tyler was buried, Bannerman announced that the posse was returning to Rimrock. There was some token protest, but the men were glad to go back to the comforts of hearth and home.

"I know you hate to quit," Simms said to Bannerman as they rode away from Tyler's grave.

"I do, but I take some comfort in the idea that if the last two of those skunks don't kill each other, the desert will likely do the job for them."

• • •

Burke spent the rest of the day coughing, and Stratton didn't fare much better. By the time they got the horses clear of the sand, it was after noon, and the air was thick with dust for a while longer. The going was slow where the loose sand had drifted, and both the men and the animals were tiring rapidly.

"How much longer 'til we stop?"

"You can stop any time you like," Burke said. "Me, I plan to keep going to the next cache of food and water."

Stratton cursed under his breath and kept riding. If he was sure he could get out of the desert on the water they had left, he would have shot Burke dead right then. After we reach the next cache, Stratton thought, I'm going to end this partnership.

Burke followed the compass, and near the end of the second day, they saw a stand of scrub like they'd found the day before. "There's the cache," Burke said. "Just the two of us, it ought to be more than enough to make it out of this god-forsaken desert."

Stratton slid out of his saddle to the ground. "Where is it?"

"Wasn't much brush, so Red and I buried it." Burke pulled his revolver from the holster. "Before we get to digging it up, I think this might be a good time to divvy things."

Stratton eyed the pistol. "You gonna kill me, ain't you?"

"A man always fears what he'd think to do to somebody else, don't he? No, I'm not going to kill you if you don't make me."

"Then why the gun?"

"I know I'm not going to kill you over the money. I'm not so sure about you not killing me."

"I could have killed you any time I wanted," Stratton said. "But I didn't."

"Because you didn't know where the cache was. Now you do." Burke stepped down from his stirrup. He threw the saddlebag with the money on the ground at Stratton's feet. "Suppose you sit down and count it into two piles, one for you, one for me. Even up. Then you and I will go our separate ways. But first, unbuckle your gun belt and throw it over there by the brush."

Stratton did as he was told.

"And while you're at it, toss that Derringer of Tyler's over there too."

Stratton glared at Burke.

"Why are you angry, Stratton? Because I pulled my gun before you thought to pull yours? Be happy I don't just shoot you and take it all."

Stratton hunkered down and dumped the money out of the saddlebag. In a few minutes, he had the bills divided and was separating the coins. 'That's good enough," Burke said. "Put one pile in the saddlebag. You can keep the coins for your trouble."

Stratton hesitated.

"Oh, come on," Burke said, "show some smarts. If I was going to kill you, why would I waste the time to have you count all that money? I would have just taken it all. I only want my share." In a few moments, Stratton had divided the money. He loaded the bag and Burke said, "Now step away."

Stratton eyed his gun belt, counting how many steps to reach it.

"You were going to kill me, weren't you?" Burke said.

"Thought crossed my mind."

"You shouldn't have shot Tyler. He would've backed your play." Burke picked up the bag and threw it across his saddle. "Of course, if Red was here, there wouldn't have been a play, would there?"

Burke picked up Stratton's gun belt and put it across his horse's saddle. "I'm going to ride away, and I'm taking your horse and your guns with me. I have enough water to get me to the nearest oasis. You can have the provisions in the cache all for yourself. I'll tie your horse a mile or so away from here. You follow the tracks and you'll find him and your guns. Take note of which way I go, and ride another direction. I see you again in this life, I'll figure you mean me harm, and I will kill you."

With that, Burke stepped into his saddle and rode away, leading Stratton's horse behind him.

Stratton stared as Burke disappeared over a dune. "God damn it!" He kicked a plume of sand into the air and cursed his bad luck.

Burke heard him shout and shook his head. Red should have been here. Then there wouldn't have been such a falling out because everyone was afraid of him. But Red planned for everything, including double crossers.

Stratton tugged at the brush. He'd get the food and water first then he'd set out after Burke. He dug with both hands in the fading light, throwing sand in every direction until his fingers found rough wood. It was a crate like the other one. He wrestled it out of the ground and stood up straight, backing out of the brush.

He felt something crawl under the gauntlet of his glove and looked down. His arm was covered with black, crawling things. The box was buried in a scorpion's nest.

Stratton threw the box down and saw his forearms and legs were covered with dark horrors as big as his hand. A bolt of pain shot up his arm from the one in his glove, and another scorpion crawled into his collar from his shoulder.

"Aaugh!" Stratton swiped frantically at his arms, legs, and chest while the scorpions stung him, and stung him, and stung him.

An hour later, Burke circled back to pick up the money. Stratton lay on his back, his face a swollen, pulpy mass. His tongue lolled, and his breath came in ragged gasps. Burke crouched beside him, and Stratton's head turned toward him. "Kill me," he moaned. "Please."

Burke stood. "I already told you, I won't kill you unless you make me, and right now, you ain't in any shape to make me do anything." He scooped up Stratton's share of the money, mounted his horse and rode away. I know, he thought, right now Red's laughing in hell.

• • •

The moon had all but set when Burke stopped to rest. He was already out of the posse's reach, and another day's trek would get him to Sparksville. He was glad Red took him into his confidence early on and glad too that Red taught him so much. He'd miss Red, but those were the risks you took robbing banks.

Ahead, a lone saguaro cast a long shadow across the scrub and sand. Might be good place to camp, Burke thought. Must be some water below or that cactus wouldn't look so hardy. If I was short on water, I could cut out the pulp and suck out the moisture, but there's no need for that.

The saguaro stood with arms bent upward like a parody of a holdup victim. "Relax *amigo*, Burke said with a laugh. "I mean you no harm."

He tethered the horses to a stand of brush a few yards from the cactus and opened a tin of beef. After he emptied that, he pried open a can of peaches. He speared a peach half with his knife and put it into his mouth. The moist sweetness was welcome after the long, dry day. He ate the peaches and even drank the syrup from the tin. Life was looking pretty good.

Burke dozed off about the time the moon set. The horses woke him, whinnying piteously and pounding their hooves in the sand. Then one of them let out a shriek that chilled Burke's blood. He jumped to his feet and drew his Colt. In the dim starlight, he saw dark shapes wrestling. Then one of the horses broke away and set off at a full gallop, running for its life.

The shapes separated. One fell to the ground while the other stood upright. It was a man, but not a man. Burke heard a dry rustling sound, something dragging across the grainy sand, something spreading long arms in the dark. He fired four shots, five, six into its torso as he backed away, but the creature kept coming. Burke tripped on his saddle and fell backwards.

The arms reached for him, wrapped around him and lifted him, holding him in an ungodly embrace. And then the spines punched through clothing and skin as the grip tightened, squeezing the living moisture out of him. And it drank and drank and drank under the indifferent stars.

• • •

"There's a lot to be said for taking the train." Durken tipped his head back and swallowed a mouthful of water from his canteen. He took a second pull and sloshed it around his mouth before spitting it into his bandanna and wiping the dust from his face with it. He ran his fingers over his moustache to get it away from his mouth.

"True," McAfee replied, but that would get us back to the ranch a day earlier and back under Eldridge's thumb again. I kinda like being free and easy for a day or two."

"Well, the next time General Sherman sends us on an errand, I hope it's to some place with green grass and trees."

The cowboys, foremen for Homer Eldridge's Triple Six Ranch, were from time to time conscripted by General William Tecumseh Sherman, whom they served as scouts in the Georgia campaign, to deal with matters that fell outside the regular purview of Sherman's prosecution of the "Indian Situation."

"Yeah, I confess I'd enjoy something to look at besides sand and scrub." McAfee put a hand over his eyes to shield them. "Look yonder. Is that a horse?"

"Looks like."

A hundred yards from the trail, the chestnut stallion seemed to be staggering, and when they got closer, the cowboys saw it was in a bad way. Its tongue lolled out and the poor beast could barely hold up its head. Its legs were white with sand, and its muzzle was caked with alkali.

McAfee dismounted and approached the horse carefully. "Easy, fellow," he crooned. "Easy, boy." The stallion was still wearing a halter, and McAfee took it gently in one hand and tried to lead the animal to the trail, but after two or three faltering steps, the horse collapsed and rolled onto its side.

"He's done," Durken said.

"You're right. That's too bad. From the looks of him, he was a fine animal a day or two ago."

"What a waste."

McAfee drew his pistol and put the muzzle against the side of the stallion's head. Its eye rolled toward him. "Sorry, fellow." One shot, and the horse's suffering was over.

"You know what we gotta ask," Durken said.

"Uh-huh. What happened to the rider."

"Guess we better find out."

The unlucky stallion left a meandering trail of hoof prints that was easy enough to follow. A few hours in, the trail became less rambling, charting the horse's dissolution in reverse. Finally, the tracks showed a straight line and evidence of a full gallop.

"Horse was running full tilt a while."

"I don't see any other tracks to show somebody chasing him," Durken said.

"You're right. That is strange. What would make him run like that?"

"Dunno. We keep following the trail, maybe we'll find out."

Soon they saw the vultures clustered over a pair of bodies, one a horse, and one a man.

Durken shooed them away from the corpse and recoiled at the sight of the body. "Holy Moses."

The body was definitely human, but shriveled down to a wrinkled hulk and its skin the hue and texture of jerky.

"Good Lord," McAfee said. "Never saw one looked like that before. "Horse looks the same, like they've been lying here for a month to be dried out like that."

"That horse we found couldn't have been wandering that long and belong to him."

"This fellow looks like that Egyptian mummy the traveling show brought to town last Spring."

"Look where the vultures were at him. The meat's dry and hard."

"That's another item. The vultures should've picked him clean a long time ago while he was soft and fresh." McAfee pried open one of the deep furrows on the man's face with his thumb and forefinger. "What's this?" A puncture showed in the wizened flesh. He spread the furrow further and found another hole.

Durken leaned closer. "Snake bite?"

"Don't think so. They're too far apart, unless it was a mighty big snake and it had needles for fangs. The holes aren't humped like a snake bite, either." McAfee opened a crease in the neck. "Here are more."

They opened the body's shirt to find the chest dotted with punctures. "Looks like he walked into a cactus," Durken said.

McAfee looked around. "Except there's not a cactus in sight." He turned to the horse and flapped his arms at the vultures. "G'wan." The vultures retreated to a safe distance. The horse was shriveled like the dead man, its skin stretched taut as a drum head over its ribs. It too was pocked with holes.

He stepped over the dead animal and picked up a fallen saddlebag. He opened the flap and whistled. "Durken, take a look at this." He held the flap open, and Durken saw the bag was stuffed with money.

"How much you think is in there?"

"Couldn't guess, but it looks like a lot." He rummaged in the bag and pulled out a torn strip of paper. "Here's a band for fifty dollars in ones. Says First Bank of Rimrock on it."

"That's that little town we passed through a week ago on our way out."

"That's the one. You suppose somebody robbed the bank since we were there?"

"If he did, he didn't live to spend the money. There's another mystery. Who killed this man and his horse?"

"More like *what* killed them."

"It wasn't bandits, or they would've taken this money. And another question: why did one rider have two saddled horses?"

"Maybe there was somebody with him who killed him and rode off on that horse we saw, and he's lying in the desert someplace, dead himself."

"But why didn't the killer take the money?"

"Beats me. You know, if we were dishonest types, we could live high for a long time with this much cash," McAfee said.

"But we aren't."

"No, we aren't."

"Guess we better head for Rimrock."

"What about our friend there?"

"Can't take him with us." Durken took his knife from its sheath.

"What are you doing?"

"I'm taking a sample to show the local sheriff, otherwise, he probably won't believe a word we say." He cut a small square patch with one of the holes in it from the corpse's skin. It peeled away dry, and when he felt it between his thumb and forefinger, it felt like tanned leather. "I figure the Sheriff'll want to come have a look around for himself. We'd best leave things as they are."

"What about the vultures?"

"As tough a chew as that body is, there should still be plenty left for the Sheriff."

"Maybe if we wrap him in a blanket, and throw some sand over him, the birds'll be satisfied with the horse."

• • •

Durken and McAfee rode down the main street of Rimrock late in the afternoon. Every person they passed stared at them and followed them with their eyes as they rode by. Gun hands subtly moved toward holsters, and people's heads went together in whispered conversation.

"Friendly folk in this town, eh?"

"They're leery of strangers now. Talk about locking the barn door. They probably think we came to rob the bank again."

"That's foolish. There's nothing in it to rob. It's all in that bag over your saddle.

"Dry as I am, I think we'd better go straight to the Sheriff instead of stopping at the saloon for a beer."

"You're probably right."

The cowboys tied their horses to the rail in front of the Rimrock jail, the only building besides the bank that was made of brick rather than wood. A swing sign over the door announced that Edward Bannerman was the Sheriff. McAfee slung the saddlebag over his shoulder, and the cowboys went inside.

A tall, rawboned man with a star on his vest sat behind a desk playing solitaire. He set down his cards and stood, favoring his right leg.

"You Bannerman?" Durken said.

"I'm Deputy Tom Hayes. Who are you?"

"My name's McAfee, and this is Durken. We need to see the Sheriff."

"He ain't here right now, but he should be back in a little while."

"All right. We'll just go to that cafe we saw down the street and get something to eat."

"Well what do you want to see him about?"

"Tell him we have some information about a bank robbery." Durken said. He turned to leave.

"Wait—wait. What information?"

"We'll talk to the Sheriff."

McAfee and Durken went down the street to the cafe where the inviting aroma of fried chicken wafted from the doorway. "You know, we probably won't get to finish our meal, maybe not even dig into it."

"Could be, but I don't plan on waiting around all day for the Sheriff's good pleasure, especially when we're doing him a favor, not the other way around."

"I see your point."

Supper arrived, platters of chicken, potatoes and beans with good strong coffee. Halfway through their meal, a big man with a ruddy face, bushy eyebrows, and a bigger star than the two deputies who followed him came through the door.

"I'm Sheriff Bannerman."

"I'm McAfee, and this is Durken."

"Hayes says you have information about the bank robbery." Every head in the cafe turned toward them.

"Then there was a robbery?"

"Just a few days ago. The Red Follansbee gang robbed our bank. A banker killed Follansbee and got shot for his trouble along with one of the tellers. Another one got gunned down in the street trying to get away. A third we found dead on the trail, likely murdered by one of his own. Now what do you have to tell me?"

McAfee looked around. "The story might put people off their supper. Do you want us to share it with the whole town, or do you want to take this conversation over to the jail?"

Bannerman looked around at the eager faces of the people at the tables. "Let's go to the jail."

McAfee put a silver dollar on the table, finished his coffee and stood up. "Come on, Durken.

Durken shoveled two more bites of chicken into his mouth, wiped it on his sleeve and pushed back his chair.

• • •

In the jail, Durken and McAfee stood in front of Bannerman's desk with the deputies behind them.

"So far, all you've told me are your names. Who are you, and what are you doing riding through here?"

"We're with the Army," McAfee said. "We're on an errand for General Sherman."

"You have proof of that?"

"We do. I have a letter that explains it all. I'm going to reach into my vest and take it out." He handed the letter to Bannerman, who read it and handed it back. "I'm satisfied." He nodded to his deputies, who moved around to Bannerman's desk and stood to either side like bookends. "Now, tell me what you know about the robbery."

"First, there's this." McAfee set Burke's saddle bag on the desk and opened the flap. Money poured out. Bannerman's eyes widened. "Wrapper in there says this came from the First Bank of Rimrock.

"Where did you find this?"

"Out in the desert along with a dead man and his horse."

"How much is in there?"

"Didn't count it. Figured that was your place."

Bannerman turned to Simms. "I'd guess Harriman's at home now. Go fetch him." Simms hesitated. "Don't worry; you won't miss nothing." Simms went out the door. "You say one dead man?"

"Yep," Durken replied.

"Two got killed here, and we found a third dead. That leaves one unaccounted for. Now tell me how you found this money."

They were most of the way through the story when Simms returned with the banker in shirt sleeves and an undone collar. He stared at the pile of money and heaved a sigh of relief like he might if he found his missing child. Bannerman held up the torn wrapper. "This says it's your money. How much did the robbers take?"

"Two thousand nine hundred forty-two dollars and sixteen cents."

"Count it."

For the next ten minutes Harriman carefully organized the money by denomination and counted it twice. "Three thousand one hundred twenty-one dollars and forty-two cents."

"Set the difference aside and put what they stole from you back in the vault. Leave the rest here. And thank these men for turning it in."

"Yes, yes, of course," Harriman said. "Thank you both." He gathered the money and clutched it to his bosom.

"Simms, go with him."

Through the window, Durken watched the banker and the deputy walking away. "Didn't occur to him to even ask our names."

Bannerman shrugged. "He's a banker. All he cares about is the money. You brought it here, so I'm guessing that you weren't in on the robbery. But the dead man. Why didn't you bring in the body?"

"His horse is as dead as he is, and we didn't have one to spare. We can take you to him, though. You'll want to see for yourself. He was full of holes."

"You mean somebody shot him?"

"No, somebody punched a bunch of holes all over him with a needle or some such, his horse too. He was dried up like he'd been dead in the sun for a couple of weeks, but it couldn't have been more than a day or so, based on when the robbery happened."

Durken fished in his pocket and pulled out the square of skin and laid it on Bannerman's desk. The sheriff stared at the wrinkled relic.

"I've never seen the like," McAfee said. "Have you?"

"Nope." Bannerman picked up the patch and turned it over in his fingers. "You say he was covered with holes like this?"

"A good part of him was," McAfee said. "We didn't strip him down, mind you, but from what we could see, he was poked through most of his body, even through his clothes."

Simms had returned in the middle of the discussion, and Bannerman handed the skin to him. He handed it to Hayes, who felt its texture between his thumb and forefinger and shuddered. He laid the patch back on the desk.

"The horse looked pretty much the same, holes in him and shriveled like a dried apple."

Bannerman said, "How far a ride to where you found him?"

"It took us three hours to get here," McAfee said, "but we followed our tracks back to the main trail. Using a compass, I can likely take us across the desert to the place in less time."

"We still have enough daylight to get there. We'll take an extra horse for the body. See to that, Simms. Tom, you stay here and make sure nobody kills anybody while we're gone."

Hayes stared at the patch of skin and made no protest about being left behind.

• • •

"So, your deputy was shot in the robbery?" McAfee said as they rode across the sand.

"Two of them. Tom caught a bullet in the leg. Roy Hobbes wasn't so lucky. He was dead before the robbers cleared the end of town."

"So, Follansbee was killed in the bank and one of his gang was killed in the street."

"Yep. That left three of them. One we found shot in the head within a day. The others escaped."

"Guess they didn't get very far," Durken said.

"It burns me up they were only a few hours away from Rimrock, but how could we find them out here?" Bannerman made a sweeping gesture with his arm. "Hundreds of square miles of nothing."

"Based on that riderless horse we found, I'm thinking maybe the last man's dead too."

"You say he was covered with holes like this?"

"We may never know."

"And that's the hell of it."

• • •

McAfee was right. They found the vultures pecking and tearing at the horse in about two hours. The corpse was undisturbed. They uncovered the body and stripped off its clothing. Simms found a silver turnip watch in a trouser pocket with the initials J. B. engraved on the back. "J. B. Jed Burke?"

"Could be. He's one of Follansbee's regulars. Of course, he could have stolen the watch from someone else. But for now, let's just work on the idea that this is Burke."

Durken kicked at the sand and uncovered a revolver. He sniffed at the barrel. "Been fired." He flipped out the cylinder and turned it. "All six shots."

"Fired at who?" Bannerman said. "That's the question."

Burke's body was pocked with an irregular scatter of holes from his face to his shins, where his boots protected them. The most disturbing sight was the pair of holes through his eyelids, peeled back from eyeballs shriveled like dull white prunes. "Let's roll him over." Two broad bands of punctures crossed Burke's back, but while withered, most of the skin on the back of Burke's body was unmarked.

"That's strange too. If he was on his back, all the holes would be in the front of him, but they aren't."

"Just like somebody gave him a bear hug," Durken said. "Picked him up and squeezed him good and hard."

"I'm starting to think we shouldn't be saying some *body* and should start saying some *thing*," McAfee said.

"What?" Bannerman stood up to look McAfee in the eye. "What do you mean some thing?"

"I know porcupines have quills —"

"You telling me a porcupine did this?"

"Not offhand, but maybe something like it we haven't seen. An animal that moves around the desert killing others and sucking out their moisture."

"That's crazy," Simms said.

"Maybe so, but Durken and I have run across some pretty strange things working for the General."

"Such as?"

"Things we aren't allowed to discuss."

"Hmmp," Bannerman grunted. He looked to the horizon where the sun was sinking. "It'll be dark soon. I want to get back to Rimrock."

"Just a thought, Sheriff," McAfee said, "but if there is something strange out there, do you want to run into it in the dark?"

Simms spoke up, a little too quickly for confidence. "Maybe he's right, Sheriff. Maybe we ought to stay 'til first light."

Bannerman chewed at his lower lip while he pondered the thought. "I suppose we could do that."

"We have some grub," Durken said.

"All right, we'll stay, but we're going to leave at first light. I want Doc Porter to see this body."

• • •

The moon rose, pouring long patches of ink behind stands of brush and the scant desert trees. The campfire had burned low, and Simms was snoring, propped against his saddle. For the third time, Bannerman was talking his way through Burke's condition, as if repeating the details might somehow resolve the puzzle.

"Well, Sheriff," Durken said, "Burke's dead, whatever it is killed him. We may never know exactly what happened."

"I can't abide with that," Bannerman said. "All my life, things have been ordinary, regular, natural."

"And this bothers you because it isn't?"

"This happened in my bailiwick, damn it. I want an explanation. I —"

A nervous whinny from one of the horses made him stop in mid-sentence. The three stood, and McAfee said, "Wake Simms." He and Durken drew their pistols.

McAfee turned slowly, taking a long look around him. "Durken, There." He pointed behind them to a dark shape standing thirty yards away. "Did you see a cactus there before sundown?"

"Nope."

"At that size, I'm assuming it didn't spring up like Jonah's bottle gourd. How did it get there?"

"What is it?" Bannerman said.

Durken pointed. "Looks like a big saguaro out there where there wasn't one before. And mirages don't happen in the moonlight."

McAfee took a half-burned stick from the fire as a torch. "Let's go have a look."

Durken picked up the hatchet from their pile of firewood. "What's that for?" Bannerman asked, cocking the hammers of his shotgun.

"Burke's empty six-shooter tells me bullets may not be a useful defense."

"Against what?"

"That's what we aim to find out."

The four crept slowly toward the saguaro. In the dancing light of the torch, it was hard to tell what moved and what didn't, black shadows twitching behind every bush and tree. The cactus shone a sleek bright green, its skin studded with long, wicked spines. They circled around it, guns at the ready. Simms stepped within six feet of its firelit side, and suddenly two slits opened, revealing a pair of golden eyes.

Simms sprung back, startled, but he was too slow. The cactus swung and one of its limbs caught the deputy's arm and wrapped around it. Simms screamed in pain and terror.

McAfee fired into the thick trunk as Durken swung the hatchet. The blade bit deep and a shrill cry came from what could only be described as a mouth below the glowing eyes. Durken chopped at it again and the cactus whirled and swung another limb at him barely missing his face.

"Get out of the way," Bannerman shouted and fired both barrels. The buckshot tore through the fleshy pulp and the limb came off. Simms fell to the ground, still screaming. In the torchlight, McAfee saw the withered flesh of his hand.

The saguaro turned and ran away from them, skimming over the sand on what must have been feet.

"Get it off me!" Simms screamed. "Get it off me!"

Durken put his foot on Simms' arm and pushed the blade of the hatchet between his arm and the piece of cactus. He levered upward with both hands and twisted the handle. The spines came free with a wet sucking sound.

"Lord in Heaven," Bannerman said. "What was that?"

"Burke's killer, I'd reckon," McAfee said. "And we've got to catch it now or we may never find it again." He and Durken ran for their horses. Bannerman put a shoulder in Simms' armpit and half-dragged, half-carried him back to the campfire. The Sheriff ripped the sleeve from Simms' shirt and stared in horror at the wounds that covered the exposed arm.

"You stay here," Bannerman said. "We're going after that thing."

Simms nodded and lay back on his saddle. Bannerman dug in his saddle bag and pulled out a tin flask. He uncapped it and poured most of it over Simms' arm. The rest, Simms swallowed in one pull.

Bannerman saddled up and he and the cowboys rode off into the moonlit desert.

• • •

"What do we do if we catch it? Shooting didn't stop it." Bannerman shouted over the pounding of the horse's hooves.

"We'll surround him and lasso the bastard from three directions," Durken said. "We tie the ropes to the saddle horns and keep them taut from three directions, it won't be able to reach any of us or the horses."

"Then what?"

"Then we figure out how to kill it."

The tracks were difficult to follow, but as the moon crept toward the horizon, they spotted their quarry, still running, but slower now, as if fatigue and injury were wearing it down. Durken spurred Sweetheart and the big bay circled ahead and to the left of the cactus man while McAfee overtook it to its right. Bannerman closed the triangle by coming up behind.

Durken threw his rope first. It landed over the running cactus man's head and slid halfway down his trunk where it caught on a projecting limb. McAfee roped it from the other side, and Bannerman, after three tries, managed to loop his rope over the green trunk as well.

"All right," Durken shouted. "Dig in."

Bannerman reined his horse to a stop and Durken and McAfee side stepped theirs to pull the nooses tight. The braided ropes bit into the green flesh, and the cactus man found itself unable to move. It began to howl in rage and frustration.

"Now what?" Bannerman shouted over the wailing.

"We know shooting it didn't work" McAfee replied. "Taking off a limb didn't do the trick either. I'd say burn it, but we don't have any kerosene. Besides, with all the moisture in its flesh, it may not burn anyway."

"And if we just keep it here," Durken added, "it can put down roots and find water underground. The damned thing lives in the desert; it can just wait us out."

"Then what do we do?"

"We have to keep it moving."

"We can't do that forever either. I don't know about you," Bannerman said, "but I'm getting tired and so is my horse."

McAfee thought for a moment. "Are there any *salinas* near here?"

"*Salina?*"

"A dried-up lake bed, a salt flat."

"About five miles to the north if my bearings are right," Bannerman answered.

"Then that's where we're taking this devil."

• • •

The sun came up to a bizarre sight, the trio dragging the cactus man across the sand as it twisted and squirmed in the ropes. When they stopped to rest, the creature tried to saw through one of the lariats with its spines but only managed to fray the braided rope before its captors realized what it was doing and started moving again.

Durken peered ahead into the golden light of dawn and saw a stretch of desert even more barren than the one they were crossing. No vegetation so much as poked a stem through the cracked alkali. Beyond lay a bed of glistening crystals of salt sparkling in the rising sun.

The creature sensed what was ahead and, desperate, renewed its struggle, nearly pulling Thunder off his feet. The cactus tried to push its roots into the ground, but found the hard white crust unyielding. As they dragged it onto the lake bed, it began to wail piteously like a trapped animal. The cries continued through the early morning hours, and McAfee feared that their canteens would run out of water before the monster expired. Then it slowly sank on its side, and its cries became more feeble. It seemed to shrink, to collapse into itself, and McAfee shuddered to think that this must be what happened to Burke.

By noon, the cactus man was still and silent. Durken dismounted and patted Thunder's shoulder. "Hold, boy." The horse dug in and kept the tension on the rope as Durken carefully moved across the *salina*, the hatchet in one hand and his Colt in the other. When he was a few feet away from the green devil, its trunk twisted, and its golden eyes stared into his with an imploring look. Durken raised the hatchet and brought it down, biting deep into what would be the neck of a human. He struck again and again, until the light went out of those eyes and finally, the cactus man's head fell away from its neck. The trunk quivered for a moment, then was still. "It's over," he called to McAfee and Bannerman.

The three stood around the dead monster, staring at it in wonder. "Do we take this thing back, or what do we do with it?"

"We leave it where it is," McAfee said. "Take it off that salt and let it get wet, who knows what might happen. I, for one, don't want to run that risk.

"What do you think it was?"

"I couldn't say for sure," McAfee said. "I read in some book once about creatures in Europe called vampires that lived by sucking the blood out of people. Maybe this is America's version."

"Dear God," Bannerman said. "Nobody's going to believe this. They'll think we're liars or crazy."

"My advice is don't tell them," Durken said. "McAfee and I've found that's usually the best way."

"How many times have you run across something like this?"

Durken grinned. "You wouldn't believe me. You'd think I'm a liar or crazy. Let's go get your deputy."

• • •

Simms was alive but weak. His arm was slowly fleshing out as his body pumped moisture back into it. After some discussion, Bannerman agreed with the cowboys that the best thing they could do was bury Burke's desiccated corpse and say no more about him. The money was returned, and while the dead could not be brought back, there was satisfaction in knowing that those responsible paid for their crimes.

Durken and McAfee rode out of Rimrock each with a fifty-dollar reward in his pocket for recovering the stolen money and a promise from Bannerman that neither he nor Simms would ever breathe a word about the cactus man.

"Do you think he'll ever tell the story?" Durken said as they rode out of town. "I guess we'll never know."

"We'll know—if we read it someday in a dime novel."

THE END

C.O. Jones is a former member of a special OSS team who spent World War II tracking down Nazis procuring occult artifacts and grimoires for Hitler's war effort. Jones, like his counterparts, is trained in every aspect of soldiering, and in dealing with supernatural entities. His marginal psi gift is what he calls The Sight, a random ability to see things a second or two before they happen. His torso is tattooed with runes and wards for protection and aggression, and they glow in the presence of magic. Stateside following the war, he finds work with the Mob and later moves to Los Angeles to become a Private Investigator. But the magic and his secret past follow him wherever he goes, for magic is everywhere. In "Shiners," Jones is sent by his boss to head off a moonshine war that threatens to decimate two mountain clans in rural Pennsylvania.

C. O. JONES: SHINERS

An hour past midnight, the tanker bumped and jostled down the rutted lane that led from Jesse Fisher's moonshine still to the dirt road that led to the gravel road that led to the two-lane State highway out of Wharton Township. To the untrained eye, the humpbacked '39 Ford sedan looked like any working man's family car, but under the hood was a souped-up flathead V-8 and in the trunk was a baffled stainless-steel tank full of corn liquor. The weight gave the car some sway, but beefed up springs and truck shocks made up for it.

Hedge Bryner, named for his bristly hair and warty face, was driving the shipment. Three miles of ruts, rocks and mud before he got to the dirt roads that connected the mountain farms, then two lane asphalt all the way to the drop off site. He was driving along one of the single lane farm roads when headlights came out of nowhere behind him, and the chase was on.

Hedge figured he had Revenuers on his tail. He knew the roads in Wharton Township well enough that he could drive them eyes shut or blindfolded, and he saw the situation less as a peril and more as a challenge. If those badged up city boys thought they could catch him, their asses were twisted. He'd outrun them two times before, and he wasn't about to get caught tonight.

A half mile down the road, the first bullet went through the rear glass and punched a hole on its way out the windshield. Something wasn't right; no red spinner, no siren, just bullets. The high split window in the back of the Ford made Hedge's head a tough target, but that was small comfort. He reached a fairly level straightaway through a cornfield and gave the motor all the gas it could drink. The twin pipes roared, and Hedge pulled away as more bullets whined off the roof and trunk.

The corn was harvest high on either side of the road and all his pursuers could see was the back of his car. Sixty miles an hour. Seventy. The car behind was closing. Hedge took a last look and cut his lights. He counted the seconds down and when he got to one, he wrenched the wheel hard left and slewed off the road into the cornfield. The driver of the chase car had pretty quick reflexes, but not quick enough to keep him from smashing through a cross buck fence where the road ended with the corn and landing his car up to the windows in a pond on the other side.

Hedge popped out of the cornfield and onto the road and didn't look back. He made it to Morgantown, West Virginia, just south of the state line an hour later and pulled up to the doors of a riverfront warehouse. The sign overhead said, Ames Wholesale Produce. He flashed his lights three times then two and waited. In a moment, the bay door swung upward, and he rolled the car inside. A pair of men in work greens stepped out of the shadows as the door closed behind him. Mickey, the shorter of the two said around his cigarette, "You got holes in the car. Any in you?"

Hedge climbed out of the Ford. "Nope, but it was close." He lit a cigarette of his own. "I'd say something's up. A week and a half ago, somebody took a shot at Buddy Hendry, missed him but blew out his back window. We all thought it was Homer Varndell because Buddy was fooling around with Homer's wife. Tonight changes everything."

Mickey's partner Elroy dragged a heavy rubber hose around the back of the car. Hedge unlocked the trunk and Elroy fitted the hose coupling onto the drain at the bottom of the tank. While the pump droned, Hedge told Mickey and Elroy an animated version of his evening's adventure. In a few minutes, the tank was dry. Mickey shined a flashlight into the trunk. "You were lucky. No holes in the tank. That special steel's expensive."

"The cost of doing business," Hedge said. "All things considered, I'd rather they hit the tank than the engine."

Mickey handed Hedge a packet of bills with a red rubber band around it. He slipped it into the pocket of his coat without looking at it.

"Aren't you going to count it?"

Hedge shook his head. "No need. If it comes up short, you'll hear from Bud and Grover."

Business done, Hedge drove across town past the University campus, up the long hill to the Mile Ground, and then to Route 857. Taking 119 through Point Marion may have been a quicker route, but Hedge was hungry and there was an all-night diner named Ruby's near Cheat Lake where they served up a good breakfast. Besides, there was a waitress there named Cassie who didn't mind his looks so long as he didn't mind hers, and Hedge figured, with a face like his, a man makes the most of what's available.

He pulled into the parking lot under the neon sign that said RUBY's DINER in big letters, and underneath, GOOD FOOD DAY AND NIGHT. The place was crowded, although it was still dark outside. The booths and stools were filled with working men in tan canvas coats or checkered hunting jackets, heavy boots and overalls; truckers, miners, loggers, and others whose days began while genteel people were still dreaming.

He stepped into the diner and inhaled the aroma of hot grease and gravy. The noise in Ruby's was its usual riot of argument, laughter and the incessant clatter of silverware on china and the rattle of pots and pans. A few nodded to Hedge as he came in, not because they knew him personally, but because he was a regular, and his was a face people never forgot.

Hedge took a stool at the counter and waved to Cassie, who was pouring coffee for three men in a booth. She smiled and gave him a nod. He flipped through the screens in the countertop jukebox station until he found the song he wanted, dropped a nickel into the slot, and punched the buttons for J-6. In a moment, Hank Williams' voice rose over the racket, singing "Hey, Good-Lookin'."

As if on cue, Cassie came down the counter with a coffee cup in one hand and the pot in the other. "Hey, Hedge," she said with a smile.

"Hello, Sweet Thing." Hedge eyed her up and down as if she were a bathing beauty, not a thick-waisted broad with a lantern jaw and one eye a little askew of the other. "Bring me the special."

"On the way, honey." She sashayed away with a little extra swing in her substantial rump for Hedge's benefit. She never got any better looking, but to be fair, neither did he. She was back in no time with a plate of ham and eggs and home fries, and Hedge suspected she brought him someone else's order so he wouldn't have to wait. She leaned over the counter and said, just loud enough for him to hear. "Eat up. My break's in ten minutes."

Eight minutes later, Hedge gulped down the last of his coffee, threw three dollars on the counter, and headed out the door. He lit a cigarette and leaned against the Ford. The lot, lit by one lamp on a pole near the entrance, was dark where he was parked. It was chilly enough that he could see his breath without the smoke. Hedge put his hands in his pockets to warm them. Cassie didn't like cold hands. In his left pocket, Hedge felt the packet of money, and in the other, the snub-nosed revolver he carried when he made his runs.

Cassie came out a minute later, craning her neck looking for his car. Hedge wasn't sure why, since he always parked in the same place. She stepped around the front of the Ford, her rayon uniform swishing under her coat. Cassie grabbed a handful of Hedge's hair and pulled his face to hers, fierce and hungry. "Come on; I only have fifteen minutes."

They climbed into the back seat, and in no time, Cassie's skirt was over her waist and Hedge's pants were around his ankles. Hedge had his big hands on her hips and was pulling her on top of him when she said, "Hedge honey, my ass is cold. Can you turn on the heater?"

"Oh, hell, I'll have to climb up front." Hedge fumbled in his trousers for his keys and rolled clumsily over the seat. He turned the key in the ignition and when he stepped on the starter switch, an explosion erupted that turned the sedan into a fireball, blew all the glass out of Ruby's windows, and woke every dog for five miles.

• • •

Two hours later, Bud and Grover Lytle sat alone at the bar of their backwoods gin mill. Little more than an oversized shingle shack with a tin roof and a neon sign that said only BEER, it stood at the end of a set of parallel ruts three miles off the paved highway in the Allegheny Mountains, Appalachia's backbone.

The Lytle brothers shared a strong chin, straight nose, and deep blue eyes. Both wore their hair in duck tails, Bud's streaked with grey. He hung up the telephone and set it on the bar. "Mickey says Hedge's car had bullet holes in it when he unloaded. Hedge said he ditched them at Ellis's farm, and he didn't think it was T-Men."

Grover nodded his agreement. "Agents might shoot, but they sure as hell don't blow shit up. I figure they'd want the car for evidence if nothing else."

"You're right about that. Who do you figure'd do something like this?"

"Monroe?"

"We stay off his turf. Besides, he knows if he starts a war he'll lose."

"What about the Tompkins clan?"

"They're strictly Hawkins Hollow, Bud. I'm not sure those inbred crackers even know there's a world outside Fayette County."

"Outsiders trying to muscle in?"

"Could be." He downed his beer. "First Buddy, now Hedge. I ain't heard of anybody else's men being shot at. Maybe the others're all in it together." He opened his wallet and took out a card with a phone number scrawled on it then picked up the phone and started dialing.

"Who are you calling?"

"Skitch Mottola."

• • •

C. O. Jones didn't exactly report to Skitch, so much as he made himself available in case the mobster needed him. He left his room in the Brownsville Hotel and walked down the hill to Snowdon Square where Skitch ran his operation out of a building with a pool hall on the street floor, a boxing gym on the second, and the real business of the joint on three and four. Jones sat, as he often did, on a sidewalk bench across from the pool room. There, he'd sit and read the newspaper, smoke a cigarette or two, and wait for Skitch and his brother Dodie to arrive. If something was up, they'd call him in. Otherwise, he'd read his paper and leave, returning after lunch. By now, the locals knew who he was and who he worked for, and for the most part they left the bench empty the same way they never parked in the four spaces in front of the pool hall.

The Uniontown newspaper was full of big news. The war in Korea, although officially undeclared, was going full-tilt. MacArthur pushed across the border into Commie territory, and the South Koreans took an airfield after heavy fighting. Some vets were re-upping, but Jones didn't think they'd want him back. His unit, which didn't officially exist, was disbanded after VJ Day and wouldn't be reformed unless the Reds hired a sorcerer.

Jones, when he was still called Randall Simmons, spent World War II in a special OSS team that tracked Nazi operatives procuring occult books and artifacts for Hitler's war effort. When he was discharged at the war's end, he took the only job that matched his unique set of skills: cleanup man for the Jersey Mob, settling internecine squabbles before they boiled over into shooting wars. Returning the teen-aged daughter of one mobster from a fake kidnapping by the son of another, Jones killed the boy in self-defense and went on the run from his vengeful father, landing in Brownsville, Pennsylvania where he found work with the Mottola Brothers. Skitch and Dodie ran the county-wide rackets and for that matter, Fayette County in general.

At the last chime of ten, the cars rolled in; Jack Mozzo's Cadillac, Skitch's Buick, and Dodie's new ride, a shiny red '50 Ford convertible with a cream-colored rag top. Jones watched the men climb out of their cars, Jack with his fake leg, Skitch, immaculate in his three-piece suit, and Dodie in his pegged pants, silk shirt, and pompadour hairdo. Skitch looked across the street to Jones and motioned with his hand. Jones folded his newspaper and started across the street to the pool hall.

Bucky, the gangly counterman in the pool room was raising the shades when Jones walked in. "Skitch says go on up."

Jones climbed the stairs and the scent of tobacco smoke and talc was replaced by the smell of sweat and leather as he entered the boxing gym, complete with a regulation ring on the second floor. In a far corner was a brass cage elevator that led to the third floor where card and dice tables stood and the fourth, where tables were piled with "policy" slips from numbers betting and a tote board with results from Pimlico hung on a wall over Richie Traficante's desk, a desk arrayed with six telephones.

At the far end of the top floor, Skitch's office door was open. Jones tapped at the frame.

"Come on in, Jones." Skitch had a hale-fellow persona that endeared him to everyone but his enemies. Like a political ward-heeler, Skitch had a smile and a handshake for everybody, and seldom turned down a request for help from anyone in the community. He was a short man, compact like a gymnast, and had no grey hairs on his thinning scalp. The blue on his jaw from a heavy beard followed him from shave to shave. "Sit down."

Jones sat. Skitch's office, unlike the rest of the building, had drapes on the windows, thick maroon carpet on the floor, and a desk as big as a dining room table. Today, the only things on it were the telephone, a humidor full of cigars, and a cut-glass ashtray. Jones didn't speak. Skitch would get to the point when he was ready.

"Hell of a thing; a lot of local boys are getting 'Greetings' letters from the Draft to go to Korea. All the way back to World War I, this part of the state's always had more than its share of combat dead. I guess they figure all the immigrants are better fodder than those blue noses from Boston or the redneck aristocrats from the Carolinas and Virginia. I'm glad my boy isn't old enough to send over."

Jones nodded agreement. "How is Frankie doing? He started school this year, didn't he?" Two years before, Jones had rescued the boy from a kidnapper.

"Yeah. Learning his ABCs and 123s. He's smart like his mother. He'll do good." Skitch pulled a pack of Chesterfields from his pocket, offered one to Jones then lit one for himself. "Got a call this morning from Bud Lytle. Seems somebody's shooting up their moonshine runners. Blew up a car last night, killed the driver and his girlfriend. We talked it over and agreed that you were the likeliest person to sort it out."

Jones took a long drag on his cigarette and let it back out. "Okay, what do I need to know?"

"Bud and his brother will fill you in with the details. You know them, right?"

"We've met."

"They won't be paying you, I will. This is a favor to them."

Whatever Skitch is paying me, thought Jones, he figures the favor he'll get in return is worth five times as much. "All right."

Skitch reached in his pocket and took out a roll of bills. he counted five hundreds from the outside and laid them on the desk. "That's for the next couple days. If it runs longer, I'll give you more."

"No problem." He got up to leave.

"And Jones —"

"Yeah?"

"These mountain boys may be hillbillies, but don't underestimate them. They'll kill you just as dead as a big-city hit man."

"Thanks for the tip. I'll let you know what I find out." He folded the money and slipped it into his pocket. As he walked to the elevator, Skitch's warning rattled around his brain, don't underestimate them.

• • •

"People who kill for a cause, people who kill for a living, and people who kill for pleasure have one thing in common; they'll all leave you just as dead if you underestimate them." Colonel Reynald Hennessey, commander of what was simply called the Unit, paced back and forth in front of the trainees, Randall Simmons, a newly minted lieutenant, among them, impressed into service because of his very real albeit slight paranormal gift. Randall Simmons had, since childhood, what he called the Sight, an ability to see things a second or two before they happened.

The Sight was random, and uncontrollable , but it had saved his life many times and remained a useful advantage.

"You men have all completed basic training, and probably think that you're pretty tough. By the time we're finished with you, you truly will be. But remember, the human mind never quits. For every tactic we teach you, by the second time your enemy sees it, he will have a counter tactic. The trouble is, that the first time you see a new trick on his part, it may well be your last. Never underestimate your enemy."

What followed was a month of intense training by Brit commandos at the legendary Camp X, where Simmons and his fellow trainees were taught more ways to kill than there were enemies, as much to anticipate and defend against a tactic as to employ it oneself. The result was an elite pack of killers, but the worst was yet to come.

What followed Camp X was intensive training in the occult and supernatural at the hands of Duke University's Institute for Paranormal Studies, where Jones learned as much about magical warfare as he did military. And there he was tattooed over most of his arms and torso with runes, symbols, wards, and incantations to protect him from enemies who would use magic against him, tattoos that glowed with heat in the presence of the supernatural. It didn't happen often anymore, but it did happen because magic was everywhere.

So, Simmons became Castleman became Tate became Lassiter as he cycled through identities, less to bury his past than to simply survive in the present. And for now, he was Jones, but always looking over his shoulder, wary of what might catch up with him.

Jones crossed Snowdon Square to the drug store where a phone booth stood in a back corner. He bought a pack of Camels at the counter to change a dollar and slipped into the booth. The number was outside the Brownsville exchange, and he didn't want it showing up on the pool room's phone bill. Jones dialed the operator, gave her the number, and lit a cigarette while he waited for the connection. The phone buzzed in his ear, three times, four, then a man's voice with a nasal twang answered.

"Yeah?"

"This is Jones."

"You know where our place is. How soon can you be here?"

"Forty-five minutes." The line went dead. Time to get the car.

Jones had dealt with the Lytle brothers once before when their mechanic Earl Coakee set up his car, a '41 Ford coupe with a hopped-up engine and many of the same features he built into the moonshiners' cars. Normally, the Lytles handled their own problems with a baseball bat or a shotgun. If they were calling Skitch for help, the problem must be a big one.

The drive along Route 40, the historic National Road took him through Uniontown and up the mountain known as the Summit. A forest fire had swept over the western face during the summer, and in the gray overcast, the charred hulks of oaks, maples, and pines thrust upward like spikes. Winter would arrive in another month, and the moonshiners should be wrapping up for the season. Unless a still was in a cave or a shed, winter temperatures made it hard to control the cooking of the mash, and the denuded trees did little to help with concealment.

Past the crest, Jones turned off the highway and followed a series of roads, each worse than the one before until he reached the Lytle Brothers' headquarters. The BEER sign was unlit, but a half dozen rattletrap pickup trucks and battered cars were parked out front. In a far corner of the lot, Jones spotted Bud Lytle's new Mercury, crouched like a panther near the trees. A rangy man in a denim jacket, cigarette in the corner of his mouth, leaned against the car cradling a pump shotgun in the crook of his arm. He eyed Jones but didn't move. Jones was expected.

The place hadn't changed since the last time he was in it. A bar with pedestal stools, a dozen tables with chairs, a sawdust floor and a jukebox that was silent for the moment. Jones swept the room with a practiced eye. The men who sat at the tables were dressed in hunting gear, flannel shirts over checkered wool coats. The silent crew followed him with their eyes as he crossed the dance floor. Rifles leaned beside them against the tables. They were going hunting, but Jones figured that it wasn't for deer.

Sonny, the bartender saw Jones and tilted his chin toward a door next to the jukebox. Jones tapped on it, and as he waited for it to open, Sonny came around the bar and dropped a handful of change into the jukebox. A song came on with whiny steel guitars and an equally whiny woman singing about lost love. The door opened, and Grover Lytle waved Jones inside.

The storeroom was cramped, the walls lined with stacks of beer and liquor cases. A single bare bulb hung from the ceiling over a scarred wooden table that Jones was sure had a sawed-off shotgun bolted to the underside aimed at the guest chair. Bud sat at the table, a bottle and three glasses in front of him. The bass of the jukebox thumped through the wall. No one outside the room would hear their conversation.

"Good to see you, Jones," Bud said, pouring two fingers of the crystal liquid in each glass. "Have a seat." Jones sat across the table from Bud and Grover pulled a chair beside his brother. They raised their glasses and Jones did the same. The moonshine burned all the way to Jones' toes, but he didn't flinch any more than Bud or Grover.

"Skitch tell you why we called?"

Jones shook his head. "He said you'd fill me in."

"Seems we got us a situation. One of our drivers, Hedge Bryner, got himself killed last night…" Jones listened as Bud told the story of the unsuccessful waylay, Hedge's delivery, and the car bomb.

"Someone wants your territory?"

Bud nodded. "Trouble is we don't know who. We already know you're a tough son of a bitch, Jones, but I hear you were a private eye out in L.A. That true?"

"Yeah. That's right."

"You suppose you could get to the bottom of this before it gets out of hand?"

"Looks as if it's already out of hand."

Grover broke in. "You don't know the half of it. You saw those men out at the bar?"

"Yeah. I figured they're ready to go after somebody."

"They are. Those are Hedge Bryner's brothers and cousins. They think the Tompkins clan from over Hawkins Hollow way killed Hedge, and they're ready to go after them."

"You think they're wrong."

"Not out of hand." Bud leaned forward in his chair. "It could've been them, but maybe it ain't. What we don't want is to start a war with them. It'll get a lot of people killed on both sides."

"And it's bad for business," Jones said.

"Yep. We start shooting back and forth, the bodies pile up, and the cops and the Revenuers can't just look the other way. We'll all go down."

"And that's a good reason why it probably isn't the Tompkins family. They'd understand that too."

"You may be right, but it's going to be tough to convince the Bryners.

"I guarantee that if they go up Hawkins Hollow, I won't find out who's behind this. Can you persuade them not to do it?"

"I can try."

"Get them to hold off for a day or two. I should know more by then, and we'll take it from there. One other thing."

"What's that?" Bud said.

"I need one of your boys to work with me, somebody familiar with all

"If they go up Hawkins Hollow, I won't find out who's behind this."

your routes, everybody knows, so people'll talk to me. Got any veterans in your crew?"

"Me," Grover said, "I'll go."

Jones shook his head. "That won't be so good. Whatever happens, I want the two of you with clean hands and a solid alibi for the next two days. Give me somebody else."

Bud looked at Grover. "Leland?"

"Grover nodded agreement. "Leland."

"Who's Leland?"

"Leland Stark. He was a Marine, fought at Iwo Jima, got a lot of medals. He drives for us now."

"Where do I find him?"

"It's Friday. He'll be at Four-Door Tavern tonight."

"How will I know him?"

"He'll be the one in the spotlight." Bud hesitated. "What do I tell the Bryners?"

"Tell them I'll bring them the killer dead or alive."

"Anything else we can do?"

"Yeah, draw me a map to the pond, and call Coakee. Tell him I'm coming."

• • •

Jones followed Grover's directions to the pond and arrived as a grizzled old coot in hip waders was hitching a tow chain to the bumper of a dark green Plymouth sedan. A farm tractor whose red paint had faded to a dappled orange stood by, belching and farting pale smoke into the crisp air. Jones got out of his coupe and strolled over.

"Need a hand?" Jones shouted over the put and rumble of the tractor.

The old man looked up and squinted at Jones, decided he was all right, and said, "Sure, fellah, take the slack out of that chain and wrap it a couple times around the pull hitch. You'll find a clevis at the end to secure it."

As Jones pulled at the heavy links, he said, "Anybody get hurt?"

"Dunno. Come by this morning and seen the car. Nobody in it, so I guess whoever it was must've walked away."

Jones secured the chain, the old man tested it and climbed out of the pond and up the bank with that deliberate sidestep common to old men with rheumatism. He clambered onto the tractor's seat and gunned the throttle. The tractor rolled forward, dragging the Plymouth with it. The car heaved over the bank and onto the road, rocking on its springs.

When Jones opened the driver's door, a minor waterfall poured over the sill. A quick look told him there were no bodies, but something shiny caught his eye just under the driver's seat. It was a badge, a shield with a bronze eagle across the top and the words US TREASURY DEPARTMENT INVESTIGATOR. He slipped it into his pocket as the old man climbed down.

"Thanks for your help. What's your name, fellah?"

"Jones. Yours?"

"I'm Roy Ellis." He made a sweeping gesture with his arm. "This is my farm."

"Nobody in the car, so I guess you were right about walking away."

"I'll bet I fixed that fence twenty times in my life if I done it once. People, a lot of them kids, come down this road at night and don't see the fence 'til it's too late, especially when it's foggy. You ain't from around here, Jones. What brings you out here?"

Jones took the badge from his pocket and flashed it. "Treasury Department."

Ellis frowned. "Revenuer, huh? You put a few of my kin in jail just because folks like corn liquor."

"That's right. I heard about the accident and thought maybe it involved moonshiners."

"Let me tell you something, fellah; if it was moonshiners, they wouldn't be on this road because they know it's a dead end. They know every road up here like they was born on it."

"You're probably right."

"I am right." Ellis leaned into the passenger window. "Huh." He reached in and pulled out a brass shell casing in the span between his thumb and forefinger. "There's your culprit. Poachers. That's a thirty-aught-six. Looks as if they were watching for deer instead of the road." He threw the shell to Jones. "Take that with you, Mister Revenuer."

As Jones drove back the way he came, he noticed for the second time the flattened swath of corn stalks leading away from the dirt road. The story Hedge told Mickey and Elroy jibed with the wreck, the tracks through the cornfield, and the shell. The badge was the mystery. Agents routinely used M-1s and .45 automatics with the occasional machine gun on a raid. A thought was forming in his head, Treasury Agents hitting the runners and making it look as if rival operations were responsible. Get them fighting among themselves, and as Bud Lytle said, the Treasury boys could just waltz in and pick up the bodies.

He had to see Coakee, but first he needed to find a phone booth and call Skitch.

"What's up, Jones?"

Jones read the license number of the car from the pond. "See if your friends on the force can trace that plate."

"Okay. Anything else?"

"I need you to ask around, see if anybody can identify a badge number for me."

"State Trooper or local cop?"

"Treasury Agent."

Skitch was silent for a moment then said. "Federal, huh? I'll see what I can do."

Jones read the number to Skitch and said, "Find out as much as you can. I'll call you back later." He hung up the phone and headed for Earl Coakee's barn.

• • •

Coakee, a cousin to the Lytles, was the master mechanic who turned everyday cars into high-performance moonshine runners and track cars for the new NASCAR race circuit. His garage, housed in a ramshackle barn miles from a paved road was equipped to tune and modify anything with four wheels and an engine. He had set up Jones' '41 Ford Coupe a few years before, and the car had served Jones well. Now, he needed another car for another purpose.

Jones pulled into the bare dirt yard in front of a gray-weathered barn surrounded by head high thistles and sumac. Before he shut off his engine, Coakee's dogs, six in all, none smaller than a full-grown German Shepherd, came boiling out of their kennel, a doorless Model T sedan orange with rust. The mongrels danced around Jones' car, barking and snarling until a sharp whistle came from the barn's open door. The pack shut up and immediately gathered around a giant man in denim coveralls who stood in the doorway.

Coakee was a good six-and-a-half feet tall and at least three feet wide, his arms filling the sleeves of the coverall like sausages in a casing. His curly red hair grew to his shoulders where it flowed into his thick red beard. "Kennel," he snapped in a voice that seemed too high pitched for his size, and the dogs ran back to the Model T where they peered over each others' shoulders at Jones as he climbed out of his car.

"Six dogs now, Coakee?"

"Nobody comes sneaking around here more than once," he said with a grin that showed off a surprisingly good set of teeth. "Bud called a while ago. What do you need, Jones?"

"You heard what happened to Hedge Bryner last night?"

"Yeah, hell of a thing. I set that car up myself."

"I'm going to make a dry run and see if I can draw out the people responsible. I need a car that isn't a tanker to pass for one, and I need a few special modifications to it."

"For when?"

"Tomorrow night."

Coakee scratched his chin through his beard. "How about a tanker running empty?"

Jones nodded. "That might do the job."

"See that gray Plymouth over there? That's one of Bud's cars. I just finished tuning it up yesterday. Small rear windshield, sheet steel up the back of the trunk, reinforced bumpers; it should do you."

"But it's got to look real. It has to look like I'm hauling a full tank. That car sits pretty high empty."

"I'll see what I can do about that, maybe drop the body a little so she looks loaded. You driving this yourself?"

"No, Bud and Grover want Leland Stark behind the wheel. Is he good?"

"One of the best." Coakee hesitated. "You said there was something special."

"Yeah, I need you to cut a hole in the roof."

• • •

Back on the highway, Jones found a phone booth at a filling station outside Farmington. He dialed the operator and gave her the number for Skitch's private line in his office. He answered on the third ring.

"It's Jones."

"I made some calls. Found out a few things. The State Police say the car in the pond was stolen a few days ago two counties away."

"No surprise. What else?"

"Found out who owns the badge, or I should say owned. Name's Richard Mayhew."

"Owned?"

"Yeah. He's dead." Jones was silent for a moment. "You still there, Jones?"

"Just thinking. How long ago did he die?"

"Year and a half. He died in a car crash chasing moonshiners. Where'd you find the badge?"

"In the car that was chasing Hedge Bryner last night, the one that went into the pond."

"There's more. He has two older brothers, Kevin and Roy. They're both on the force."

"T-men?"

"Yeah."

An idea was forming in Jones' head, but he didn't want to risk saying it over the phone. "I'll handle it. I have a plan."

"Do you need any manpower?"

"No, I'm using one of Bud's boys. What I will need, though is a solid alibi for tomorrow night."

"No problem."

Jones looked at his watch: 3:55. The sun would be down in an hour or so, and by the time he drove back to Brownsville, he'd have to turn around and head back up the mountain. The Chuck Wagon was right down the road, so Jones headed that way for some chow.

The parking lot was nearly full, but Jones knew from experience that it was busy most of its twenty-four-hour schedule. He parked near the end of the lot between a stake side truck loaded with hay and an old black Buick hardtop. Inside the Chuck Wagon, Jones took a seat at the counter. Someone had left an afternoon newspaper, and Jones read the headline on a front-page article: LOCAL MAN DIES IN EXPLOSION. It was a short piece and said only that Wilbur Bryner, aged forty-two of Elliottsville was killed when his car exploded outside a Cheat Lake restaurant along with an employee named Cassie McBride of Morgantown. No details, and the police are investigating.

The waitress in the Chuck Wagon was a stringy woman with a weathered face who wore a flannel work shirt. She could have been forty, fifty, or sixty. She set a cup of black coffee in front of Jones, and since there was no saucer with it, she dropped the teaspoon into the cup. "What'll you have, bub?" she said around the cigarette in the corner of her mouth. Jones squinted over her shoulder where the day's specials were scrawled in white on a chalk board.

"I'll take the pork chops, mashed potatoes and green beans."

"Number three," she shouted over her shoulder and moved on down the counter. A customer the other side of a vacant stool said, "You want cream or sugar?" ready to slide them down the counter.

Jones shook his head. "I learned to drink it black a long time ago."

"Me too, in the Army. No milk that hasn't soured and you never know what's in the sugar bowl." He laughed then dropped his grin. "You in the War?"

"Army Air Corps. You?"

"Navy. I was a gunner on the Rhode Island. Musta shot a hundred Jap Zeroes outta the sky." Jones turned on his stool and eyed the man next to him. He was young, maybe twenty-five with a jagged part in his hair that crossed his forehead and his left eye. "Piece of shrapnel got me."

"That's too bad. I have a few beauties myself. What are you doing for work now?"

"Same thing I did before Pearl Harbor, logging with my old man and my brothers. My name's Ronnie Haggerty." He held out a work roughened hand for Jones to shake.

"C. O. Jones."

"What's the C.O. stand for?"

"Counter Offer."

Haggerty laughed. "Okay, I get it. You got one of those fancy names people laugh at, huh?"

Jones gave him a patient smile. "Fought somebody every day in grade school. People usually just call me Jones." He picked up the newspaper and pointed to the article about Bryner's death. "That's really something. Did you know the guy?"

"Hell, all of us around here knew Hedge. It's too bad. Everybody liked him."

"I guess not quite everybody."

"Yeah. Well, that's the risk moonshiners run." Haggerty downed his coffee and stepped off his stool. "Gotta get a move on. Nice to meet you, Jones."

"Same here." As Ronnie walked away, the waitress set down a plate full of steaming food. For diner fare, the Chuck Wagon food was a notch better than average. Jones might have said it was good as home cooking, but he hadn't had a home cooked meal for so long, he had no point of comparison. As he drank his second cup of coffee, Jones decided he needed to go back to the road house and talk to Bud and Grover.

So, everybody knows Hedge was a runner. Everybody knows the Lytles make moonshine. Precious few secrets among the mountain people, but Jones figured there were a few still hiding in the shadows.

When he pulled into the gravel lot of the Lytle Brothers' headquarters, except for a few battered cars and trucks, the lot was empty. The Mercury was gone. He went inside. Small groups of twos and threes sat at tables and the bar. Jones took a stool at the far end. Sonny came over and said, "Bud and Grover ain't here, Jones."

"Any idea when they might be back?"

"Not sure."

Jones turned his hand over revealing the Treasury badge in his palm. "Then you tell me about Richard Mayhew."

Sonny blinked. He stared at the badge and visibly swallowed. "You better talk to Bud and Grover." He hurried away and got busy filling the beer cooler. Then when he thought Jones wasn't looking, he huddled over the phone and dialed a number.

Two beers later, Jones heard the rumble of the Mercury's twin pipes in the parking lot. Bud and Grover came in and motioned Jones to follow them into the store room.

"Sonny said you wanted to see us, Jones," Bud said. He didn't uncork the moonshine bottle this time.

"When were you going to tell me about Richard Mayhew?"

The brothers looked at each other. Grover said, "Didn't think he had anything to do with this."

"I think it has everything to do with this." Jones tossed the badge onto the table. "Found that in the car that was chasing Hedge last night."

The Lytles stared at the badge.

"Now, unless you believe in ghosts, somebody's started a vendetta and I'm betting it's Mayhew's brothers. Tell me about it."

Bud uncorked the bottle.

"You know, and so do the Treasury boys that they will never stop moonshining. Hell, it's been going on in this county for two hundred years since Tom Gaddis started the Whiskey Rebellion and George Washington sent in fifteen thousand troops to quell it.

The Revenuers shut it down in one place, it pops up someplace else. So, we and the Treasury people have kind of an unspoken agreement to just sort of dance around each other. The County Sheriff leaves us alone, and so do the State Troopers; Skitch sees to that, but the Treasury agents still have to make a showing.

"Near two years ago, the Feds did what they usually do, raided a few stills, roadblocked a few shipments, just to make it look like they were earning their pay. We figured after a few weeks, things would die down and it would be business as usual, but this time, the agents didn't back off. Some new boys on the team decided they were going to be crusaders and make a name for themselves."

"The Mayhews," Jones said.

"Yep. The three of them would raid a still in one place or another and bring a cameraman with them so they'd get their picture in the newspapers. They weren't even about enforcement; they were all three in it strictly for glory. The newspapers called the oldest, Kevin, the Eliot Ness of Appalachia, if you can believe that."

"So how did Richard die?"

"He was the youngest of the three. The Mayhews decided that it was too much work to comb through the woods all up and down the mountains, and started going after the runners, thinking they'd be easy pickings. What they didn't count on was how good our people can drive. They caught a few, ran them off the road, shot out the tires, but most got away, then one night, one of our boys turned the tables on them."

"Hedge Bryner?"

Bud shook his head. "Billy Cobb."

Grover picked up the story. "The Mayhews never went in for roadblocks; they liked the chase, like hounds on a fox. That night Billy was taking a load to Cumberland. The Mayhews were in two cars, Richard in one and Kevin and Roy in the other. They fell in behind Billy, and he said it was pretty close.

"On a dirt road about two miles from the Maryland border, there's a one-lane bridge. Richard thought if he got ahead of Billy, he could block the bridge and they'd have him. When they got close to it, Richard pulled alongside Billy to pass him, and Billy slammed on his brakes. Richard got just past Billy's bumper and Billy floored it. He caught Richard's car in the back corner and ran it through the bridge railing and into the creek. When his brothers got to the car, Richard was dead, his neck broke."

"So, did Kevin and Roy get their revenge on Billy Cobb?"

"They never got the chance. The brothers didn't know it, but Billy was drafted. A week after Richard was killed, Billy was on his way to Korea."

"He stepped on a land mine," Bud said. "All that came home to his momma was a folded flag and a gold star."

"So, the Mayhew brothers never had their chance to get even with Cobb. Maybe they're taking it out on all of you, trying to start wars among the families, get you to do their killing for them."

"All in the name of the Treasury Department," Grover said, picking up

Richard Mayhew's badge and turning it in his fingers.

"I'm not so sure," Jones said. "I don't think the Department would sanction murder. I think these boys are running their own show."

"What can we do?"

"Here's my plan…"

• • •

Jones had to circle the lot of the Four-Door Tavern to find a place to park. The roadhouse's neon sign flashed red on the windshields of the cars and pickup trucks that packed the lot. He found a space in a far corner beside a rocking sedan with a pair of bare feet pressed against a back window.

He crossed the lot to the front of a squat building that, as advertised, sported four doors under an awning that ran the width of its porch. One of the doors opened, and a man in a suit jacket over his denim work shirt came out, half-carrying a thick-waisted blond whose head lolled on her shoulders.

The Four-Door Tavern was a step up from Bud and Grover's place, but a short one at best. At least the floor wasn't covered in sawdust. A thick haze of cigarette smoke hung over the dance floor, where sweating people wrestled with each other in time to a hillbilly band; steel guitar, a bass fiddle and a stand-up drummer with a snare drum, a cymbal and a high-hat.

The lead singer was a rawboned guy in his mid-twenties blessed with a farm boy's wholesome good looks and a head of blond hair combed back with about half a jar of Dixie Peach pomade and sideburns that reached an inch past his earlobes. He was dressed in tight black pants over cowboy boots and a red pearl-buttoned shirt with a shiny black yoke across the shoulders. The name Leland was painted in an arch over the sound hole of his guitar.

Jones shouldered into an open spot at the bar and ordered a beer. He didn't really care for country music, but he had to admit that Leland Stark had a pretty good voice. That coupled with his performer's personality made him a big hit with the crowd. A few more songs about lovin', fightin', drinkin' and cheatin' took the band to its break, and the bartender plugged the jukebox back in. The big Wurlitzer's lights blinked on, and the turntable picked up where it left off in a scratchy recording of "Blue Moon of Kentucky."

Leland stepped down from the band's dais and started across the floor to the bar with a girl on either arm. Jones waited until the singer passed by him and called out his name. Leland's eyes met Jones's and he nodded once. He leaned down and said something to the girls that Jones couldn't hear. They giggled and walked back to their table. Leland pushed into the crowded bar beside Jones and waved for the barmaid. "You're Jones?" Leland talked around a toothpick in the corner of his mouth.

"That's me."

"Bud said you'd be by."

"What did he tell you?"

"Enough. I hear you need a driver."

Jones nodded. "I do. Hard to drive and shoot at the same time."

"Understood."

"Doesn't worry you?"

"What, a couple people shooting at me? Hell, I was in the sights of a hundred or more Japs at a time in the war, and I'm still here." Leland took the toothpick from his mouth and gestured with it for emphasis. "Besides, if I'm driving, we'll be a hard target."

"Some people might get killed in the bargain. That bother you?"

"Hell, no. I'm a Marine; that's what I'm trained to do."

"I'll pick up the car from Coakee tomorrow and meet you at Bud and Grover's place around nine o'clock."

"Good enough." Leland pushed away from the bar and threaded his way across the dance floor to the table where his admirers were waiting for him. Jones left a dollar on the bar and headed outside.

When he was almost to his car, he heard a step on the gravel and a voice. "I smell something, fellows. You smell it?"

Jones turned to see three men, one in a cowboy hat, silhouetted against the neon sign. "I smell a Revenuer," Cowboy said. Jones backed between two cars to keep them from circling him.

"You boys have the wrong number."

"Why don't you pull out your badge like you did for old man Ellis? He told us all about you. You can wipe your ass with that badge. It don't scare us one bit."

One of Cowboy's companions spoke up. "We don't cotton to Revenuers coming around here wrecking stills, putting folks in jail, causing us trouble."

"That's right, Jeff," the third man said.

Jones felt a tingle at the base of his brain. The Sight showed him a fourth man coming up behind him ready to swing a pick handle. Jones twisted to the side and the bludgeon swished past him. He grabbed the pick handle and twisted it, using his attacker's momentum to throw him to the ground in a clumsy somersault and wrench the weapon from his grasp.

The man rose to a crouch, and Jones swung the club two-handed and caught him square in the forehead. One down. Before the other three could come up with an alternative plan, Jones waded into them swinging the pick handle like a Louisville Slugger. He caught Cowboy at the knee and felt bone shatter. The man screamed and fell to the ground.

One of the others pulled out a hunting knife, the blade pulsing red in the flashing neon. He charged Jones, sweeping the foot-long blade back and forth in broad figure eights. By the third sweep, Jones had his rhythm and in one fluid motion, shifted his grip and wrapped his fingers around the broad end of the pick handle to driving the narrow end into the knife man's throat.

A rabbit punch made Jones see stars and drop the club. Jeff had come up behind him. Jones fell out of his reach for a second, and he rolled aside in time to avoid a kick that would have fractured his skull.

Jeff circled Jones, fists up, his teeth showing as the light caught his face. "You think you're tough? Come on, you son of a bitch," he snarled.

Most street fighters and barroom brawlers rely on a personal trick to surprise an opponent and give them an easy advantage by doing maximum damage out of the gate. Most times it works, unless, that is, the victim has seen it before or in Jones' case, been trained to counter it.

Jeff brought his fist down, intending to knock Jones's forearm aside and take a shot at his unprotected jaw with his right. Jones dodged the blow and caught Jeff's arm in both his hands, pulling him off balance and yanking the arm behind his back to his shoulder blades. Jones kicked Jeff's feet from under him and pushed his face into the gravel. He pulled upward on Jeff's arm and felt the tendons straining. Jeff moaned in pain. Jones thought it over. Instead of breaking Jeff's arm, Jones drove his elbow into the base of his skull and walked away, leaving the hillbilly quartet sprawled among the parked cars. They were still lying in the gravel as Jones drove away.

• • •

Kevin Mayhew slumped behind the wheel of his Chevy coupe, the dashboard lights painting his features a pale green. A strip of adhesive tape spanned his nose where it had been broken on the steering wheel when the car went into the pond, but he and Roy got even with Hedge Bryner for the stunt he pulled.

It used to bother him, even more than it did Roy to sit still and wait, but he learned that that's how you catch fish. Patience. Law enforcement was all about patience, and so was vengeance. He switched on the radio. It warmed up in the middle of Eddy Arnold singing "Bouquet of Roses." It seemed that every other week he had a new hit record. Kevin turned the dial and found a big band playing "Don't Get Around Much Anymore." That was more like it.

He hated hillbilly music, hated hillbilly food, and hated everything else about them. Hillbillies were little more than animals, Jukes and Kallikaks grubbing a living out of the dirt. When he and his brothers first arrived in Fayette County to hunt moonshiners, he had nothing but contempt for the locals. Then Richard died chasing one of the degenerates, and Kevin's contempt blossomed into hatred. He and his brother Roy blamed Billy Cobb for Richard's death, but before they could make him pay, the Army snatched him up and he was killed in Korea. That's all right, though, Kevin thought. Plenty more under that rock he came from.

Kevin took a swig of the coffee from his thermos bottle. It was lukewarm now, but it would help him stay alert. The short-wave radio under the dash crackled and hissed but no one spoke. The Treasury agents were elsewhere tonight, leaving Kevin and Roy a clear field for their unsanctioned activity. The Tompkins clan didn't have much imagination. They used the same routes and the same cars over and over. If not tonight, the next night or the next night, but the Mayhew brothers would be ready. Patience.

• • •

Ardell Tompkins slid behind the wheel of the big black Dodge sedan and stared through the windshield. Beyond the square of light from the barn door, the night was black as a tar bucket. Behind him, the trunk slammed shut, and he heard the gallon jugs of shine rattle in their wooden crates. In the rearview mirror, he saw his daddy, Cameron Tompkins, talking to his younger brother Travis, hands on his shoulders, forehead to forehead, the way fathers do when they have something important to say.

In the mirror, he saw Cameron hand what the boys called simply Daddy's Gun to Travis. The gun was a double-barreled Remington with the stock cut off and carved into a curved handle like his grandfather's old flintlock pistol that hung over the mantel in the farm house's living room. The barrels were sawed off short, making the weapon look like an old-time pirate gun he saw once in a book. Tonight's run wasn't just business, it was about family pride. The Bryners made threats and boasted all up and down the mountain that they were going to get even for Hedge's death, unfairly accusing the Tompkins clan for blowing up Hedge's car. Well, they'd show those Bryners that the Tompkins boys ain't afraid of nothin' nor nobody. Just let them try something tonight. They'd see what's what.

Travis climbed into the front seat. "Ready, big brother?"

"Yep."

Travis patted the shotgun cradled in his lap. "Me too."

Cameron stepped up beside Ardell's open window. The seams in the patriarch's face were deep furrows in the harsh light. Daddy looks old and tired, Ardell thought. It won't be too much longer 'til I have to take over.

"Don't have to tell you to be careful, son."

"I will, Daddy. Don't you worry. I'll be to Accident and back before that old rooster crows sunup."

Cameron nodded, then reached into the window and ruffled Ardell's hair with a work roughened hand. He stepped back, and Ardell started the engine. The Dodge had been a cop car once, and its already hefty motor had been stroked and bored, the heads milled. A full race camshaft plus a special manifold to accommodate two carburetors made the motor half again as powerful as before. He revved the engine, and the snapping roar of the exhaust filled the barn.

Ardell gave his father a two-finger salute and rolled out into the night.

Cameron watched the tail lights disappear down the lane and around the bend. He was never much for church or religion, but that night, he wished he knew how to pray.

Ardell's eyes flicked back and forth between the road and his rear-view mirror. He was confident, having made the run over the Maryland border to Accident dozens of times, but the possibility that the Bryner clan might be lying in wait somewhere along the way made him watchful. Beside him, Travis slouched in the seat, cradling Daddy's Gun in his lap.

"Light me up a cigarette, Little Brother."

Travis shook out a Lucky and lit it. He passed it to Ardell, who never took his eyes away from the road. "You think the Bryners'll try something?" Travis said.

"Too soon. All that talk and chest beating's like the howl of a scalded dog. In a week, maybe, give 'em time to plan something, but not this soon."

"You're probably right," Travis said, "but if they show up for the party, —" he patted the shotgun "—they'll dance to our tune, not theirs."

Ardell nodded. He'd been shot at more times than one, and had shot back in the bargain, but unlike Travis, he didn't think it was exciting or an adventure, just dangerous. He'd had enough of that in the war. Travis was too young to be drafted then, and he still thought he missed something glamorous. If the fight keeps up in Korea, Ardell thought, he may get his chance to find out firsthand that he's wrong.

The pair were driving on a two-laner just short of the Maryland border when a car fell in behind them, its high beams blazing through the rear windshield. Travis twisted in his seat to look out the back.

"Keep your head down, damn it." Ardell snapped.

Another hundred yards down the road, Ardell felt a jolt. The driver behind sped up and rammed him then dropped back. Ardell watched his mirror. The car started moving in again, and at the last second before he hit, Ardell cracked the gas and the Dodge accelerated, minimizing the impact. Travis started rolling down his window.

"What are you doing?"

"Gonna give those Bryners a taste of lead." He started pulling himself through the window well with one hand, the shotgun in the other. Ardell grabbed Travis's belt and yanked him back inside. "Stay in here, you fool. You need two hands to shoot that gun. You can't hold on. I hit a bump or he rams us while you're hanging out of that window, you'll fall on your ass — if you're lucky."

Ardell knew the road. In half a mile it dipped into a long downhill stretch that ended in an almost right angle left turn where a narrow bridge crossed a creek. This late at night, both lanes were empty, and he could power slide around the curve and into the bridge. If the driver behind him misjudged by one second, he'd end up in the creek.

A bullet shattered Ardell's outside mirror. He looked in the rear-view and saw a muzzle flash outside the driver's window. He was shooting a handgun left-handed but not hitting much. This definitely wasn't a Revenuer; he was alone in the car.

The Dodge swooped over the rise, nearly leaving the road, and started the descent into the valley. The chase car hung on. That's it, Ardell thought, keep close so you don't see what's coming. Halfway down the slope, Ardell's eye twitched to the mirror. The chase car suddenly fell away. He looked back to the road just as Travis cried, "Ardell look out!"

A dark shape burst from the trees a few yards ahead. A stakeside truck rolled across the road in Ardell's path, blocking both lanes. Ardell slammed on the brakes and tried to broadside into the truck, but his pursuer rammed him again, and the Dodge plowed up the embankment to roll onto its roof and come to rest against a thick-boled oak.

Ardell woke a few minutes later. He smelled gasoline mixed with the sharp tang of moonshine from the broken jugs in the trunk. He tried to move. The steering column was bent downward, pinning him to the seat with the steering wheel. When he tried to push with his feet, Ardell realized that he couldn't feel his legs. "Travis," he said. "Travis, are you all right?"

In the dashboard lights, he saw his brother lolled against the driver's door, his head too far down on his chest to still be locked on his spine.

Lights. Two flashlights, their beams bobbing in the darkness. Ardell saw Daddy's Gun lying on the floor by Travis's feet, just out of his reach.

One of the men spoke. At first, Ardell thought they were talking to him, then realized they were talking to someone who wasn't even there.

"For you Little Brother," the gruff voice said. "It's all for you."

"Who are you?" Ardell shouted. "What do you want?"

"An eye for an eye," the voice intoned. "And an eye, and an eye, and an eye."

Ardell heard the scrape of a striker, and a bright red flame lit the scene with a hellish glow. The speaker held the railroad flare over his head. Ardell saw a thick mustache and a pair of rimless glasses, their lenses ovals of flame. Roy Mayhew. With a flick of his wrist, Roy tossed the flare through the window into the back seat of the Dodge into the puddling mix of gasoline and alcohol.

● ● ●

When he got to his room in Brownsville, Jones pulled off his shoes and flopped fully dressed onto the bed. In less than a minute, he was asleep, but it didn't last long. Knocking at the door of his room yanked him out of his dreams like a rabbit in a snare. He rolled off the bed with a squeak of its springs and reached for the revolver on the night stand. In the thin bar of light under the door he saw one pair of feet.

"Jones, you in there?" The voice was almost a whisper, but he recognized it at once. It was Danny Hayes, one of Skitch's men.

"Yeah, I'm here." Jones unlocked the door and let Danny into the room. The sandy-haired Marine stepped inside and Jones closed the door behind him. He looked at his watch: two-thirty. "What's up?"

"Skitch got a call from the Lytles. Another moonshiner got killed tonight. They want you up there right away."

Jones nodded. "I need you to drive me up and bring my car back."

"Okay. Out of curiosity, just tell me why."

"Because my car has to be in front of the pool room from about six tonight on."

"Got it."

Jones dozed in the passenger seat as Danny drove his car through Uniontown and into the mountains. In an hour, they pulled into the parking lot of Bud and Grover's bar. In the Ford's headlights, Jones saw bullet holes, broken windows and a big bare patch where a shotgun blast had blown away a chunk of the building's shingle siding.

"Want me to wait?"

Jones shook his head. "Just let me get a few things out of the back." He walked behind the car and opened the trunk. Under the spare tire, he worked a hidden catch that opened a storage well Coakee had built in for him. In it was a canvas duffel bag, He lifted it out, slung it over his shoulder by the strap, and closed the trunk.

"Take off. I'm good from here."

Danny nodded, eyeing the bullet holes. "If you say so, Jones." He fish-hooked the car in reverse and drove away, bumping and lurching down the rutted lane.

The door to the tavern opened, and in the rectangle of light, he saw one of the Lytles — it was hard to tell them apart in silhouette. "Come on in, Jones." He recognized the voice: Grover.

The tables and the bar were empty. Sonny was pushing a broom around the dance floor, sweeping up broken glass, the butt of a revolver sticking out of the waistband of his trousers.

"Must've been some party. Anybody hurt?"

Grover shook his head. "Nobody, but not for lack of trying. We were closing up, no customers in the place, when we heard a car pull up outside. Then the shooting started. It was over in less than a minute."

Bud came out of the storeroom. "It was the Tompkins clan."

Jones wasn't so sure but didn't say so. "You saw them?"

Bud shook his head. "It was over so fast, all we saw was tail lights pulling away."

"Then how do you know it was them?"

"Ardell Tompkins and his brother Travis were killed tonight making a moonshine run out of Hawkins Hollow. Their car was run off the road and burned. Who else could it be?"

"And you're sure it wasn't the Bryners did that."

"As sure as I can be. Practically the whole clan was in here at the same time it happened, drinking to Hedge's memory. But the Tompkinses won't listen to me or anybody else."

"You're lucky this was a knee jerk action."

"What do you mean?"

"If they'd taken the time to plan, it would've been much worse. You're lucky they didn't have a couple sticks of dynamite handy."

Bud nodded. "I see what you mean."

"Can you arrange a meeting tonight between the families?"

"Are you crazy?" Grover said. "Both sides are ready to shoot each other on sight."

"You're going to have to do it. I can't deal with the Mayhews while I'm dodging bullets from some cracker feud."

"I'll try," Bud said. "But I can't guarantee anything."

"Tell them I'll meet with both sides together. Who're the heads of the families?"

"Anson Bryner and Cameron Tompkins."

"Get word to them. Pick a location that's out of both your territory and theirs, somewhere the law can't listen in."

"I know just the place."

• • •

The sun was about to rise when the cars rolled up to either side of the rusted railroad trestle over the Youghiogheny River, an unofficial dividing line between the Tompkins' territory and the Lytles'. Bud was right. The trestle was a good place for the meeting. Seventy feet over the river on cut stone pylons, its dual spider web of girders made sniping from the sidelines difficult, and the only way to get to the middle of the hundred-foot span unless you had a train or a handcar was on foot. The floor of the trestle was little more than railroad ties spanning the steel understructure. Below, the white water swirled and boiled as it rushed to a nearby waterfall. The rush of the river would cover any conversation past ten feet.

Jones waited alone in the middle of the bridge. He'd mediated between warring families in Jersey. Mobsters, hillbillies, it was all the same. Revenge for lost family, turf, and maintaining a swinging dick posture were the primary issues, and not always in that order. The trick was to satisfy both sides without either losing face.

The parties arrived within a minute of each other, two cars for the Bryners, and one car and a pickup load of the Tompkins clan. Bud and Grover arrived in their Mercury. Bud came onto the trestle first, hands out at his sides and empty. He knew both clans and would introduce them to Jones. Bud patted down the three Bryners and Grover the three Tompkinses to make sure there were no guns. When he was finished, Bud came to the middle of the trestle. "Ready, Jones?"

"Let's start the show."

Bud beckoned with either hand to both sides, and three men came from each of the clans, leaving the rest of their respective parties at the ends of the trestle. Anson Bryner walked ahead of two of his sons. He was a good three inches taller than Jones, and half again as broad, but by Jones' estimation none of it was fat. He was bald to his crown with thick white hair that swirled in waves around his ears like busts of Benjamin Franklin Jones had seen. The patriarch's thick brow shielded dark eyes, making his face hard to read.

Cameron Tompkins was a short man, lean and wiry. His face was shadowed by a slouch hat but Jones could make out gray stubble along a sharp jaw line. Tompkins was half the size of his counterpart, but Jones decided he didn't want to bet on either of them in a one-on-one fight. Behind Tompkins, two young men followed. All had their hands out and empty.

"Boys," Bud said, "this is C. O. Jones."

"Heard you was a Revenuer," Tompkins said, cocking his head back and studying Jones with one eye.

"Old man Ellis tell you that?" Bud said.

"Said Jones here showed him a badge and all."

"A badge I found in the car that was chasing Hedge Bryner and ended up in Ellis's pond. I'm about as much a Revenuer as you are, Tompkins." Murmuring broke out among the men. "I work for Skitch Mottola." The buzz of voices suddenly ceased. "I see you know the name. He sent me to get to the bottom of this. First, let me express my sympathy at your losses. You've both lost family, you've both lost equipment and you've both lost merchandise —"

"And you shot up my place tonight," Bud said, pointing an accusing finger at Cameron Tompkins.

"The hell we did. That's a god damned lie," Tompkins snarled, throwing his chest forward.

Bud started for Tompkins. "You scrawny bastard, I oughta —"

"Hey!" Jones' voice cracked like a whip, freezing everyone. "All of you shut up and all of you listen. I don't think anybody on this bridge did anything to anybody else on this bridge. Let's start with that."

"What are you talking about?" Anson Bryner said.

"None of you are fools. None of you is stupid enough to start a war that neither side will win. There's a German proverb that goes: *Wenn zwei sich streiten, freut sich der dritte,* when two are fighting, the third rejoices."

Jones let that sink in before he continued. "Things have gone smoothly for you all for a long time. Skitch keeps the Sheriff and the State Police off your backs, and the Feds don't seem to try too hard, because it's too much work. If you all start shooting each other and blowing up each other's stills and cars, who benefits?"

"They do," one of the younger Tompkinses said. "Those Lytles think they'll put us out of business and they're stirring up those Bryners to do their dirty work. Show them what you found, Daddy."

Cameron held out a metal ferrule with a spike at its end. "I found this in Ardell and Travis's car. It didn't burn on its own. Those sons of bitches lit it up."

This started a shouting match that threatened to derail the whole business. Jones pulled his automatic and fired a shot in the air.

"I thought there was no guns allowed at this shindig," Anson said angrily. He pointed at Jones' pistol. "What's that?"

"That, my friend," Jones said coldly, "is the referee."

A shout came from the Tompkins side of the trestle. "Daddy, is everything all right?"

Cameron eyed Jones. The wrong word from him would bring his clan shooting and the whole scene would go to hell. "Well, Tompkins," Jones said, "Is it?"

Tompkins hesitated for a second or two then shouted over his shoulder. "It's okay. Stay put."

Jones turned to Anson. "Tell your boys. They need to hear your voice. Now."

"Nothing wrong," Anson called. "Stay where you're at."

Jones reached into his pocket and pulled out the badge. "This is the badge I found at Ellis's farm. I checked on the number. It used to belong to Richard Mayhew."

"Mayhew?" Anson said. He spat.

"That no-good bastard. Him and his brothers," Cameron added."He got what was comin' to him."

"His brothers disagree. I believe they killed Hedge and your boys," Jones turned to Bud, "and shot up your bar to get you all blaming each other."

"The Feds would never sanction something like that," Bud said.

"Then they've gone rogue and they're running their own show."

"How do we know you're telling the truth?" Anson said

"You don't. You just have to trust me. All I ask is twenty-four hours to put an end to this. Take a breather, cool off, and wait. You'll know soon enough."

"Cameron?" Bud said.

Tompkins nodded. "I'll give it a day."

Anson hesitated but finally said, "We'll hold off, but twenty-four hours is all."

Both sides went back to their cars and drove away. Bud leaned over the railing and stared down into the swirling water. He shook his head. "Whew. I can't believe you got them to agree."

"It wasn't that hard. Neither of those families wants this to go on. They know what feuds are all about. All I did was show them a common enemy and offer an alternative that let them keep their pride."

"You know, Jones, if you don't deliver, they'll all want to kill you, and Grover and me too."

Jones put a foot on one of the rails. "We'd better get off this trestle. There's a train coming."

• • •

Late in the afternoon Bud's driver dropped Jones off at Coakee's garage. Coakee was waiting outside, his mongrels on their haunches surrounding him like a phalanx of guards. Coakee handed Jones the keys. "Did what you wanted. It was a chore, but she's ready."

Jones looked the Plymouth over. The alterations were seamless, and the paint a perfect match. "I see it's riding lower. Will it still handle all right?"

Coakee laughed. "You got Leland driving. He could outrun Revenuers with a tractor trailer." Then his expression turned serious. "Watch your ass, Jones. I'd hate to lose a customer."

• • •

Jones grabbed a few hours of sleep on a cot in Bud and Grover's backroom, and he woke to the thump of the jukebox through the wall. He looked at his watch: 19:04. He sat up and stretched. It was always a marvel

"All I ask is twenty-four hours to put an end to this."

to Jones how something as simple as a canvas cot could be as comfortable as a double bed with a feather tick.

Jones sat at the table in the backroom and set his duffel bag on the floor beside him. He reached inside and pulled out a leather zip case. In it was a disassembled Sten machine gun. Jones carefully examined every component as he fitted them together. American gangsters and the FBI preferred the Thompson submachine gun but Jones found it too cumbersome, and the hundred-round drum magazines heavy and difficult to conceal.

The Thompson had its utility but was too often a crutch for people who were poor shots or didn't want to bother aiming for a close grouping. "The bludgeon, not the rapier," as Jones' British MI-5 counterpart Treadwell, code name Iago, once said. "If you can't kill a bloke with thirty-two bullets, you likely won't succeed with a hundred."

The intimidation factor played into the attraction as well. A man with a pistol or even a shotgun would think twice before going against a Tommy-gun wielding opponent.

Jones didn't bother fitting the stock, little more than fancily bent tubing, onto the Sten's frame. It made the Sten too long to fit under his coat. Stens had two bad habits; jamming, and going off when dropped or bumped the wrong way. Jones had neither worry with his. It was a gift from MI-5, manufactured in Line Brothers' London toy works. The weapon had been tested, tweaked, and refined to perfection by MI-5's armorers.

Jones loaded a second magazine, just in case, but tonight's job, if it went as Jones hoped, would be quick and dirty, and he wouldn't need the second one.

The door opened and Grover looked in. His eyes widened at the sight of the machine gun. "Leland's here."

"I'll be right out."

Jones measured a length of rawhide thong and tied it to the Sten behind the trigger guard. He looped the thong over his shoulder and adjusted it so that it would swing naturally into firing position. The last touch was a red and black plaid hunting coat, borrowed from Grover, long enough to cover the muzzle of the gun. To the casual observer, it made Jones look like one of Bud and Grover's gang, or for that matter, like half of the population of Wharton Township.

As an extra measure, Jones slipped his .45 into the game pocket in the back of the coat. "Never rely on one weapon," Hennessey had taught him. "Keep your options open."

Jones buttoned the coat over the Sten and opened the storeroom door. Bud and Grover's bar was crowded with drinkers and dancers hopping to a two-step fiddle tune on the jukebox. The Lytle brothers sat at a table at the edge of the dance floor and would be there until closing time, in case anybody questioned their involvement in what was about to happen.

Leland was crouched beside the Plymouth, checking one of the tires. He had traded his cowboy shirt for a denim Eisenhower jacket over a chambray work shirt, and his fancy boots for steel-toed work shoes. His blond pompadour was tucked under a snap brim cap, but the toothpick was still in the corner of his mouth.

"Everything okay?" Jones said as he opened the passenger door.

"Time to find out," Leland said with a grin that belied the killer behind it. "Hop in."

"Take this." Jones offered Leland an automatic identical to his own. Leland opened his jacket to show Jones a big cowboy Colt tucked in the waistband of his jeans. "Thanks. Got one of my own."

Leland started the car, and unlike so many of the drivers Jones had seen, didn't race the engine and let out a raucous blast from the exhaust. Leland let the engine idle for a moment, listening to it rumble and feeling the throb through the floorboard. He nodded, approving, but made no move for the gearshift.

"What's wrong?"

"Nothing," Leland said. "Just letting the oil warm up before I put her in gear." He pushed in the clutch and backed the car out of its spot. He gently touched the gas and the Plymouth rolled quietly out of the parking lot and onto the rutted lane beyond. No noise, no flair, no attention.

They reached the blacktop a few minutes later, and Leland said, "Let's see what she'll do. Hang onto your teeth, Jones." He floored the gas pedal at the same time he popped the clutch, and the car came alive with a roar like an angry lion. In seconds, the car was pushing eighty.

Tail lights ahead. They came up on a car in their lane, and Leland twitched the wheel, sending the Plymouth around the car and back in their lane in a blur of motion. The tires barely chirped.

"Handles good," Leland said in the same matter-of-fact tone he would use discussing the weather or a song on the jukebox. On a long, empty straightaway, he pushed the speed over a hundred. "Brace yourself." He stomped the brakes and whipped the wheel left, sending the car into a broadslide and finally turning it a hundred eighty degrees, a move Jones recognized as a "bootlegger turn."

"Oh, yeah," Leland said, driving back the way they had come, "She handles real good."

Jones was trained in evasive driving, but he had to admit that Leland was at least as skilled as he was, and probably better on the country roads. The alternative would have been for Jones to drive while someone else handled the gunplay, and if there was killing to be done, it was better that he handle it.

"Let's go to the still."

Leland drove in a completely different manner now, running up the RPMs and blasting the exhaust, showing off and attracting attention instead of stealthily slinking around the back roads. "What happens if the Mayhews don't take the bait?"

"Then I have a problem with the Bryners and the Tompkins clan."

The Mayhews had hit Hedge, then the Tompkins brothers. Now it was Bud and Grover's turn. Neither family was running tonight, and Jones was counting on the rogue agents chasing the one tanker on the road.

The still, one of several the Lytles operated, was tucked into a hollow that was one road in and out, and generally otherwise inaccessible except by a difficult trek over rough terrain. The car bumped and jostled over ruts and rocks.

"I guess the Mayhews figured they'd better not wait to kick the kettle over."

"Why's that?" Jones said. He had a good idea, but he wanted to hear Leland's take on it.

"Another month, it'll all be shut down. Too hard to cook in the snow, and all the leaves fall off, there goes your cover. Most everybody around here lays off 'til Spring."

And with time on their hands, thought Jones, two vengeful families could focus on a feud that promised to put most of them in the ground. The Mayhews were clever, diabolically so.

Jones lit a cigarette and shook one out for Leland. "Smoke?"

"No thanks. I quit not long ago. Bad for my voice. That's why I'm always chewin' on a toothpick. Gotta think about my future."

Jones stared out the windshield, marveling at the confidence of a man who might be driving himself straight into the jaws of death.

Leland stopped the car beside a clump of mountain laurel and flashed his lights. Like a magic trick, the bushes swung away on a hinged gate to reveal another lane to the left. Leland pulled onto it, and the gate swung back into place. In the red glow of the tail lights, Jones saw two men with long guns.

Even with the windows up, Jones could smell the scent of wood smoke mixed with an odor he couldn't place.

"Sourdough bread," Leland said, anticipating the question. "Good cooking mash smells like sourdough bread baking. You get the mix wrong, it can smell like anything from puke to paint thinner."

It was necessary to go through the motions as if they were actually loading moonshine into the Plymouth's tank so that if the Mayhews were watching the still or the route, the whole act would look real. Leland pulled the car into a clearing beside a cylindrical tank in a wooden frame. Below the tank, a fire glowed. "Stay in the car, Jones. We don't know who might be watching." Leland climbed out and shook hands with two dim figures, one in overalls and sporting a long beard; the other in a jacket similar to the one Jones was wearing and a leather cap.

Jones watched in the side mirror as the men dragged a heavy hose from a holding vat to the back of the car. Leland opened the trunk and Jones could hear the clanking of the hose coupling, then feel the vibration of the pump, even though nothing was coming through the hose. In a few minutes, the operation was complete. Leland slammed the trunk shut, waved goodbye to the still tenders and climbed into the driver's seat. "Ready, Jones?"

"One second." Jones took a metal tube from his pocket and shook out two white tablets. "Benzedrine," he said. "Want one?"

"Our sergeant called them 'sleep in a bottle,' a gallon of coffee in a little white pill." He held out his hand. "I'll take two." He dry-swallowed the bennies. Jones crunched his between his teeth to start the drug moving faster.

"Let's do it."

They rolled through the camouflaged gate and onto the bumpy lane. Except for their headlights, the forest was totally dark. Once or twice, Jones saw the luminous eyes of deer staring back from the curtain of trees and brush, but besides that, nothing and no one.

• • •

The Mayhew brothers sat in the parking lot of the diner listening to the chatter on the police band radio, Kevin behind the wheel. He was the better driver, and in spite of his glasses, Roy was the better shot. Kevin looked across the seat to his brother. Roy was stroking the mustache he'd recently grown; he thought it made him look sexy to women, like an old

West desperado. Kevin thought it made him look like a horse's ass, that and the flat-brimmed hat with the round crown he taken to wearing lately. What next? Twin holsters with pearl handled Colt .45s; maybe spin them on his fingers?

"Any coffee left, Kev?"

Kevin shook the thermos bottle. "Some." He handed it to Roy who unscrewed the cap and poured out the last of the coffee. Roy put his forefinger across his mustache to keep it from getting wet. Kevin rolled his eyes.

"I'll go inside and get the bottle filled. We may need more later." Roy reached for the door handle and stopped short as the radio buzzed, "Got a gray sedan haulin' ass east on State Route 381. He got away from me, but maybe you can catch him before he makes Farmington. Over."

Another voice responded, "I'm headed that way now. I'll watch for him. Over."

"Won't have to watch. You'll hear those loud pipes of his a mile away. Over and out."

"Think that's our boy?" Roy said.

Kevin nodded. "Good chance." He started the engine. The tip they got earlier that evening was that the Lytles were making a run to Morgantown, and that Leland Stark was driving. The Mayhews wanted to hit the Lytle operation again, ramp up the hostility between them and the Tompkins clan, but bringing down that cocky pretty boy Stark sweetened the pot. Being Treasury Agents gave the Mayhews the equipment, the intelligence, and the opportunity to set the moonshiners at each other's throats and foment a feud that would decimate the clans and fulfill the oath the brothers took at Richard's funeral: vengeance.

Kevin put the Chevy in gear and switched on the headlights. "Let's go get the bastard."

• • •

Leland pulled the Plymouth onto the two-lane that led across the border to Morgantown. It was late, and the road was empty. Leland ran the Plymouth up to seventy, his forearm resting on the sill of the open window. The Mayhews knew the still, they knew the route, and they knew the car. Two miles, three, then a pair of headlights appeared in the rear-view mirror.

"Company," Leland said, cocking his eye to the mirror. "They're closing fast."

Jones nodded and turned to kneel on the seat. He slapped the magazine into the Sten and ratcheted back the bolt. Through the divided rear windshield, he could see their pursuer in a split image. The headlights were gaining. Closer, closer, until they disappeared below the windshield's rim. A crash jolted the Plymouth. The chase car dropped back, and ran up for another strike. Leland cracked the gas and the Plymouth surged ahead, avoiding the hit.

"Stay steady," Jones said. "Don't get too far ahead."

The chase car went into the left lane and started to pass. Jones recognized the car as a late model Chevrolet coupe. As it moved alongside, Jones saw the passenger window roll down and framed in it he saw the head and shoulders of a man with glasses, a mustache, and a pistol. Jones raised the Sten to fire across Leland's chest, but before he could Leland hit the brakes and wrenched the wheel hard left, the Chevy shot past, skidding to a halt, and Leland was already speeding up the road in the opposite direction.

The Chevy's lights disappeared around a bend. "Don't lose him," Jones snapped, and Leland replied. "I won't tell you how to shoot, Jones. Don't tell me how to drive."

Leland held a steady seventy, and soon enough the Chevy's headlights were back in the mirror. "We got a long straightaway coming up, Jones. Might be a good place to make your play."

"Try to keep him behind you."

"No problem."

Leland moved the car to the left until its hood was centered over the white line in the road, as if the clipper ship ornament were sailing up a narrow white river. The trees were close at either hand, and the soft berm made it unlikely that whichever Mayhew was driving would chance running off the pavement at high speed.

A muzzle flash; a bullet sang off the roof of the car. A second shot, and glass exploded in the left half of the rear windshield. The Chevy was closer now. Thirty yards, twenty.

Jones sprang upward, shoulders against the car's ceiling. The false panel Coakee had put in the hole he cut in the roof popped out and rattled over the back of the Plymouth and under the Chevy's wheels. He raised the Sten and fired a burst, spraying the Chevy's windshield. The glass spidered, but the bullets didn't go through.

Bulletproof glass.

Another shot from the Chevy, and Jones felt a blaze of pain in his shoulder. Thinking quickly, he emptied what was left of the Sten's magazine into the Chevy's grille and hood, hoping to hit a vital spot in the engine. The Chevy slowed, and another bullet bounced off the Plymouth's roof as Jones dropped back inside.

"You're hit," Leland said.

"Yeah, but I disabled their car."

"Leave it to me." Leland did a U-turn and started back to the spot where the Chevy sat at the side of the road, steam and smoke billowing from under its hood. The Mayhew brothers were crouching behind the Chevy, aiming guns over its hood like cops on the cover of a pulp magazine. As the Plymouth got closer, they opened fire. The windshield shattered, spraying Leland and Jones with shards.

Leland turned the wheel and aimed the Plymouth diagonally at the disabled car. The Mayhews kept shooting and realized too late what was about to happen in the next two seconds. The left front corner of the Plymouth struck the Chevy at its weakest spot, the rear edge of the door, and the car bent upward in a shallow vee. The nose of the Plymouth dug in under the Chevy, and its momentum tipped the coupe, rolling it on its side, trapping the gunmen underneath.

Blood from a cut where Jones' forehead hit the dashboard flowed into his eye socket. He tugged at the door handle and his door groaned open on bent hinges. He tried to step out of the car, but fell sideways onto the glass strewn pavement, his head spinning. His only thought was to finish the job.

He got two steps before he pitched forward and Leland caught him by his armpits. "Sit down, Jones. I'll take it from here." Leland drew the long-barreled Colt from his waistband.

"No . . . no." Jones shook his head. "I have to. It's the deal."

"I won't tell." Leland lowered Jones to the ground and propped him against the side of the Plymouth. He took the toothpick from his mouth and threw it aside. "Sit tight. I'll be right back."

As Jones slipped into unconsciousness, the last thing he heard was a shot, a scream, and another shot.

• • •

Sound, and scent, and color washed over Jones' brain as he struggled to swim at least to wakefulness. It would be so easy to just let go and slip back under, but his nature wouldn't permit it. Bread—baking bread —moonshine brewing? Was he at the still? The clatter of pots and pans, voices. It was a toss-up which hurt worse, his head or his shoulder.

Jones forced his eyes open and the room around him came into focus. He was in an old four-poster bed under a quilt of bright colorful squares. Jones turned his head and in the rectangle of light from the open door he saw Leland dozing in a ladder backed chair, feet propped up on the night stand.

"Leland." Jones' voice was a croak.

The runner's eyes opened and he yawned and stretched. "Welcome back, Jones."

"Where am I?"

"My mama's house."

Jones reached his hand across his chest and felt bandages. "She patch me up?"

"No, I had that privilege. You learn a lot doing combat triage. You were lucky. The bullet went in one way and out the other. I had more trouble stitching up your face."

"What time is it? How long have I been out?"

"It's almost six. You've been out half a day."

"The Mayhews, the cars —"

"Taken care of. Cars're out in the tall weeds behind Coakee's barn, and in a day or two, Coakee's boys'll salvage what they can and scrap the rest."

"The bodies?"

"Feeding the pigs at my uncle's farm."

"But I told the Tompkinses and the Bryners I'd deliver them."

"You got the next best thing, Jones." Leland reached into his pocket. He pulled out a pair of badges, two shields that said TREASURY DEPARTMENT.

• • •

For the second time, Jones waited in the middle of the railroad trestle as the clans came together. Jones was leaning against the railing, but when Anson Bryner and Cameron Tompkins arrived, he pushed himself away and fought to stay upright unaided. Bud and Leland stood on either side.

"Jones has news," Bud said.

"The whole business was a scheme to start a feud between you. The Mayhews hoped that you'd kill each other off."

"To stop us moonshining?" Anson said.

"No, to get even for the death of their brother."

"And the Mayhews?" Cameron said.

"Dead. Both of them."

Anson cocked his head in skepticism. "I don't see no bodies. Where's your proof?"

Jones handed Anson one of the blood-stained badges. "Proof enough?" he handed Cameron the other one.

Leland spoke up. "I was there. Jones is telling the truth. He took a bullet over it."

"An eye for an eye," Jones said. "It's over."

Anson stared at the badge for a moment and closed his huge hand over it. "I'm satisfied."

Jones looked to Cameron Tompkins. The little man nodded.

"Now, Bud said, "let's bury our dead and put things back the way they were."

No handshakes, no parting words. The Tompkinses and the Bryners went in their respective directions, leaving Bud, Jones and Leland on the trestle.

"And this is for you," Jones said, handing Richard Mayhew's shield to Bud.

Bud studied the shield for a moment and threw it off the trestle into the swirling river below. "You did good, Jones. I hope I never have to call on you again."

"That makes two of us." Jones turned to Leland. "Give me a lift to Uniontown?"

"Glad to, but first, I thought maybe you'd stop by my Mama's. She's got fried chicken, yams, and beans on the table. Said she'd be pleased to have you by for supper."

"It'd be a pleasure. I haven't had a home cooked meal that I can remember, and who knows when I'll have one again."

THE END

IKE MARS is a '30s Pittsburgh Private Eye who has the distinction of being struck twice by lightning. As a result, he can change his face at will, an ability that gets him into as much trouble as it gets him out. Along with his wise-cracking fiancée Marge, he chases bail skips, blackmailers, bank robbers, Nazi spies, crooked cops, sleazy politicians, and murderers all over the pre-war Steel City. In "Sole Heir," Mars is hired to keep an heir alive long enough to inherit a fortune before his family kill him to grab it for themselves.

IKE MARS: SOLE HEIR

Marge was right, as usual. We've been engaged for a year and a half, and she can read me like the newspaper she works for as a reporter. "Your problem is you're getting bored, Mars," she said over breakfast. "Too many mundane cases."

"Mundane?" Her vocabulary reaches a whole arm past mine and she's always trying to teach me new words — part of what she calls "civilizing" me.

"Run of the mill, ordinary, pedestrian."

"What's walking down the street have to do with being bored?"

Marge threw what was left of her toast across the table and bounced it off my forehead. "Nothing, you dope." She stood up laughing and sashayed off to get dressed for work. I followed her with my eyes, appreciating how her hips moved under that silk robe I bought her for her last birthday — I know how many, but I'm not telling — and I wished we both had the day off.

But like I said, Marge was right. Being a private eye isn't all guns and gams and gangsters like you read in the pulps. Most of the time it's standing on a street corner waiting for some cheating spouse to come out of a hot pillow joint, or pounding the pavement looking for some bail skip, or digging through mounds of paper in the City Records Office, or following some thieving employee to see where he — or she — fences the swag. Yeah, it gets to be routine, and yeah, I was bored. I thought about it while I finished my coffee and Marge's piece of toast.

Maybe what bothered me was the thought that I hadn't used my unique talent for a while. I was struck by lightning, not once but twice within a year, and after the second strike, I woke up to find that I could change my face to look like anybody I wanted from Clark Gable to Boris Karloff. Not my hair, not my build, not my voice, just my face.

That talent got me into lots of places and got me out of lots of places where my own mug could've gotten me killed, and I can't say it hurt my business. But that talent is a secret I can't share with the world. Marge knows, and Mason Cutter, my old partner from the Pittsburgh P.D. knows, and that's it. Maybe six, eight months had passed by since I had to use my special ability, and like a kid with a squirt gun, I was itching to pull the trigger.

Marge came out of the bedroom dressed in one of her tweed suits, the green one. Hats were still fashionable for women, but Marge seldom wore one anymore. Lately she wore her sandy hair shorter and smoothed to one side down to her eyebrow. She leaned over and gave me a quick kiss on the cheek. "Gotta run, Mars. See you tonight."

I concentrated on Randolph Scott and gave her a big smile. "Sure you don't want to stick around, baby?"

"Sorry, Randolph, duty calls. Got bills to pay."

I wanted to wrap my arms around her and pull her onto my lap, but I knew better. I let my face slip to my own. "Hey, how about going to the Blue Flame tonight for a steak?"

"Sounds great," she said, and she was out the door.

I share an office in the Pratt Building on Sixth Street with my old partner Mason Cutter. We're just office mates now, as Mason always points out to anybody who walks in. Not partners, but neither of us makes enough scratch to pay the freight on his own. Roosevelt keeps telling us that the Depression's on the way out and prosperity's returning, but in January of 1939, it hasn't found its way to the detective business yet. So, we share one room, two desks, one phone, and all the bills.

I try to get in early in case somebody calls. Mason and I have an understanding: whoever gets the call gets the job. Today, I didn't even have to wait for the phone. A hefty guy in a long topcoat and a fedora was pacing outside the office door when I got off the elevator on the third floor. He was about my size, a little narrower around the shoulders and a good bit thicker around the middle.

He was too well dressed to be a bill collector, so I didn't turn around and head for the fire stairs. Instead, I walked right up to introduce myself.

When he heard me coming up behind him, he spun around and put a .38 revolver in my face. "Who are you?"

Startled, I put up my hands. "I'm Ike Mars. This is my office. Who are you?"

He lowered the pistol. "I apologize for the gun. My name is Arthur Osborne, and people have tried to kill me twice in the last three days." His breath told me that he'd drunk his breakfast.

I made a show of looking up and down the hallway. He put the pistol back in his pocket, and I thought about punching him in the mouth for pulling a gun on me, but I decided I needed the work. "Well, nobody's around now. What do you say we go inside and talk about it?"

He nodded. "Yes. That's a good idea." I unlocked the door and ushered him into the office. I pushed one of the two client chairs, the one with the least stuffing showing, in front of my desk and told him to have a seat. His cashmere Burberry topcoat had a hundred-dollar pin striped suit under it and a shirt with monogrammed cuffs but no cuff links.

I tried to casually bring the phone from Mason's desk to mine as I said, "So, Mister Osborne, someone's trying to kill you? Who is it?"

Osborne took off his hat and I got a good look at his face. His mug looked like somebody hooked it up to an air compressor and left the hose on too long. All of his features were exaggerated; big fleshy nose, boulder of a forehead, eyes like hardboiled eggs and a lantern jaw. His lips were the worst. They looked as if somebody glued on a pair of miniature hot dogs.

"I'm not sure. It could be any one of five people." he spread his open hand for emphasis.

"Five? How'd you make so many enemies?"

"I was born to it. Let me explain. Is the name Charles Hollister familiar to you?"

"Like in Hollister Industries? The millionaire? He just died a few months ago, didn't he?"

Osborne nodded. "Yes. My mother was Daphne Hollister Osborne. Charles Hollister was my uncle."

"And the five people who want you dead?"

"My cousins, Uncle Charles's children."

"I'm guessing here, but does this have anything to do with Uncle Charlie's will?"

"It has everything to do with it. Do you mind if I smoke?"

"Go ahead," I said, opening a desk drawer and pulling out my ashtray. Mason isn't a smoker, and he gets annoyed if I smoke when he's in the office. Osborne took a pack of Chesterfields from his pocket and scratched a match on the side of one of those little boxes you find on the table in a night club.

The box had "Club La-Ja" in fancy letters on its face. Matches from a cheap coochie joint instead of a gold-plated Zippo to light a half-penny cigarette. His prosperity must be a recent event, I thought. His vices haven't caught up with his wardrobe.

He blew out a lungful of smoke and flicked a little bit of ash into the ashtray. When he did it again in a few seconds, I realized it was a nervous habit, and Osborne was definitely nervous.

"So," I said, "tell me about the will."

"He left me everything."

"Everything, as in —"

"Stocks, bonds, money, the company, like I said, everything."

"And nothing to his children."

"Right."

"Did they contest the will?"

"Unsuccessfully."

"I can understand why they'd like to see you dead. I'd be pissed off myself in the same situation, but your uncle's been gone a while. Why the sudden run at your life?"

"Because the estate isn't mine yet. I inherit it all on my thirtieth birthday, three days from now. If I die before then, it reverts to the five of them. It's pure greed on their part."

"Makes sense. But how could they think they wouldn't get caught? They'd be the first people the cops'd haul in."

"There are five of them. Any one of them could kill me and the other four would give him — or her — an airtight alibi. They're all in this together, I'm sure of it. But I think they'd rather pool their money to pay a professional than get their own hands bloody."

"I don't exactly understand. You said they tried twice already. How did that happen?"

Three days ago, I was on the street getting into my car when a truck came speeding around the corner aimed right at me. I dove into the front seat. The truck tore off the driver's door, and kept going. It's a shame. The car was a brand-new Packard."

"And nobody got the license number?"

Osborne shook his head and flicked ashes into the tray again. "No one. The police wrote it off as a hit-and-run accident."

"What about the second try?"

"Last night as I was walking out the door of my town house, a chunk of the terra cotta cornice fell from the roof. If I hadn't stepped back to make sure I'd locked the door, it would have pushed my head through my shoulders. Again, the police said it was an accident."

"How long have you lived there?"

"I moved in two months ago."

"A new car, a new town house, new clothes; if you don't mind me asking, did you have money before? After all, you haven't inherited anything from your uncle's will yet, have you?"

Osborne shook his head. "Not a dime, but my attorney Wilbert Mackenzie was very persuasive about arranging credit for me with different people, anticipating the windfall."

"So these attempts on your life are all to prevent you from inheriting the money. What do you need from me? Protection? I could be your bodyguard for the next couple of days."

"I'm afraid that's not enough, Mister Mars. Even if I live to inherit the money, they'll want to kill me for spite. I want you to keep me alive, but I also want them caught in the act. I want proof of their intent. I want them punished so they won't ever try again."

"My regular fee is —" I began.

Osborne held up his meaty hand. "I have very little ready cash at the moment, Mister Mars. I can't pay you in advance."

That's what happened to the cuff links, I thought, they're in the window of some hock shop to refill his wallet. "What about your lawyer?"

"Getting people to agree to future payment is much easier than getting them to advance cash, unless, of course he went to a loan shark, and he won't do that. What I will do is promise you a thousand dollars if you keep me alive for five days, and five thousand dollars if you catch my cousins trying to kill me."

"A grand is a drop in the river if you're inheriting millions."

"Very well. Let's make it two thousand for five days and ten to bring down my cousins."

I pulled out a sheet of paper and a pen. "Can I have that in writing?"

I don't usually take clients on a contingency (Marge's word) basis, but this gamble was too good to pass up.

Osborne signed the agreement, and I scrawled my moniker under his. "Congratulations, Mister Osborne. You just bought yourself a three-day shadow."

The door opened, and Osborne's hand jumped for his gun. I put up my hand. "Easy, pal."

Mason came in carrying a cardboard diner tray with two cups of coffee and a couple of donuts. "Hey, Ike. Sorry there's only two coffees. If I'd'a known you had company, I would'a brought three." Mason's about my size, better dressed, and better looking. According to Marge, I'm lucky she didn't see *him* first.

"Mason, this is my client Arthur Osborne. Arthur, this is Mason Cutter, the other name on the door."

"If you want, I'll go downstairs and drink my coffee in the lobby 'til you're done."

"No need. We were just finishing up. I'll be spending a lot of time with Arthur the next few days, so I won't be around here much. You hold down the fort."

He grinned. "I'll be waiting by the phone."

We left the office, and as we were waiting for the elevator, I said, "Give me your gun."

Osborne blinked. "My gun? Why?"

"You won't need it. You have me to protect you, and I don't want to have to worry about you hitting me while you're shooting at someone else. Besides, you're a little too quick to pull. That causes its own set of problems."

"I'm not —"

"Then I'm not." The elevator bell dinged and Tommy, the operator slid open the brass X-gate with a ratcheting noise. "You do things my way, or you're on your own, pal." I turned to start back for the office.

Osborne did a three count then said, "All right," and handed me his piece. Tommy's eyes bulged, but he didn't say a word except "Lobby?"

I nodded and put Osborne's .38 in the pocket of my overcoat, wondering whether he had another gun on him. I had an inkling that this case was going to be a colossal pain in my ass, but with as much as twelve grand on the line, I figured I could sit on a block of ice for a few days.

We stepped into the lobby just as a tall man in a trench coat came through the revolving door. Osborne's hand twitched for his pocket, and I was satisfied that I made the right decision taking his gun. He was ready to shoot at anybody he didn't know.

Outside, the cold air bit my nose. If Pittsburgh's number one product is steel, its number two product has to be slush. As we walked down Sixth, it splattered from under our shoes and flew from the gutters as cars passed by. I got the worst of it because I kept myself between Osborne and the traffic. Osborne's eyes twitched in one direction after another.

"Relax," I said. "Nobody's going to shoot you on the sidewalk."

"How can you say that?"

"Because if you're right, they've already tried to off you twice. They're doing their best to make it look like an accident to avoid suspicion. The last day they might try for a desperation play, but this morning? Nah."

"Where are we going?"

"We're going to your place. First we're going to get my car." I didn't tell him, but I wanted my car because it gave me more control of the situation than I'd have riding in a cab. I was taking the whole thing seriously; I just didn't want to make him more nervous than he already was.

We walked to the public garage on Liberty Avenue where I keep Old Faithful, my Clipper Blue '34 Plymouth coupe. I bought it new when I was still pulling down a good buck on the force. It doesn't look as good now as did then — Pittsburgh's number three product is rust — but it starts when I turn the key, stops when I step on the brake, and goes where I point it. What else do I need? The unplugged bullet holes in the door give it character.

Barney, the old guy who usually works the night shift was in the booth. "Hi, Mister Mars."

"Hello, Barney. Isn't your shift over?"

"Yeah, but Eddie's wife went into labor last night, and he's at Mercy Hospital. He called and asked me to stay 'til he can get here."

"I see. Well, can you get the Plymouth for me?"

"Right away." He reached behind him and took the keys from the board in the booth. He locked the door behind him. "Be with you in a jiffy."

I always hold my breath when Barney's driving my car around the garage. He's a little nearsighted, and I'm always listening for the telltale sound of scraping metal or the tinkle of broken glass. In a minute, Barney returned with the Plymouth. He pulled up to the booth and set the hand brake with a sound like wringing a turkey's neck. "There you go, Mister Mars."

"Thanks, Barney." I turned to Osborne. "You drive."

"Me? Why?"

"You know how to get where we're going. Besides, it's tough to steer, shift gears and shoot all at once."

Osborne nodded. "Right." He got behind the wheel and I climbed in the passenger side. Osborne was a decent driver. He managed the early morning traffic better than average and drove us out Fifth Avenue through Oakland and into Shadyside. His town house was on a side street lined with them, standing behind rows of bare trees. It was easy for me to pick out which one was his. A chunk of terra cotta the size of a bowling ball was lying on the stoop beside the front door. A quick look overhead showed me where it came from.

As we climbed the steps, Osborne kept his gaze upward, as if he expected another piece of the cornice to drop. "Don't worry," I said. "They won't try the same stunt again. Besides, it's daylight."

In the foyer, I told him to wait. I went from room to room to make sure someone wasn't hiding in one of the closets or under the living room sofa. The place was pretty nice. Based on the quality of the furniture I guessed Osborne rented it furnished. "All clear," I called down the stairs from the second floor.

I came down to find him in the living room pouring three fingers of Old Overholt into a glass. I put my hand over it. "Not now. I need you sensible." I opened my notebook to a fresh page. "Tell me everything you can think of about this business."

Osborne lit a cigarette off the butt of his previous one, and for the next hour or so told me a disjointed tale of family squabbles, disinheritance, accusations of fraud, theft, and disloyalty and about the reading of a will that nearly erupted into a fistfight. It gave me a headache to keep it all straight because there were so many players.

What it amounted to was this: Charles Hollister became irritated with his children's impatience over his impending death and began pushing the old man to hand out some money all around before the main event. When he didn't come across, things started disappearing from Hollister's mansion; a Tiffany lamp here, a sculpture there, an antique sword, a gold watch, nothing big, but worth some quick cash from a fence. The old man got cranky and had his will rewritten a week or so before he died.

"I never asked him for a thing," Osborne said. "He was always generous on my birthday and at Christmas; no complaint there. And after my father died, he saw that Mom never wanted for anything while she was alive. But when I'd go to visit him, he'd always ask, 'Do you need anything?' and I'd tell him no because I didn't. I made a decent living as a bookkeeper, and I was proud of the fact that I paid my own way and didn't go to him with my hand out every week like my cousins. Maybe that's why he left it all to me, because I never asked for it."

"Now, let's talk about these cousins. Who are they, and what can you tell me about them?"

"Maude, Clarence, Robert, Millicent, and Charles Junior."

"Junior's the oldest?"

"No, Maude's the oldest." He counted them down his fingers to his thumb. "Then Charles, Millicent, Robert and Clarence."

"Which of them work for the company?"

"All three of the boys."

"Then they ought to be pretty well off."

"You'd think so, but no. Did you ever work in a family business?"

"Nope, my dad was a mill Hunky."

Then you don't understand how it works. Dad starts a business and makes it a success. The kids work in it for low wages and the promise that 'someday this will all be yours,' the carrot that keeps the mule pulling the cart. The old man lives like a king and the kids just have to be patient 'til he dies for a piece of it."

"And the sisters?"

"Their husbands work for the company on the same promise by proxy."

"I can see why they'd be angry. They keep their eyes on the prize all their lives then have the door slammed on them."

Osborne nodded.

"Did you ever consider sharing?"

"It crossed my mind, but after trying to kill me, they don't deserve any consideration as far as I'm concerned."

"Which one of them do you think is trying to do you in?"

"Any of them, maybe all of them."

"Okay, then which of them is the most likely to hire a hit man?"

Osborne took his time thinking about it before he answered the question. "Charles. He always had the attitude that being first-born and named after his father entitled him to everything and anything."

"So, was Junior treated any better?"

"Not really. As far as I know, he made about the same salary as the others, even though he was vice-president of the company. But if he wasn't the most angry when the will was read, he was the most vocal, and the most threatening. He said he'd like to kill me."

"And he's got three more days to get the job done." I shut my notebook. "You can have that drink now. I have to make some calls. Oh, and find me a photo of you I can use."

Homicide Detective George Czap is one of the few people in the Pittsburgh Police Department I trust. He's no angel, but he and his partner Mike Montrose have somehow managed to stay above the murk and mire of politics and pay-offs. Maybe Cap Agronski, the City police Commissioner kept those two on the force after the infamous Purge of '36 when Cap rid himself of anybody — me and Mason included — who didn't kiss his ring, his feet, or his ass because he needed a pair of virtuous tokens to point to when the press yelled "corruption." Anyway, it was Czap I called from Osborne's phone. He wasn't in, so I told the sergeant who answered at the desk to have him call Bill Thompson and I read him the number off the dial.

Osborne walked in and handed me a black and white eight-by-ten in a cheap cardboard fold over frame like you'd get at the photo booth at Kennywood Park. It showed Osborne at a night club table, I guessed the La-Ja, with a painted floozy on each knee. He was grinning broadly, and so were the girls. I saw cuff links with diamond chips at his wrists. "How's that?"

I nodded. "Perfect."

"What do we do now?"

"Now, we wait."

• • •

Osborne wasn't bad company; he was no company. I've never seen such a dull person. He sat like a lump in his easy chair, chain-smoking and drinking for the next two hours. He was a big guy, but it surprised me how much booze he could take and still keep his eyes open. I decided he was one of those guys like my old man whose sense of reality was based on being half in the bag all the time. After two tries at conversation, I gave up and turned on the radio. It was a big Emerson console the size of the old Heatrola my folks had in the living room of our company house.

After a few big band numbers, the news came on. *You Can't Take it with You* won the Academy Award for Best Picture. Marge and I saw it at the Stanley Theater, and we both thought it was okay, but I wasn't so sure about it being the best of last year's crop. I like Jimmy Stewart — he's a Pennsylvania boy — but I liked *The Adventures of Robin Hood* better.

In another item, the Brits did something new. They used the new gadget, television to show a boxing match live in three packed theaters in London. That'll be the day, I thought, when any red-blooded American would cough up a buck to watch a fight on a movie screen.

The door bell rang. Osborne started out of his chair, and I waved him back down. I walked into the hallway so that he couldn't see me, concentrated on his face in the picture for a minute, and looked in the mirror. It was all there; the flushed skin, the rubbery lips, the puffy cheeks, the works.

I looked through the lace curtains to the side of the door and saw a man in a green service uniform with a visored cap and a waist-length jacket holding a basket by the handle. I opened the door with one hand and slipped the other inside my jacket close to my shoulder rig. The little fellow gave me a big smile. "Mister Osborne?"

"Yeah."

"Delivery for you."

The basket was about a foot in diameter, wrapped in red cellophane and piled with fruit; a small bunch of bananas, apples, a cluster of grapes, a few pears, and even two peaches.

"Who's it from?"

The little fellow read the attached card. "Birthday wishes from Hollister Industries." He held out the basket. I took it from him with my left hand, keeping my right where it was. I set the basket down to fish a quarter out of my pocket for a tip, never moving my gun hand. The delivery man smiled again. "Thanks, buddy." He gave a two-finger salute to the shiny bill of his cap and walked away whistling. The street was nearly empty, and there was no delivery van in sight.

I shut the door and put my face back before I brought the basket into the living room and set it on the coffee table. "Has Hollister Industries ever sent you a birthday present before?"

"Not even so much as a card."

"Let's take this out to the kitchen." I set the basket in the sink and slit the cellophane with my pocket knife. I speared one of the pears with the tip of the blade and pulled it out. I took it to the window and looked it over carefully in the light. "I don't see any punctures."

"Punctures?"

"Needle marks. Hypo."

"Poison?"

"Or drugs. A good load of hop would make you a lot easier to manage."

I did the same with one of the peaches and an apple. No sign of tampering. I was beginning to think that the basket was an innocent gesture. The grapes came next, and I threw them in the trash. Too many

I looked through the curtains to the side of the door...

to look at and too hard to see. Then I reached in for the bananas. When they cleared the cellophane, an ugly black spider the size of a silver dollar scuttled out of the bunch and made a beeline for my hand.

I gave my wrist a hard snap and the spider flew into the sink where I beat it to death with the bananas. If I had any doubts before then, the spider scared them away. Czap still hadn't called, but I decided that I shouldn't wait to get Osborne away from the town house and stash him someplace safe 'til I could get the whole situation under control.

"Pack a bag," I said. "I'm getting you away from here."

Fifteen minutes later, Osborne came down the stairs carrying a Gladstone bag that clinked when it bounced off his knee from the bottles of hooch inside. Some days, prohibition doesn't seem like such a bad idea. Against my better judgment, I gave his pistol back to him. What I didn't tell him was I took out all the bullets but one and set it up so he'd have to pull the trigger twice before the round fired. Small insurance that he wouldn't shoot me by mistake, but better than nothing.

I went out first, gun in my hand in my overcoat pocket. Nobody in sight on the street except a woman lugging a double armload of grocery bags and a guy in a mackinaw smoking a pipe and walking what looked like a mix between a bulldog and an Irish wolfhound on a leash.

Osborne followed me out a minute later and started for the driver's door. "Uh-uh. I'm driving." As much as he drank the last hour, I wasn't trusting him to drive my car, no matter how well he held his booze. I started the Plymouth and took a last look up and down the street. No cars coming or going, and no tell-tale steam from an idling engine in the bitter cold. I pulled away from the curb and took Fifth across Oakland into downtown and the Liberty Bridge.

"Where are we going?"

"I'm taking you to a motor hotel about twenty miles south of here. I'll hide you there while I try to sort out this mess."

Traffic was light and we got through the Liberty Tunnels without any problem. To keep Osborne occupied, I turned the rear-view mirror so that he could watch behind us to see whether the same car followed us too long. When we got to Route 51, I headed South a few miles and got on Route 88, Brownsville Road. It's a snaky two-lane that pretty much follows the winding and twisting of the Monongahela River through a smoky valley of steel mills, coke ovens, and coal mines.

My destination was the Blue Moon Motor Hotel in Charleroi, one of those joints where you pay for your room and the clerk hands you your bed sheets and a six pack of Iron City. About halfway down the road I saw the flashing lights for a Pennsy crossing, and before I could get to it, the wooden barrier swung down like a head chopper's axe. I slowed to a stop and heard the blare of the train's horn coming from my left.

"Mars," Osborne said, looking out the back window. "There's a truck coming, and I don't think he's going to stop."

I looked in my side mirror and saw a big green panel van bearing down on us. Two seconds later, it rammed the back bumper of the Plymouth and pushed us through the safety arm and onto the tracks. The engineer blew his horn frantically. My first instinct was to slam on the brakes when we rolled forward, but I got over that pretty quick when I saw the cowcatcher heading for my running board. I popped the clutch and floored it. The tires squealed and we smashed through the crossing arm on the other side with a foot or so to spare as the train roared past.

I kept rolling, and Osborne said, "Why aren't you stopping? Why don't you turn around and chase him?"

"There's a mile of coal cars between us and him. By the time the train's gone, I'm betting he'll be gone too. On the other hand, he can't follow us 'til the caboose rolls by. I'm making tracks."

The car made a scraping sound that had to be my bumper dragging on the pavement. Later, I thought, when I can find a coat hanger. I turned off 88 at the first intersection I found and spent the next hour navigating one lousy back road after another until we finally rolled into the Blue Moon. There was a phone booth outside the office, and I used it to call Mason. I was lucky. Mason answered the phone on the second ring.

"Mason Cutter, Private Investigator," he said.

"Mason, it's Ike."

"What's up?"

"Somebody just tried to kill my client and send me along with him."

"Where are you?"

"The Blue Moon. I'm going to stash him here for a day. I need you to run down some info on a couple of people for me."

"Who do you need me to check on?"

"Five people." I read him the list of Osborne's cousins.

"This'll take a while. My usual rate?"

"Yeah, sure." If I was going to make a minimum of two grand on this caper, I could afford fifty bucks, I mean, you gotta spend money to make money, right? And if I was going to score the big tab, I needed all the help I could get.

I read him the phone number from the dial. There were no phones in the Blue Moon rooms. "I'll check back with you in a few hours. If something pops up, call the booth and let it ring. I'll hear it."

"You got it."

I hung up the phone and stepped into the motel office. The guy behind the counter looked like he had about a quart of motor oil on his hair that he didn't put there himself. I guessed he and the bathtub weren't intimate acquaintances. He had a bag of peanuts on the counter and a pile of empty shells lay in a heap beside it. "Room for you, bud?" he said around chewing.

"Yeah." I put a five on the counter and he walked through an arch then came back with the bed linens, although the word "linens" is probably stretching things. He took the five and gave me a buck in change. He didn't ask me how long I'd be staying. Nobody stays more than one night at the Blue Moon.

"Fridge is busted," he said. "I got the beer outside keeping cold in the snow." He stepped out for a minute, and I guess he must have seen Osborne in the passenger seat. He gave me a funny look as he set the beer on the counter. Then he grinned and said, "Enjoy your stay."

Some things never change; one of them is the Blue Moon. Somebody must have had big plans for the place because the room numbers start with A-1, which tells me they expected to build onto the place as they made money. I guess that dream crashed when the Depression hit, because the highest room number in the place is A-16; they never made it to B.

Room A-7 was the same as others I'd seen in the Blue Moon; ten by fifteen with a double bed, a ratty carpet, a greasy looking orange armchair, and a bedside table with a lamp and a beat-up radio that was attached to the table top with a piece of porch swing chain. A door at the back opened into a bathroom that I wouldn't use if I had dysentery. The place smelled of body fluids, Lysol, and of course, Iron City.

Osborne wrinkled his nose. "How long do we have to stay here?"

"Not we," I said, "you. Maybe until tomorrow. Nobody'll think to look for you here."

"And what are you going to do?"

"Go back into the city and do some legwork. There's a diner down the road. I'm going to get you some food to hold you for a while. Do you want a newspaper?"

He nodded. "Yes, and a couple packs of Chesterfields."

Your cousins missed the boat, I thought as I walked out the door. If they wanted you dead, all they had to do was keep you supplied with booze and smokes; nature would take care of the rest.

I stopped at the phone booth to try Czap, but I missed him again. I came back from the diner in half an hour with a sack of cheeseburgers and French fries. Osborne had spread a sheet over the blue striped mattress and was lying on his back on the bed snoring like a motorboat, his pistol clutched in his hand. I took it away from him before I shook him awake. I would have preferred to let him sleep, but I needed him to lock the door behind me and set the burglar chain.

I took a burger for myself then handed the sack to him. "There you go; burgers and fries. Don't eat them all at once. Save some for later so you don't have to go out for food."

"They'll get cold."

"So, set them on the radiator. If you want to stay alive, don't leave this room. I'll be back sometime tonight. Stay put. By the way, what's your favorite restaurant in the 'Burgh?"

"Uh, Meloni's on the South Side, why?"

"A hunch. Trade me top coats." I left without further explanation.

On the road, I ate the cheeseburger. It was pretty good, and I wished I'd taken two. On 88 I drove across the tracks through the ruined crossing gates, sweating all over again at the close shave we'd had. The people who were trying to kill Osborne were determined to make it look like an accident, which worked to my advantage. Tonight, I'd go to two places, Meloni's and the La-Ja, wearing Osborne's face and see whether they'd take a run at me. It was risky, but the prospect of an extra ten Gs for nailing the conspirators made it seem worth the try.

• • •

When I got back in town, I called Marge at the office. "Won't be home tonight, babe."

"Oh yeah? And to what do I owe this vacation from your snoring? Something newsworthy?"

"You'll get the scoop when it all comes down; all your favorites: murder, intrigue, betrayal, millions at stake."

"Sure it is." She laughed, then her voice got serious. "You keep your head down, Mars. And you come home to me."

"Always, darlin'." I hung up before the conversation got any further on the subject.

I found Mason at the office on the telephone. He finished his conversation and hung up. "Nice top coat, Ike. You mug your client?"

"It's a loaner. I'm going out on the town tonight as Osborne. Have to look the part."

"Need company?"

"Yeah, I'd like you to watch my back. I'm going to a few of Osborne's haunts and see who might show up. How does dinner at Meloni's sound?"

"Great, if you're buying."

• • •

We took Mason's Ford since my car was in danger of the bumper falling off. On the way across the Tenth Street Bridge, I put on Osborne's face. Meloni's is a block off Carson Street on the South Side. It's not Maxwell's but it's pretty pricey for an Italian joint. Word is that half the mobsters in Pittsburgh ate there, but every spaghetti joint in town liked to float the same rumor.

Mason and I walked in the door at eight o'clock. Beside the *maitre d's* station was a fountain and a pool with goldfish swimming around in it. Mason looked at it for a second and said, "I don't know about you, but I'm not ordering fish." We didn't even have the snow stomped off our overshoes before a round little fellow in a tuxedo with a handlebar moustache like a circus ringmaster came running over.

"Oh, Mister Osborne, so good to see you." His accent was maybe five years off the boat. He pumped my hand like he was filling a horse trough. "Table for two?"

"Uh, yeah, sure." I coughed into my fist to cover the fact that my voice was about an octave lower than Osborne's. "Got a cold."

"Oh my," the *maitre d'*, whose name I learned was Carlo, tutted. "We'll get you some wine, fix you right up." Carlo led us across the dining room to a table for four and snapped his fingers. A waiter in a short white jacket hustled over and took away the extra plates and utensils. "Would you and your friend like to see a menu, or would you like to have your usual order?"

"Yeah," I said. "The usual for both of us. Is that okay with you Mason?"

He shrugged. "Sounds good." As Carlo scurried away, Mason said, "Somebody else may want your client dead, but they love him here."

"Money talks."

He said under his breath, "The face is working. The little guy didn't blink."

A waiter brought a basket of hot bread sticks and rolls while another brought us steaming bowls of minestrone. I'm no expert on Italian food, but the soup was rich and delicious and could've made a meal all by itself. Then *antipasto* arrived. I'd had it once before, and it gave me heartburn, but if I was going to make a believable Osborne, I had to do as he would. I ate the whole thing down to the last olive. Mason ate half of his, and he was lucky he didn't finish. Next came two huge bowls of spaghetti and meatballs in a thick tomato sauce laced with anisette and loaded with chunks of yellow pepper. A strolling violinist in a gypsy head scarf and a hoop earring stood by our table as he sawed his way through "Isle of Capri."

Mason grinned across the table at me and waggled a finger. "Every bite, now, Sonny; people in Europe are starving."

The pasta was delicious. I can shovel in a lot of food, but it took all I could do to finish, washing the last three bites down with a glass of sweet red wine. I was getting the picture of how Osborne got to be the size and shape he was. If Marge cooked like this for me every day, I'd look like the Hindenburg.

As I was finishing the spaghetti, a different waiter arrived with a pitcher. "More water, gentlemen?"

"Yeah, sure," I said, twirling the last of the pasta on my fork. He refilled the glasses and stepped away. A man at the next table said, "Could you refill ours too, please?" He smiled and said, "Certainly, sir, in just a moment," and retreated into the kitchen. The pitcher was still three-quarters full. Mason reached for his water glass. "So, *tiramisu* for desert, and then I'll call for a wheelbarrow to roll you out of here."

I caught his hand just as his fingers closed on the stem of his glass. "Hold it. You see that waiter with the pitcher around anywhere?"

Mason scanned the room. "No, I don't."

"He didn't serve us any of the food."

"You're right. You don't suppose —"

I stood up. "Be right back." I walked toward the front and stooped beside the fountain. I pushed my sleeve back and after two tries, came away with a goldfish wriggling in my hand. I sat down at the table and dropped the little fellow into my water glass. He swam around for about three seconds, convulsed, and floated to the surface where he lay on his side as his mouth worked for another three seconds then quit.

"Holy mackerel."

"No," Mason said, "I think it's a Koi."

This all went unnoticed because of the commotion in the kitchen that spilled into the dining room. It seems that somebody cold cocked one of the waiters and stole his jacket. I stood up. Carlo saw this and came running.

"May I have our check, please."

"Oh, Mister Osborne, apologies, apologies," the little fellow said, wringing his hands. "I am so sorry for the disturbance. Please stay."

I smiled and patted him on the shoulder. "It's quite all right, Carlo. Not your fault. Please bring the check."

He was back quickly with the check and a pen. Apparently, Osborne had a line of credit here, too. I scrawled his name at the bottom of the slip and left a five on the table as a tip. "Don't worry, Carlo," I said, I'll be back again soon. I promise."

As we left, Mason said. "I guess that's why when you go to Europe everybody tells you, 'Don't drink the water.'"

• • •

As we drove out of the South Side, I let my face slip back to my own.

Mason said, "That's five tries, Ike."

"One for each cousin."

"Think they're coordinated, or is each one running his own show?"

"Osborne thinks the Hollister clan is working in tandem, and he may be right. Professional hitters don't work cheap, and they don't operate on a contingency basis. From what Osborne tells me, the old man worked all the cousins like he was Simon Legree for next to nothing on the basis of the pie-in-the-sky promise. On the other hand, the waiter wasn't the same guy who delivered the fruit basket today. Maybe each one hired his own hitter — or hers."

"So, are we headed for the La-Ja?"

I belched. "I've had enough of Osborne's life for one night. I'm so full I can barely move. That banquet was Osborne's 'usual'; if he eats like that all the time, coupled with his smoking and drinking, I'm surprised he hasn't keeled over dead already."

"Maybe he couldn't afford it 'til now."

We crossed the river and I looked over my shoulder at the huge octagonal clock, the largest in the world, on a lighted billboard that said "Drink Coca-Cola" nestled in the side of Mount Washington. Twenty after ten. "Drop me at my car. I'm going back to the Blue Moon to babysit."

• • •

The drive to Charleroi was uneventful, which was a relief. Keeping Osborne alive for a few more days may not be easy, I thought, but it was doable. The problem was roping his cousins in to charge them with attempted murder for the big payoff. I was inclined to believe they were all in it together, but how to drag them out from behind the curtain?

I got back to the Blue Moon around midnight and parked the car. The lights were off in the office except for the neon Vacancy sign in the window. I wanted to call Marge from the pay phone, so I grabbed a couple of nickels from the roll I keep in the ashtray and went into the booth.

The phone rang five or six times before Marge answered with a drowsy "Ike?"

"Yeah, honey. It's me. Just called to let you know I'm okay."

"Glad you did. When are you coming home?"

"Tomorrow, I hope."

"Be safe."

"I promise. Go back to sleep."

"Fat chance, Mars." We hung up, and as I put the phone in the cradle, I saw a dark shape creeping between two of the cars. I pulled my revolver and slipped out of the phone booth. I kept the parked cars between me and the shape, and in the flash of light from a passing truck, I saw the guy standing on tip toe looking through one of the windows two doors down from Osborne's room.

I snuck behind him, crouched down, and grabbed his ankles. I yanked his feet from under him and he went face down in the snow. Before he could push himself up, I put the muzzle of my .38 behind his ear and my knee between his shoulders. "Vice Squad." I flashed my P.I. buzzer at him, and in the dim light he couldn't tell the difference.

"Uh, uh," he stammered.

"What's your name, pal?"

"Uh, Jones, Bill Jones."

This was no hitter. A pro wouldn't stutter around while he thought up a fake name. He'd have one ready.

I hauled him to his feet. "Are you a peeper, Billy?"

"Uh, no, I'm — looking for my wife."

"Uh-huh. And you think she's in there?"

"Maybe. I don't know where she is. I thought she might be in one of these rooms shacked up with her new boyfriend. I mean where else would I look?"

"This is your lucky day, Billy. I'm going to let you walk. Don't come back here again."

"Yessir, yessir," he said and almost tripped over his feet scurrying away. I was kinda sorry to spoil the poor sap's evening, but I couldn't have him distracting me, prowling around all night. Besides, I never really thought of sex as a spectator sport.

I turned the key in A-7's lock. The door opened an inch and the chain stopped it. I could hear Osborne snoring, and in the light from the bathroom, I saw his bulk under the blankets looking like a beached whale. I made an executive decision and closed the door, locked it again, and spent the night in my car.

I woke up stiff and cold around seven to see the Blue Moon's manager looking through the windshield and shaking his head sympathetically. I walked to the diner for two cups of coffee, and by the time I got back to the room, Osborne was awake. I noticed the six-pack was empty and so was a bottle of scotch, but the heir apparent looked no worse for it.

"Where were you all night?" he said.

"Right outside your door in my car, making sure nobody threw a stick of dynamite through your window."

He looked startled. "Oh, I didn't think of that."

I told him the goldfish story, and he turned pale. "You see?" he said. "I wasn't making it up. I really am in danger."

"Yes, Arthur. Yes, you are. The other tries could be shrugged off as coincidental accidents. Last night was outright attempted murder. Finish dressing and we'll go get some breakfast then I'll try to reach a homicide detective I know and fill him in."

"Wait a minute. You don't look like me at all. How did you fool the people at Meloni's?"

"The wonders of disguise. A magician never reveals his secrets." He frowned, so I lied. "I have a woman works for me sometimes. She does theatrical makeup. A little face putty here, a little greasepaint there. The killers never saw you up close; maybe they worked from pictures. The only people I had to strain to fool were Carlo and the waiters. Besides, Meloni's is basic candlelight. They never really saw me that well anyway."

He grunted acceptance, but I didn't think he really bought my explanation. "Let's go eat. Oh, and give me back my Burberry."

• • •

At the diner, I had a Western omelet while I watched Osborne finish off two plates of flapjacks smothered in butter and syrup along with a hubcap sized slab of ham and fried eggs. I paid the tab since he had almost no cash left in his wallet, but I figured that once he had a couple of million in the bank, he wouldn't quibble over reimbursing my expenses.

On the way back into town, he kept checking the mirror and swiveling his head right and left every time we went through an intersection. "Take it easy, Arthur," I said. "They don't know where you are. Since I passed myself off as you at Meloni's, they probably think you've been in Pittsburgh all this time. When we get to town, then you can start worrying. We get past today, then tomorrow at midnight, your worries will be over."

"I can't rest easy until I know that they won't try again anyway," Osborne said, his eye drifting again to the rear-view mirror."

"The trouble is," I said, "there are five of them. That's a lot of doors to watch."

"I wish I could just get them all into one place and deal with them all at once."

"What, shoot them? You'd get the Chair before you could spend your first million." Then something happened in the back of my head, like the last piece of a jigsaw puzzle falling out of the sky and landing in the empty space. At that moment, I knew how I was going to nail all five of them.

I spotted a phone booth at a crossroad Texaco station and pulled over. "Be back in a few minutes," I told Osborne. "I have to make some calls."

Mason answered on the first ring. "Mason Cutter, Private Investigator."

Someday, I was going to have it out with him about answering the phone without mentioning my name, but today wasn't the day. "Mason, it's Ike. Do you have the addresses for Osborne's five cousins?"

"Yeah, right in front of me."

"Good. Grab a pencil. You remember the printer who did our business cards last year? What was his name?"

"Roth."

"Right, Roth. As soon as you hang up, get him on the phone and tell him we have a rush job for him, a set of engraved invitations. This is what I want them to say. . . ."

When I got back to the car, Osborne was frowning, his thick lower lip sticking out. I looked in his lap and saw his pistol with the cylinder flipped out. "You took my bullets."

"Not all of them."

"How could I defend myself with one bullet?"

I snapped my forearm and stopped the edge of my hand an inch short of his Adam's apple. "Would five more bullets have saved you from that? A professional hit man would kill you three different ways and be walking

"...then tomorrow at midnight, your worries will be over."

away before you pulled the trigger. If it'll make you feel better —" I reached into my coat pocket and pulled out the missing five bullets. I threw them in his lap. "Go ahead, load it up. Just watch where you aim it. If you shoot me by mistake, you just lost your last defense."

Osborne relatively sober was a little more sensible than Osborne with half a fifth of rye down his gullet. He sighed. "You're right. I don't have a chance against someone who kills for a living." But he loaded the empty chambers anyway.

"Can Mackenzie get you access to your uncle's mansion?"

"I suppose so, why?"

"Because you're going to throw a birthday party."

• • •

We arrived at the office around eleven. Mason was out, but the note he left me said that he'd be back in a few minutes. Osborne sat in one of the client chairs and I pushed the ashtray across the desk with one hand and the phone with the other. "Call your lawyer."

Based on one end of the conversation, I could see that Wilbert Mackenzie, Osborne's mouthpiece was giving him a hard time and asking a lot of questions.

I reached over the desk and took the handset from Osborne. "Hey, Mackenzie, this Ike Mars. I'm working for Arthur Osborne, and so are you, just in case you forgot. That can change in a heartbeat. Arthur takes my advice seriously. I have a phone book full of ambulance chasers who'll be happy to take over his affairs starting now. He told you what he wants. Just do it."

Mackenzie didn't say anything, but I did hear him gulp. "You still there, Shylock?"

After more silence, Mackenzie said, "Put my client back on the phone, please."

Osborne listened for a minute and nodded at me. "Okay, we'll get the keys tomorrow morning."

He hung up the phone, and I pulled the Pittsburgh directory out of a drawer in Mason's desk.

"Who are you calling now?"

"A bakery."

• • •

Mason came back with a small bundle under his arm. "Didn't have time for engraved invites, but these look pretty ritzy." He untied the string on the package and handed each of us a cream-colored card with an embossed panel that gave the look of a frame around the printing. The message, spelled out in a fancy script, read:

You are invited
to celebrate the 30th birthday of

Arthur David Osborne

on Thursday January 19
at the Charles Hollister mansion
213 Hunter Court,
Pittsburgh, Pennsylvania
Please arrive at 11:45 p.m.

"Looks good." I handed back the invitation and Mason said, "They were costly because of the rush, but I decided to spring for an extra touch. One of the women who works in the shop is a calligrapher. I paid her five bucks to hand address the envelopes." He held one up, and I could see Charles Hollister, Junior's name and address flowing across the matching envelope in fancier script than the invitation.

"Looks classy."

"Too late for the mail."

"You're right, and we want to be sure everyone gets the invitation. I suppose we'd better find a courier and have them hand delivered this afternoon. You take care of that little detail. I have to talk with George Czap."

Like the man says, third time's the charm. Czap was at his desk when I called the precinct. I filled him in on Osborne's situation, and when I spelled out my plan, he said. "If it was anybody but you, Mars, I'd say you were nuts, but that's already an established fact. Okay, I'll play along. I want to see if this gambit will really work."

• • •

That evening, Osborne and I sat in my car across the street from Junior's house in the South Hills. It wasn't a bad place, but no mansion; a lot less than you'd expect the vice president of Hollister Industries to live in. At seven-thirty he walked out the front door and climbed into his car. I followed him across town to a house in Squirrel Hill where he pulled his car into the driveway behind two others. The house belonged to the widow Maude Hollister Pritchard. Within five minutes, two more cars parked on the street in front of the house.

"That's Clarence," Osborne said as a short man in a long coat rang the bell. "And that's Millicent behind him."

"Hail, hail, the gang's all here," I said. I started the car.

"Why are we leaving?"

"We've learned all we're going to learn tonight. They got their invitations, and they all came here to pow-wow. I'm more convinced than ever that they're all in it together. I thought Junior would be the ringleader, but Maude just became top contender. Let's get out of here."

I called Marge and told her I wouldn't be home and got adjoining rooms at the Mingott Hotel on the edge of Oakland. The Mingott was a slim notch higher than flop house status, but it was as good a one-night hideout as I was going to find on short notice. I'd put clients up there once or twice when they didn't want to be found by process servers or angry wives. Maybe the best way to characterize the joint was the sign in the lobby window: These fifty-cent-a-night rooms must be seen to be appreciated.

Ronnie, the night manager sat behind the counter guarding the board that held the room keys on hooks. I don't know why they bothered to number them, since any one could probably open all thirty doors with a little educated jiggling. I've come to the conclusion that Ronnie died about ten years ago and nobody bothered to tell him. The scrawny little weasel had a cancer cough that could scare a man to death if he didn't croak first from laughing at Ronnie's bad toupee.

"What's up, Mars? Old lady toss you out?"

"Nothing so melodramatic, Ronnie. Got two that connect?"

He turned around and made a show of studying the board. "How about 303 and 305?"

"They're connected? What about 304?"

"Odd numbers on the east side of the hall, evens on the west."

I laid a dollar on the counter as he lit a Lucky Strike and took a drag. He coughed like his lungs were going to jump out of his chest.

"You really ought to quit with the smokes."

"Been puffin' on 'em forty-three years. Ain't killed me yet."

I had Osborne wait in the lobby while I parked the car two blocks away. It would be just my luck to have one of the Hollister hitters drive by and spot it parked in front of the Mingott. I went back inside and climbed the stairs to the third floor, Osborne wheezing behind me. I unlocked both doors and let him look inside and choose which one he wanted, not that there was much difference between them; a single bed with a blank wooden headboard, a ladder backed chair, and a beat-up dresser with a mirror over it.

He took 303 and I got the other one. The interconnecting door was a convenience; the wall between the rooms was so thin I could probably have kicked through it without much effort. I left it ajar, but an hour later, after trying to fall asleep while Osborne snored like a buzz saw, I shut it.

• • •

We went to Mackenzie's office just before lunch. His secretary gave us a look like we were lepers and handed over the keys to the Hollister Mansion.

"Let's go look the place over."

I've been in a few bigger houses, but not many. Maybe the best way to describe the place is a museum with carpets, couches, and armchairs. The ground floor had paintings and sculptures in every room, and the furniture and rugs were so expensive that I half expected to see velvet ropes across the doorways to keep people from wandering in and touching anything. Every once in a while, as Osborne walked me around the place, I noticed an empty niche here, a light rectangle on a painted wall there, where the Hollister kids had lifted something to fence.

The formal dining room looked like the best bet to stage the caper. A set of doors opened to the sitting room on one side and to the kitchen on the other. A pair of pocket doors opened onto the main hallway. A French window I could drive my car through led to a patio and the garden. The French window was at the center of the fourth wall behind the head of a fifteen-foot dining table. Thick green velvet curtains were pulled back to let in what light the winter sky allowed, but they could be shut to prevent a potential hitter from spotting a target from outside. Perfect.

Mason came early in the afternoon and we went over the place securing every door and window while Osborne secured the bar in the study. The last thing we wanted were party crashers, especially those with guns. The grounds had plenty of evergreen shrubbery to give Czap's crew places to hide while they watched the outside. The cake arrived at three. It was three tiered and done with all kinds of fancy swirls and decorations in the icing. Thirty candles ringed the top layer.

Marge arrived at nine with a travel bag full of makeup. All we had to do now was wait.

"This is your makeup artist?" Osborne said, working on a gin and tonic.

"Shh, not so loud. She's kind of a secret weapon." I don't know why I said shh; Marge and I, Osborne and Mason were the only people in the place. Czap and Montrose would come in for the party, but at the moment they were outside getting their men into position.

"I suppose it's time for you to earn your keep, girlie," I said. Marge gave me what I call her gun sight look for the comment and said. "Sure, Mars. Let's find a room with good light."

Upstairs we set up shop in a bedroom suite that could have had basketball nets at either end. I never really cared much for that spindly French furniture — Provincial, Marge called it, but she oohed and aahed over every gold edged stick. She opened her bag and set a handful of bottles and brushes on the vanity table. Then she pulled out a maid's costume. When she asked earlier in the day why she'd need one, I told her someone had to answer the doorbell and wheel in the cake.

I closed my eyes and concentrated on Osborne's face. In a few seconds, I had the beetled brow and the rubbery lips. Marge made a face of her own.

"Good job?"

"You look just like him."

"We'll have to wait about a half hour before we go downstairs to make it look like you really worked at it."

"Did you bring a deck of cards? We could play Gin Rummy."

I looked across the room. "You know, we never made out on a canopy bed before, and you have to get undressed to change into the maid's costume anyway, so . . ."

She eyed the quilted satin bedspread. "Okay, Mars, you talked me into it, but first, put your own face back. I'm not making love with Frankenstein."

• • •

At eleven, everything was in place. Czap and Montrose covered the side doors to the dining room in case someone got past the uniforms outside. Mason was across the main hallway with Osborne in the study. We had drawn every drape, curtain, and blind on the ground floor so that nobody could look in and see what was up.

Osborne nearly fainted when he saw me wearing his face. Maybe he believes in the old Kraut superstition of the *doppelgänger* like my grandmother did: if you see your double, it means your death is coming. It was my job to see that didn't happen. Osborne would just have to live with it.

The doorbell rang promptly as the grandfather clock in the hallway chimed the three-quarter sequence. Instead of arriving separately, the five Hollister cousins showed up together. Marge took their hats and coats and led them into the dining room. I watched them from a telephone alcove behind the staircase. No spouses, just the siblings. They didn't come empty-handed, either. The one I recognized as Robert carried a box about a foot square with a big blue bow on the lid.

Marge had set up a makeshift bar on the dining room sideboard, and I heard her tell the guests to help themselves. She told them I would be joining them shortly and came back into the hall, shutting the doors behind her. She tiptoed to the alcove and I whispered, "Ready?"

She nodded and hiked up her skirt to show me the pistol strapped to her thigh. "Ready." Her face softened for a second, and she said, "Be careful, Mars," then scooted off to the kitchen.

At ten to twelve, I stepped from the alcove and waved to Mason, who was watching from the study.

Showtime.

I slid the pocket doors apart with a bang and all five heads jerked around. "Good evening," I said, as close to Osborne's voice as I could get. "And thank you all for coming to my little celebration." I closed the doors behind me and walked around to the head of the table so that my back was to the French doors.

The eyes that followed me around the room were filled with more hate than I've ever seen. Everyone had a drink in his hand or hers. The men were dressed in suits and the women in street length dresses, Maude in green and Millicent in purple; envy and rage. The gift box sat on the table opposite me.

No one spoke, so I said, "Nothing to say?"

"I have a lot to say, but I can't say it in mixed company." Junior gestured to Maude and Millicent who stood glaring at me from one corner of the table.

"Did you invite us here to rub our noses in it?" Maude said.

I grinned. "No, I invited you here to make you an offer."

"What kind of offer?" Charles stepped forward.

"I'll give each of you a hundred thousand dollars." Eyebrows rose. "Tomorrow." I strolled down the table toward them. "Of course, I can't do that if I'm dead, can I?"

"What do you mean?" Clarence asked.

"In the last few days people have tried to kill me five times, one for each of you. Well, we're down to the last turn of the minute hand now. If a hail of gunfire comes through the French doors from the garden, I won't be the only one who's hit. If you're not all in it together, maybe just one of you knows when to duck so that as many of your siblings as possible will go with me and up your share of the loot."

None of them flinched. None of them looked to the others. Whatever would happen, they were all in it together.

"You're deluded, Arthur," Maude said. "You're a drunk and a wastrel, and a paranoid to boot."

"And a greedy son of a bitch," Robert spat. "You could give us each a million and never miss it."

"I'm greedy?" I said. "You want it all, don't you? Every dime."

"We deserve it all," Junior said. "Our whole lives we slaved for the company while Father lorded over us like Zeus from Olympus, and he leaves it all to you."

I stole a look at my watch. Seven minutes to midnight.

"You said an offer," Millicent said. "In exchange for what?"

I smiled. "Letting me live, of course." No response. "Hey, this is a celebration. It's no birthday party without a cake, now, is it?" I raised my voice. "Bring in the cake."

Marge pushed a serving cart with the cake on it through the swinging door to the kitchen. She was smiling, but I could see the tension in her eyes. "Right over here," I pointed to the head of the table. Marge rolled the cart over, curtsied, and left.

I stood beside the cake and made a show of lighting the candles. I looked at my watch. Five minutes to go. "Aren't you going to sing 'Happy Birthday'?"

"Before we do," Junior said, "we brought you a present." He lifted the lid from the box and all five of them reached a hand inside. All five came out holding revolvers. All five aimed them at me.

"You can't possibly get away with this. All five of you will get the Chair."

"There's where you're wrong, Arthur," Maude said, thumbing back the hammer of her revolver. "Four of these pistols have blanks; only one has a live round, and none of us knows which one it is. We all shoot on the count of three, and nobody knows who did the deed. We'll tell the police it was a birthday party prank gone wrong. We should be able to afford the best attorneys money can buy, since we'll have so much of it."

"Clever." I plucked the handkerchief from my breast pocket. "But before you shoot, there's something you need to see." I put the handkerchief to my face and rubbed at it while I put my own mug back. Everybody gasped when I took the hankie away and shook it out; dumping the gobs of face putty I'd hidden in it earlier on the table.

The pocket doors slid away behind them. "Looking for me?" Osborne stood in the doorway.

The siblings spun around as if they were wired together, raising their guns, but they stopped short when Mason popped up behind Osborne aiming a sawed-off twelve gauge over his shoulder.

He grinned. "Pull your trigger, and I'll pull mine."

The doors to the kitchen and the parlor opened. Czap came in through one and Montrose through the other, badge in one hand and service revolver in the other. "Police. Drop the guns."

I found out who was the brains of the outfit when everyone but Maude obeyed the order. She turned and aimed her pistol at me. "You bastard." She knew which gun had the live round.

She fired at me, and I would have caught the bullet if it hadn't ricocheted off the concrete under the icing on the cake.

A second shot, and Maude fell to the floor. Marge stood in the kitchen doorway, a wisp of gray smoke curling from the muzzle of her .38.

Osborne stepped around Maude and put the table between himself and the would-be heirs.

"Did you hear enough, Lieutenant?" I asked Czap.

"More than enough to put this gang away."

I heard a commotion at the French windows, and the curtains parted with a gust of cold air. Four uniforms were wrestling two men into the room from the garden. I recognized the faces of the waiter from Meloni's and the delivery man.

Osborne looked as if he was going to faint. He picked up the handkerchief I dropped on the table and started mopping sweat from his forehead.

"Well, Osborne, that's twelve large you owe me."

"Yes," he said. "I—I—" His mouth opened in a big oval. Osborne clutched-ed his chest and fell on his face on the Aubusson carpet. Before any of us could get to him, the grandfather clock started the Big Ben song.

• • •

It's been six months, and I still haven't gotten a dime for the caper. The attorneys are wrangling over whether Osborne was breathing or not at midnight, since none of us could take his pulse fast enough to prove he was still alive and they'll probably be fighting over it for years. Osborne died intestate and Mackenzie's in no rush to pay me from his estate. The last time I called him on the phone, he said, "You're not working for Arthur Osborne, in case you forgot, and I am, and I will be for a long, long time."

The Hollister siblings are lawyered up and are slated to go to court soon, including Maude, who recovered from Marge's bullet. I hear their attorneys are all working on a contingency basis with that same promise of big rewards for faithful service.

I did get one thing out of it all, though. After we packed up our act at the Hollister mansion, on the way out, it seems I took the wrong topcoat. I may never see a check for the case, but when the weather turns and the Pittsburgh snows fall again, that cashmere Burberry will be a great comfort.

THE END

Ming and Hong, the Smith Brothers are conjoined Oriental twins, the sons of a British shipping magnate and his aristocratic Chinese wife, who died giving birth to them. I was interested in exploring what may have happened to Chang and Eng Bunker, P.T. Barnum's world-famous Siamese Twins had they been born into a wealthy household and enjoyed the best of education and culture rather than being sold to a circus at the age of nine years. The brothers take over their father's business at his death, but soon tire of the day to day tedium and follow their true passion, investigation, which pits them against pirates, smugglers, the Tong, crooked politicians and the Municipal Police Department in *fin de siecle* San Francisco. In "Bronze Dogs" the Smith Brothers have to solve a mysterious shipboard theft of a valuable statue.

THE SMITH BROTHERS: BRONZE DOGS

When the telephone rang, the Smith Brothers were sitting in the conservatory playing a Bach sonata for flute and cello. Ming played the cello because being the left half of conjoined twins, he enjoyed the best angle for the bow, while Hong played the flute. They continued the piece for a few more measures, then gave up as the raucous jangling persisted. At last, Raphael, their butler and man servant answered the call and the ringing ceased.

"There are times when I wish we had never installed a telephone," Hong said.

"Its convenience never outweighs its intrusiveness," Ming agreed. "A telegram seems no less urgent, but it at least can be opened and read when one is prepared for bad news."

Raphael appeared in the doorway. The little Honduran bowed slightly at the waist. "My apologies, sirs, but Mister Montrose is calling. He says it is urgent."

The brothers set aside their instruments and rose from the wicker bench as one person. "The Shanghai Empress was due in port this evening," Ming said. "I hope she is still afloat."

Edward Montrose was the general manager of the Oriental Trading Consortium, a shipping company founded by Reginald Smith, the brothers' late father a few years before their mother, Ling-Tao died giving birth. The Smiths had progressively less to do with the day to day operation of the inherited business as they pursued what they believed to be their true calling: investigation.

Their heels clacked on the marble tiles of the foyer in a synchronized rhythm born of a lifetime of walking in tandem; when one stumbled, both fell. "You take it," Hong said, reaching into his jacket for a cigar.

Ming put the receiver to his ear. "Yes, Edward," he said into the mouthpiece. "This is Ming."

Hong snipped the end from his thin cheroot, and before he could fumble a match from his vest, Raphael silently appeared at his side to light it. Hong watched in the mirror above the telephone stand as his brother's face folded into lines of concern. "I see. We will be there as quickly as possible." He said over his shoulder, as he hung the receiver in the cradle, "Raphael, please ring for Taylor. We need the carriage at once."

"Yes, sir." Raphael disappeared down the hallway.

"Well, Ming? What is so urgent?"

"The Shanghai Empress has docked, and when the customs officer entered the hold, a crate was missing. Customs and the Police have impounded the ship and are holding the crew."

"Things disappear from time to time; items are misplaced, not loaded from the dock. What crate is it?"

"One of Robert Cabbel's temple dogs."

Hong's eyebrows raised. "That is impossible. They weigh a half ton each."

"But true nonetheless. We should leave at once."

• • •

The carriage rolled to a stop under the *porte cochere*, and the double doors of the mansion's entrance swung open to throw a rectangle of light across the wide stone steps. Taylor, the Smith Brothers' driver and bodyguard dropped from the seat and despite his size and bulk, landed lightly on the bricks. He opened the door of the carriage and let down the cast iron steps then stood back to wait for his passengers.

Ming and Hong stepped through the double doors and into the night side-by-side. The twins shared Oriental features, a Van Dyck beard, and a tailor and looked each to be the mirror image of the other. Ming, the left-hand twin deferred to his brother, and the pair sidestepped up and into the carriage. They settled into the seat and Raphael spread a lap robe over them against the chill and fog of the San Francisco night.

"You will get word to Darby?" Ming said to Raphael.

"Yes, sir. I shall have him meet you at the wharf," the wiry Honduran replied. "Excuse me; I must open the gate below."

Taylor climbed onto the driver's seat, the springs sagging under his weight. A flick of the reins, and the matched grays pulled the carriage away from the portico, its wheels clattering on the bricks of the driveway. When they reached the wrought iron gate, it swung noiselessly aside, melting into the thick fog like a parlor trick, and the carriage rolled away down the gas lit street.

"I was so looking forward to playing the Bach sonata this evening," Hong said.

"As was I, Brother. For all its convenience the telephone can be a damned nuisance. It is so insistent a demand on one's attention."

"Based on the urgency in Edward's voice, I suspect he would have beaten down our door shortly anyway. It all seems so far-fetched."

"I agree. A half-ton crate disappearing from a ship's hold in transit — where could it have gone?"

"He said Pendleton is beside himself. Maritime Indemnity insured the pair of crates for six hundred thousand dollars. But I would wager that Cabbel is shouting louder."

Robert Cabbel, millionaire timber baron had purchased a pair of bronze Chinese Foo dogs to flank the gates of his Nob Hill mansion, statues that reputedly had once graced the Forbidden City. Like so many of California's *nouveau riche*, Cabbel believed acquisition was an avenue to legitimacy.

"Perhaps one of the crates was left on the dock in Hong Kong," Ming said.

"Wishful thinking, Brother; Occam's Razor. We will find out soon enough."

The clock in the Custom House tower tolled eleven times as the carriage entered the harbor district. As they approached the Oriental Trade Consortium wharf, the brothers saw a crowd of people belly to belly with a phalanx of uniformed police officers at the gangplank of the Shanghai Empress. Stacks of crates sat on the ship's deck under netting and police guard.

The crowd shifted its attention from the ship to the carriage as it pulled up to the dock. Taylor vaulted from the driver's seat to open the door and let down the steps for the brothers to alight. As he did, three men in suits pushed through the crowd to confront Ming and Hong.

"I need my shipment, Smith. When'll it be released?" shouted one of them.

"How long will our goods be tied up?" demanded another.

"What are you two doing about it?" said a third. He reached for Ming's arm, but before he could close his hand, Taylor seized him by his coat and lifted him from the ground, slamming him into the other two and knocking them down.

One of the three was quickly on his feet and about to rush at Taylor when the uniforms stepped between them, Billy clubs raised. "Here now," a sergeant called. "Step aside, all of you. Let these men pass." The crowd grudgingly parted, and Ming and Hong walked in tandem to the cargo ramp with two officers ahead of them and Taylor behind.

"When's our men getting off that boat?" a woman with a child in her arms cried. "Yeah, when?" others chimed in.

"Why is the crew is being held?" Hong said, leaning forward to be heard by the officer in front of him.

"Detective Harcourt thought it best to keep a hand on them 'til all this is sorted out."

"I see."

They climbed the cargo ramp, the gang plank being too narrow for their easy passage, and stepped onto the deck of the ship. The Shanghai Empress was a steam and sail freighter; oak hulled, she ran two hundred fifty feet and three thousand tons. She was not the fastest ship in the Pacific but could make ten knots under full steam. Her sails were furled now, and her idle stacks pointed upward like twin cannons aimed at the stars.

Captain Amos Bingham, a long-time employee of Oriental Trading, crossed the deck with three other men. Ming and Hong recognized them all; Richard Broadwater, the head of the San Francisco Customs House, Detective Lieutenant Abraham Harcourt of the San Francisco Police Department, and Robert Cabbel.

The Captain took off his cap and held it in his hands. "Sirs," Bingham said. "I don't know what to say."

Hong raised a hand. "Please. Just tell us what happened."

"I'll tell you what happened," Cabbel snarled. The broad-shouldered millionaire leaned forward to put his thick red nose and mustache an inch from Ming's face. "You lost one of a pair of priceless sculptures. That's what happened. They were a matched set, and one without the other is worthless."

"A pleasure to meet you, too, Mister Cabbel," Ming said. "And we are not 'you two.' I am Ming Smith, and this is my brother Hong." Ming nodded toward him. "I am the sinister one."

"First," said Hong. "My brother and I have lost nothing. An error was made, perhaps, and we will do all we can to rectify it. As for worthless? I hardly think an ancient statue, even if part of a pair, is worthless."

Cabbel showed his teeth. "We're not talking salt-and-pepper shakers here, Smith. Foo dogs are an inseparable set, just like you and your brother."

"I would be offended were not Foo dogs really lions. Please be patient, Mister Cabell." Ming said. "We will discuss this when all the facts are known. In the meantime —" he turned his head toward the Captain. "Where is Edward?"

"He's in the office with Walsh, Mister Cabbel's man. They're going over the paperwork."

"Please send someone for him and ask him to bring the ledger. Now, please take us to the hold."

The ship's stairwells and ladders were too narrow to accommodate the Smiths, so the whole party was lowered on a platform by the ship's davit. The chugging of the steam-powered motor and the clanking of the mechanism made further conversation impossible. The platform touched down, and the brothers saw in the light of kerosene lanterns the remaining crate of the pair standing amid others of various sizes. The crate's lid had been removed and leaned against the bulwark.

"We opened this crate as soon as soon as we found the other one was missing." Bingham said.

"It was intact?" Hong asked.

"Yessir," a burly sailor answered. He was nearly the size of Taylor and sported a pair of bushy mutton chop sideburns. His muscles strained the seams of his jersey.

"This is Pettigrew," Bingham said. "My First Mate."

"I pried the lid off the crate myself, sirs, the Mate said. "And I did it in front of the Customs man and the Copper, here."

"And the statue was inside?"

"Yessir. Ugly devil it is."

"Mister Cabbel, is there anything unusual about the crate or the packing?"

"It was built around the statue on a dais reinforced with timbers to handle the weight. Otherwise, it's an ordinary crate. The packing is common excelsior to prevent incidental damage."

"The other crate, the missing one was identical?"

"In every detail."

"Detective," Ming said. "Have your men searched this crate?"

"Well, no, once we saw the statue was in it, we left it as is."

"Mister Pettigrew, would you please remove the sides and the packing?"

"Yessir," Pettigrew said. He picked up a crowbar and with a screeching of nails began prying the pieces apart. In a moment, the statue was revealed in all its grotesque magnificence.

"Remarkable," Ming said, then added, "the female."

"What?" said Bingham.

"Foo dogs are paired, female and male, Yin and Yang. The male traditionally has a foot resting on a ball; the female, on a cub." He pointed. "As you see there."

"Well, that's all very interesting, I'm sure," Harcourt said, "but we have a theft to solve here."

"Perhaps," said Hong. "Perhaps simply an incident."

At that moment, two men came down the ladder into the hold, one a thick-waisted man in a vested suit, and the other a thin man with a sharp nose and chin dressed in a cloth coat. The heavy man was carrying a leather-bound ledger with the corners of papers protruding from its edges. "The papers are all in order," the heavier man said. "Both statues were loaded into the hold in Hong Kong. The papers are signed by the British Officer at Hong Kong and initialed by Captain Bingham."

"Thank you, Edward," Ming said. "That eliminates one possibility." He said to the thin man, "And you, sir are?"

"Jonathan Walsh; I am Mister Cabbel's secretary."

Ming's eyes dropped to Walsh's waist. "And do you always carry a pistol, Mister Walsh?"

"What?' said Harcourt.

Ming pointed with his chin. "The telltale bulge under his coat."

Without blinking, Walsh opened his coat to reveal the butt of a pearl handled pistol in a cross-draw holster. "I carry it whenever circumstances warrant, Mister Smith."

Ming nodded. He looked around the hold. "Captain, apart from the hatchway overhead and the one to the other side of the davit, are there any other openings a crate the size of this one could be removed from the hold?"

"No, sir," Bingham said. "The other hatches are small ones for the crew to come and go; nothing that large. Aside from a few portholes, there are no other openings into the hold from outside the ship."

"What is that stain on the deck?" Hong said, pointing to a dark patch on the wood.

Pettigrew crouched to put a finger in the stain then held it to his nose. "Machine oil."

"Are there any drums of oil in the cargo hold?"

Bingham shook his head. "No."

"And the missing crate was placed where?"

"Two feet to the left of the other one."

"And when was the last time that both crates were seen together?"

"Last night," Cabbel said. "Walsh and I checked on them every night of the voyage."

Ming pointed to the darkened area beyond the lantern light. "And you have searched the entire hold, detective?"

Harcourt nodded. "Of course we have. Give us a little credit, Smith. You pair aren't the only ones that solve crimes in this town."

"I think we have seen as much as we will tonight. Mister Broadwater, is there any reason to hold the remaining cargo now that the ship has been thoroughly searched?"

"No," the customs officer said. "I suppose not."

"Detective, what about releasing the crew?"

"Not until we question each and every one of them and I'm satisfied that none is responsible."

"Very well," Hong said. He took a small leather-bound notebook from his pocket and scribbled a note on it. He tore it out and handed it to Montrose. "Take this to Macintyre at Cliff House. I want the crew wined and dined with nothing but the best. Tell him to put it on our account and bring it to the ship this evening, no matter the hour. If these men are to be sequestered, at least they will be well fed. Captain, will you please take us back to the deck. We're finished here for the moment."

"But what about —" Cabbel blurted.

"We can meet with you tomorrow, Mister Cabbel. Right now, we have enquiries to make."

Bingham signaled the crew on deck, and the platform was lowered into the hold.

"What a racket," Ming said, hands over his ears to shut the clank and rumble of the davit.

"Yes," said Hong, "and one reason that I find it difficult to imagine how the statue was stolen from this ship."

• • •

Darby was waiting in the carriage when Ming and Hong sidled aboard. "So, gents, what's in the wind?" The little man was dressed in a pinch-backed suit and pork-pie hat, making him look like a race track tout. The ex-reporter from the *Chronicle* was the leg man for the brothers' operation, gathering information from myriad sources around the City.

"Three hundred thousand dollars." Ming said. Darby whistled. The brothers told him all that they knew about the disappearance of the statue as the carriage rattled through the darkened streets.

"What do you need from me?" Darby said.

"Get out your notebook," Hong told him. "We'll make a list. Start with Robert Cabbel."

• • •

As the grandfather clock in the hallway struck three, the brothers sat as they often did in one of the broad settee-like chairs designed and built for their comfort at the round table that rested in a nook off the kitchen. Joined by a trunk of flesh and bone at the chest, they looked as if someone had set a mirror at an angle beside a single man. Ming and Hong had declined Raphael's offer to make tea for them and opted instead for a pot of his strong, dark coffee.

"It seems impossible that a thousand-pound statue could simply vanish from the closed hold of a ship."

"Yet it apparently has," Ming said. "According to the bill of lading, both crates were on board when the Shanghai Empress left Hong Kong. Somewhere between there and San Francisco, the statue disappeared."

"But why steal one and not both?"

"Interesting question." Ming looked into the bottom of his coffee cup as if to find the answer there before saying, "Perhaps the thief intended to steal both but didn't have the opportunity."

"I find it difficult to believe the opportunity existed to steal even one of them." Hong unrolled a nautical chart across the table and set their coffee cups on the curling edges. "The Empress' course is plotted in red. You can see that she sailed directly from Hong Kong; no other ports of call. If they

He looked into the bottom of his cup as if to find the answer there..

met another ship en route, it would have to have sailed from an island along the way. According to the chart, there are no islands within two hundred miles of the shipping lane.

"That is possible, but such a ship couldn't dock with the Empress even in the dead of night without being noticed. Particularly if that clanking davit were used to transfer it from one ship to the other."

"Unless the Captain and the entire crew were complicit."

Hong nodded slowly, "But that many hands in the kettle would spread even three hundred thousand dollars very thin. And remember the wisdom of Benjamin Franklin: Three can keep a secret if two of them are dead."

"Quite so. And Cabbel and his secretary were on board the entire voyage."

"Could the statue have been destroyed or simply dropped into the sea?"

"To what end?"

"Perhaps to stab at Cabbel. To make so much money in so few years, he surely has made enemies."

"But there is no way to destroy a bronze statue without making more noise than the davit. Also, what of the crate? It could have been reduced to pieces small enough to force through a porthole, I suppose, but you heard the racket Pettigrew made dismantling its mate. There is no quiet way to do any of it."

"It is a puzzle."

"And neither of us will be satisfied until it is solved."

"Let us see what Darby brings us in the morning."

• • •

After breakfast, Darby arrived. He used his own key after ringing a code on the doorbell to alert Raphael that he was entering. Darby knew that the Honduran, once the man servant and bodyguard of an assassinated dictator could kill an intruder with as little effort as clapping his hands, and with as little remorse. He stood just inside the door and a voice came from behind him. "Take your coat, Mister Darby?"

Darby was long past the point at which Raphael's sudden appearance startled him. "Thank you, Raphael. Are the Brothers in their office?"

"No, sir, they are at table. Please follow me."

He found the Smiths once again at the round table amid notes, ledgers, and charts.

"Coffee, Mister Darby?"

"Yeah, please. I could use it. Been up most of the night."

"Please sit down, Darby," Ming said. "What do you have for us?"

"I ran checks on Captain Bingham and his crew. The Captain, Pettigrew, his First Mate, and Pike, the Navigator came up clean. Almost all of the crew have arrest records locally, most for drunken brawling on shore leave, but two of the sailors served time; Peter Beckley and Orville Bright, both for theft."

Raphael brought the coffee and Darby pulled a flask from an inside pocket and poured a dollop of whiskey into the cup. He took a sip, smacked his lips, and said, "Here's the significance: the two of them, Beckley and Bright served time for the same crime."

"Partners?" Hong said.

"Yep. They burgled a couple of houses the night before they were to set sail on a freighter to Argentina, but bad weather set in, they boat didn't sail, and they were picked up before they could get away."

"We'll look into their story," Ming said, "but of course there's more, correct?"

"You bet," Darby said with a nod. "I got the real lowdown on Cabbel from some people I know. Turns out that he's in some financial trouble. His creditors are all sharpening their knives."

"If that is so, why would he purchase anything so expensive as the Foo dogs?"

"Why else? Keeping up appearances. You know as well as I do that ninety percent of business posture in this town is image. If you look successful and prosperous, you must be. Start looking shabby and you lose a lot of customers."

Hong looked at his notes. "What about that man Walsh, Cabbel's secretary?"

"Turns out that Walsh isn't his original name. Jonathan Walsh used to be Aaron Bailey. He's got a past too. Used to be connected with Black Stone Coal in Pennsylvania. He was head of their company police when eight miners were killed in riots during a strike in eighty-nine. The company tried some shenanigans to wriggle out of their obligations in the Panic and their principals went to jail. Bailey served a short sentence, changed his name to Walsh, and took Horace Greeley's advice. He came west and ended up working for Cabbel's timber operation. Seems he's as much a bodyguard as a secretary."

"But he's Cabbel's man, so it is unlikely that he would try such a bold theft. Beyond the difficulty of stealing the crate from the ship, people don't buy ancient statuary off the back of a wagon at Market Square. He would need contacts to fence the piece and sell it to a wealthy collector."

Ming broke in. "And the collector could not put the statue on display or be found out as complicit in the theft after the fact; aiding and abetting, as it were."

"Besides that," Hong said, "the dogs are a set, and a collector would have the Devil's own time trying to quietly buy the mate."

The telephone rang in the foyer. In a moment Raphael appeared. "Sirs, Mister Montrose is calling."

The brothers rose. "Is there anything more I can do for you?" Darby asked.

"Keep poking about. Dig a little deeper at Walsh, and try to learn just how much debt Cabbel has accrued. You have done well. Keep at it."

The brothers went to the telephone, and this time, Hong took the call. "Edward. What news?" He held the receiver so that both could hear the reply.

"Customs has released the cargo, and Harcourt has released the crew."

"I see. We will be there shortly." Hong hung the receiver in the cradle. "Our friend Harcourt has acted precipitously."

"Yes," Ming said. "Foolish and regrettable."

"It is time to return to the Empress."

• • •

When the brothers reached the wharf, the crowd of the night before was gone as was the police cordon. The Shanghai Empress had been unloaded, and longshoremen were lifting bales and crates onto wagons. Captain Bingham saw the Smiths stepping from their carriage and came down the gangplank to greet them with Detective Harcourt close behind.

"Captain, Detective," Hong said. "I see that Customs has cleared the cargo."

"Yes," Bingham said. "Early this morning Broadwater released it."

"So, the hold is empty now?"

"No, the remaining statue has been re-crated and Cabbel intends to ship it back to China."

Both brothers were surprised at the news but smart enough to not let their faces betray them. "And you have released the crew as well, Detective?" Ming said, changing the subject, "before your investigation is through?"

Harcourt's lip curled away from his teeth. "Our investigation is ongoing, thank you, Smith. We took statements. There was nothing more to be learned keeping the crew on the ship. I say turn them loose and see where they go, what they do, and who they meet. My men are shadowing them. Something I suspect you can't do so well. Hard to be inconspicuous when there's two of you joined at the hip, eh?" He chuckled at his own joke.

"I take it there was little learned from the crew," Hong said.

"Enough," Harcourt said with a smug grin. "Enough." He turned on his heel and strode away.

Bingham shook his head. "I don't understand his antagonism. You all want to solve the case."

"There is resentment toward us from the San Francisco Police Department. To them we are upstarts, rank amateurs. They despise us, not so much for our intellect or even our success at solving cases that they could not; they are jealous of our freedom to operate outside their prescribed bounds. The detective is limited by procedure, politics, and pecking order."

"Your shooting of the Police Commissioner fuels the sentiment," Ming said.

"Point taken. Now, Captain, is it convenient for you to answer a few questions for us?"

"Of course, please come to my cabin." He turned toward the ship. "Pettigrew! Take over here."

Bingham poured three snifters of brandy and settled into the chair behind his desk. His account was concise.

"The night was quiet and the sea calm. I passed the helm to Mister Pike at the start of First Watch and retired to my cabin. According to the duty rotation, Culley was on watch in the engine room, and Kadish on deck. They were relieved, respectively, by Doolan and Beckley at Middle Watch. I believe that whatever happened to the crate occurred during that time, because it was at the end of morning watch that Mister Cabbel raised the alarm."

"What time was that exactly?" Hong said.

"By the clock, seven-thirty in the morning."

"The rest of the crew were asleep at that time?"

"As far as I know, yes."

"And neither Kadish nor Biggs saw anything suspicious."

"According to their word, no. And the men below wouldn't hear Armageddon over the sound of the engines."

"How long have the men on watch that night been with you?"

"Culley, five years, Kadish and Doolan, three. Beckley has been on the crew a little more than a year."

"He signed on along with Orville Bright, correct?"

"Uh, yes. How did you know?"

"Because the two of them spent time together in jail for theft. Were you aware of that?" Ming asked.

"Yes. They were young and foolish at the time — and drunk. They've mended their ways since, and their behavior under my command has been exemplary."

"And Mister Cabbel; did he regularly go below during the voyage?"

"Either he or his man Walsh went at least once a day or in the evening. I suppose he went early that morning because we were going to arrive in port later in the day, and that was when Cabbel discovered the crate was missing."

"Do you know of any way that crate could have been removed other than through the main cargo hatch?"

"None. It's a complete mystery to me."

"And, I must confess, a complete mystery to us."

• • •

When the Brothers arrived at the mansion, Darby was drinking coffee in the foyer.

"You have news?" said Hong.

"A little."

"Then come with us." He handed Raphael his coat and hat and the three crossed the foyer to the corner where a brass elevator car waited like a gilded bird cage. "Raphael, please bring tea for us and more coffee for Darby."

As the car ascended with a whir and hum, Darby said, "I spoke with Chang, He knew of the theft of the Foo dog, but nothing of its whereabouts." Chang Tzu, the leader of the Chinatown Brotherhood, rival to the Tong, was what the Brothers called a "paid ally," a source of information and occasionally forceful action. "He gave his word that he will contact me if he learns anything about it."

"And how much will his word cost us this time?" said Ming with a laugh.

"Probably a lot."

"The cost of doing business."

The elevator stopped at the third floor and the three crossed the hallway to the office where Raphael was already adding coal to the fireplace from a scuttle. "The tea will be ready soon, sirs," he said.

"So, Darby," said Hong, "what else have you learned?"

"For the past year, Cabbel has been buying art; paintings, sculptures, a Fabergé egg. He appears to be trying to own one of everything, yet an entire wing of his mansion is still unfinished. He's become an obsessive collector at the expense of everything else."

"Or a clever investor," said Ming. "If his business is failing, he may be accumulating items to convert to quick cash to save the company and in the meantime give the outward appearance of prosperity, like a gambler who wears a diamond ring as a hedge against bad luck."

"Or as a portable escape fund if his creditors pounce," Hong added. "He could likely flee with a wagonload of his baubles, sell them through a fence to another like himself, and live well from the proceeds for the rest of his days while his creditors whistle into the wind."

Darby nodded. "That sounds right to me. Plenty of lumber businesses went under in ninety-three, and Cabbel would have gone down with them if he didn't have the government contract to supply timber for Hunter's Point. That saved him, but just barely, and although Cabbel denies it, he's had a toe or two over the edge ever since."

"But the temple dogs don't fit the pattern of acquisition. They are anything but portable."

At that moment, Raphael appeared with the tea cart. Hong frowned, disapproving, as Ming dropped extra cubes of sugar into his cup. "Brother, the body is a temple, and I will thank you to remember that ours is shared. What you drink flows through my veins as well."

Ming smiled. "Indeed, Brother, as does what you breathe — your cigars."

A bell tinkled faintly from the ground floor. Someone was at the gate. The brothers rose and crossed to a window overlooking the front of the estate. Beside it, a brass telescope rested on a tripod. Hong turned it toward the gate and squinted into the eyepiece. "It is our friend Detective Harcourt and the sergeant from the wharf last night."

Raphael appeared in the doorway. "Sirs —"

"Please let them in, and bring them up here."

In a moment, the Brothers heard the clump of heavy shoes on the stairs and in another, Detective Harcourt and the uniformed officer entered the room. Harcourt was wearing the same suit and the same smug grin he had the night before.

"What a coincidence," said Ming. "We were hoping to speak with you today to perhaps pool our resources to solve this perplexing theft."

"No need," said Harcourt, his grin widening. "The sergeant and I just dropped by to let you know the case is solved — or I should say on the way to solution — with no need of your help."

"Is that so?" said Hong. "And who was the perpetrator?"

"That ex-con Beckley. We've got him in custody now. It won't be long before he cracks and gives up the men in the boat that took it away."

"Beckley was on watch during the night, and he is a likely suspect, but how could he get the statue out of the hold without rousing the entire ship? That davit makes enough noise to wake a cadaver."

Harcourt tilted his head back and thrust out his chin. "The davit may, but its pulleys don't. You two think you're so damned smart, but you didn't figure this one out."

"You're dying to tell us," said Darby. "Spit it out."

"The way I reckon it, a sloop under sail came alongside the Empress in the dark. Beckley slipped the cable off the pulleys and put a heavy rope in its place. Wind it over three pulleys, and a few strong men could lift the crate free and clear and lower it into a waiting boat with nary a sound. That oil on the floor in the hold? Come from oiling the pulleys so they'd make no noise."

"But how do you know it was Beckley and not Kadish, the man on First Watch?" Ming said.

"Because we got Beckley dead to rights." Harcourt's eyes gleamed. The sergeant nodded agreement. "We followed the men who weren't asleep that night once they left the ship, and guess which one of them turned up in a saloon later in the day drunk and buying round after round of drinks: Beckley. We took him home and searched his flat, and tell these fellows what we found in his duffel, Sergeant."

"The better part of five hundred dollars."

"I don't run no shipping company, but I know for a fact that no sailor makes that kind of wage on a voyage."

"How does Beckley account for the money?'

"Says he found it." Harcourt snorted. "What a fairy tale. He's guilty, and by day's end, I'll wager we'll have the names of his accomplices out of him."

"Your theory is interesting," said Hong. "Did you find a rope?"

Harcourt hesitated, as if grasping for an answer. "Plenty enough of 'em on board."

Hong nodded. No one spoke. Harcourt leered. "Nothin' to say? Eh? Eh?

Let's go, Sergeant. We've got a prisoner to interrogate." They left and the Brothers waited until they could see them walking down the driveway to the gate before either spoke."

"This could mean trouble," Ming said.

"I fear you are right."

"Trouble?" said Darby. "How?"

"Because if a crewman in our employ is found guilty of the theft, Marine Indemnity International, who insured Cabbel's shipment can make a case that the loss is our liability and not that of the insurance company. We may be forced to pay three hundred thousand dollars in settlement."

"That wouldn't sink your business — no pun intended," Darby said.

Hong chuckled. "No, it would not. But recall what you said earlier about image. Image is not confined to money; it includes reliability. This case will make headlines around the world, and if we are found liable by the courts, our reliability will be called into question. That will hurt our image and cost us customers and money."

"That includes our investigative business. I do not believe that the solution to this matter is so simple as Harcourt paints it. The idea of the rope is one possibility, but not the only one. He has seized on this theory and will cling to it doggedly, at our expense."

"You two sound pragmatic," Darby said. "But I think there's just a little bit of pride involved."

"You are probably right," Ming said. "I can speak for both of us when I say that we hate to be beaten."

• • •

The next morning Ambrose Pendleton arrived at the mansion. The insurance agent's stout build was testimony to his eating habits, and he was delighted to accept the coffee and chocolate éclairs that Raphael offered. In return, he gave the Smiths copies of all the documents concerning Cabbel's insurance of the temple dogs. Included was a photograph taken in the Hong Kong warehouse with Cabbel standing between the two statues, a hand on the head of each.

"I understand that the police have a man in custody," Pendleton said.

"Yes," Hong replied, "for the moment, but it remains to be seen if the charge will hold."

"Detective Harcourt seems confident."

"You have spoken with him?"

"Read it in the papers."

"Ah, yes, the papers," Ming said. "Of course, they also reported the authenticity of the Cardiff Giant, the Diaphote Hoax, and the Mammoth Potato of Loveland, Colorado."

Pendleton blinked. "Are you saying that the police report is a hoax?"

"Not at all," Ming replied. "I am merely suggesting that the prudent course is to wait for further developments; to not count one's geese, as it were."

"Some of them may be wild," Hong said, with a smile, picking up the metaphor.

"Hmmph." Pendleton put the last bite of his éclair into his mouth and wiped his fingers on a napkin. Time for business. "Whatever you gentlemen may think, I fear that the police will never find Cabbel's missing statue, and there will be a hefty price to pay."

"Yes," Hong said. "Three hundred thousand dollars is as you say, a 'hefty' sum."

"My company has authorized me to make an offer to you, in the light of recent developments in the case, to eliminate costly litigation and unpleasantness by sharing the cost between yourselves and us."

"Share?"

"Fifty-fifty; a hundred fifty thousand dollars each."

"And why would we agree to such an arrangement?" Ming asked.

"Because your crewman facilitated the theft, which makes Oriental Trade liable."

"Allegedly."

"But the police have every confidence that their theory is correct and that it is only a matter of days before it is proven beyond doubt."

"You rely on the newspapers once again." Hong said. He and Ming looked to each other, and both shook their heads. "No."

"No? You're willing to risk paying it all instead of half?"

"If you were so assured that Harcourt is correct, you would never have come here." Ming said. "Our answer is no, and it will remain so."

"You're acting like fools," Pendleton sputtered. "I can tell you this, the next time we talk, you'll be coming to me, and it won't be fifty percent anymore." He jumped to his feet, his voice rising. "Every day you wait, the gap will widen. Good day." Pendleton turned and almost collided with Raphael, waiting with his coat and hat.

"We need to talk with Beckley," Hong said. He called for the carriage, and in half an hour, they arrived at the Broadway Jail. The ugly three-story building had no windows on the ground floor, and a railed staircase from the sidewalk to the second floor balcony and entrance. Its stern façade abutted another as tall that sported a sign at the top of the second floor and another at the top of the third that read: FOTOGRAPHS. Hong looked up the narrow flight of stairs and said, "This climb never gets any easier."

"Perhaps we should file a petition to the Mayor's office to widen the steps."

The Brothers found Peter Beckley alone in a cell in handcuffs, sitting on the iron bunk. He was still wearing his ship clothes, although they were ripped and blood spattered. Beckley's lower lip was split, and his left eye was purple and swollen shut.

"Ten minutes," the guard said.

"I see Harcourt's investigation was vigorous," Ming said through the bars.

Beckley grinned to show a missing tooth. "I gave as good as I got. A few of them blues'll remember me a while."

"You know who we are?"

He nodded. "Who wouldn't recognize you? The Smith Brothers. What're a couple of rich lads like you doing here?"

"You are our employee," said Hong. "We are attempting to arrange bail for you and we will provide legal counsel for your defense."

"Oh yeah? And what do I have to do for all that?"

"Simply tell us the truth."

"I told the truth," Beckley snapped, jumping to his feet and wrapping his hands around the bars. "You see where it got me. My story ain't changed a whit since that bastard Harcourt set his bully boys on me. I can't tell them something I don't know, and I'm not going to say I did something I didn't."

"Please, just tell us what happened."

"Not much to tell. I went on deck for Middle Watch, relieved Kadish, I walked the deck regular, kept an eye on things like I should. It was a quiet night, and I was relieved at the end of watch."

"And you saw no ship during the night?" Ming said.

"None. Not so much as a light in the distance."

"And at the end of your watch?"

I went to my hammock, and woke up to a commotion when that Cabbel fellow found out his crate was missing. The Captain called all hands, and I went on deck with the rest. Cabbel was raising holy hell, and we were ordered to search the hold."

"And, of course, you found nothing."

"Not a trace."

"And the five hundred dollars?"

"I went to my flat when we was let off the Empress, and when I was unpacking by bag, I found a roll of banknotes inside one of my socks."

"How do you think it got there?"

Beckley shrugged. "Maybe someone stole it or won it gambling in Hong Kong and was afraid it might be stolen from him because people knew he had it. I figured 'finders-keepers,' you know." He grinned. "I'm not one to question good luck or Divine providence."

"You said that Cabbel was raising a fuss. Was Walsh on deck with him?"

Beckley's eyes slid side to side as he pondered the question. "Now that you mention it, I —"

"Who let these men down here?" The brothers turned to see Harcourt standing at the end of the row of cells. Before he could answer, Harcourt glared at Ming and Hong and said. "What the hell do you two think you're doing?"

"Your prisoner is our employee," Hong replied. "We came to arrange for bail."

"Bail? Are you joking?" Harcourt snorted. "Not only is he being held for theft, Beckley assaulted three of my officers."

"I suppose then that the next time you interrogate him, you will shackle him to the bars," Ming said.

Harcourt's face reddened. "Get out of here before I arrest the pair of you for interfering with an inquiry."

"How could we interfere with something that has ended? It appears that you have already decided Beckley's guilt and will hear nothing to the contrary."

"Get out! Get out!" Harcourt stormed. "Guard, remove these freaks."

• • •

Back in their office, Hong said, "Do you believe Beckley?"

"As much as I believe anyone else at this point. It is a shame that Harcourt is clutching his pet theory to his bosom. He wants so desperately to be correct that he sees any skepticism as a threat."

"And he is playing into the hands of Pendleton and Maritime Indemnity."

"As we feared," Ming said.

"Yes, the heat rises."

"We need to ponder this problem."

"Beethoven's Fifth Piano Concerto?"

Ming nodded. "The challenge will put all of this out of our minds and allow us to start fresh."

Hong rang for Raphael. "Please bring tea to the music room."

The Brothers had a pair of concert grand pianos nestled with the prow of one in the nook of the other. One had the eighty-eight keys in ordinary sequence, and the other keyboard split at middle C, placing the treble register to the left and the bass register to the right so that Ming was not doomed to play the left hand only. Both were concert-quality musicians, but Beethoven's Fifth Piano Concerto was a daunting task for the most accomplished pianist.

The brothers sat at the wide piano bench and opened the folio. Across the top of the first sheet of the score was a notation penned by their boyhood tutor and mentor, Oxford scholar Robert Fellowes: What one man can think, another can do. - Jules Verne.

"Robert was correct as always," Ming said.

"Reminds me of our case."

"I'd rather forget about that for a while. Ready?"

Hong nodded, and Ming tapped the piano with his thumb. The Brothers plunged into the concerto. Thirty-one measures unto the piece, Hong stopped playing.

"What is it?" Ming said."

"What Robert wrote on the score. Do you recall why the five concertos were not performed for nearly fifty years after Beethoven composed them?"

"The difficulty of the piano solo was beyond the capability of most pianists."

"And do you recall who was the first to perform concertos three, four, and five with the Boston Symphony?"

Ming's brow wrinkled, then he nodded slowly and said, "Robert Heller."

"The 'Prestidigitator-Pianist.'"

"Robert is still counseling us from beyond the grave."

"Yes," said Hong. "We have been studying a theft, when we should have been studying an illusion." He reached for the bell cord. In a moment, Raphael appeared.

"Yes, sirs?"

"Send Taylor with the carriage to bring Darby here as quickly as possible."

• • •

The next morning, the carriage stopped before a modest storefront on the fringe of the Theater District. The sign above the door read: Aaron Breckenridge and Sons Theatrical Construction. Darby rapped at the door with his knuckles. "You don't know how difficult it was for me to arrange this meeting. Breckenridge has a rarified clientele, and as a rule he won't meet with anyone outside that tight little circle."

"Testimony to your powers of persuasion, Darby," Ming said.

The door opened a few inches, and a bearded young man in a carpenter's apron peered out with one blue eye. "Yes?" From behind him they heard busy hammers and saws.

Darby produced a business card. "These are the Smith Brothers, Ming and Hong. We have an appointment."

"Yes, sir," the young man said. "Please step inside." He handed each of the three a sheet of paper and set bottle of ink and a pen on a stand just inside the door.

"What's this?" Darby said.

"A statement of promise that you will divulge nothing that you see here to any person outside these walls."

Darby rolled his eyes, but Ming and Hong signed the documents without comment. "Follow me, please," the young man said and led them through the ground floor of the shop past workbenches and stalls to a narrow staircase set against the back wall. He led them down a corridor decorated with blueprints and diagrams thumb tacked to the walls. At its end, he knocked on a closed door.

"Come in."

In his office, Aaron Breckenridge sat at a table rather than a desk. The Brothers immediately recognized the resemblance between the owner and the young man who led them upstairs, as true as if they were stamped from the same die. "Thank you, Charlie." Breckenridge stood and offered his hand to shake all around.

"You understand, gentlemen, that I ordinarily do business only with illusionists. I almost refused to meet with you, but I wanted the opportunity to see one of Nature's greatest tricks for myself. The two of you are an absolute marvel, and no illusion, either." He held up a hand. "I mean no offense when I say that. It is a true privilege to meet you."

"No less a privilege than for us to meet one of the profession's greatest craftsmen." Hong said. "We have seen your work on the stages of San Francisco employed by such men as Howard Thurston, Harry Kellar, and Alexander Hermann."

"Yes?" From behind him they heard busy hammers and saws.

"And now," said Ming, "we would like to employ you to build something for us."

The brothers gave Breckenridge a brief account of their situation and explained their need.

"Darby?" said Hong.

Darby set a rolled diagram on the worktable. Breckenridge put a pair of rimless spectacles on the end of his nose and unrolled the sheet. He studied the diagram for a moment, then a smile folded his face into myriad wrinkles. "This is very clever. Yes, it could be done."

"The catch is," Darby said, "They need it by tomorrow night."

"Money is no concern," said Ming.

Breckenridge removed his glasses and looked at each of the brothers in turn. "Nor is it for me. I want no money; instead, I want the right to build this gadget in the future."

"Done," said Ming. Hong nodded.

Breckenridge rose from his chair and opened the door into the corridor. "Charlie!" he called. "Clear the main bay and assemble the workmen. We have a rush job to do."

• • •

The next night, Darby arrived at the mansion carrying a box under a canvas cover. Taylor had the carriage waiting at the door. The Brothers were dressed and ready when he arrived. "Everything set?"

"Yes," said Hong. "All will be at the Shanghai Empress at eight o'clock; Cabbel, Walsh, Bingham, Pendleton, Montrose, Broadwater, and of course, Harcourt. We should leave now. We don't want to be late."

The carriage arrived at the deserted wharf. A few lanterns lit the scene, but for the most part, Oriental Trading's dock and the ship were in shadow. The Captain and Pettigrew were waiting at the head of the cargo ramp. "Is everyone here?" Ming asked.

"Yes. Everything's ready."

Pettigrew worked the davit, and the clanking crane lowered them into the hold. In a moment, Pettigrew slid down the ladder to join the group clustered around the only crate left in the ship.

"What's this all about?" Cabbel snapped.

"Have you reconsidered?" Pendleton said with a smirk.

"You'd two'd best not be wasting my time," Harcourt snarled.

"Have your handcuffs ready, Harcourt," Ming said. "If we're wrong, you can use them on us."

Pendleton pointed at the cloth covered box. "What's that?"

"The solution to a puzzle," Hong said. "All this time, we have been trying to understand how a thousand-pound statue could vanish, along with its crate without a trace and without a sound from a closed hold with no opening other than a ten-inch porthole. We admit," he said with a nod to Harcourt, "that the Detective's theory involving a rope and pulleys was ingenious, but it was regrettably wrong."

"Now just a minute, you," Harcourt said.

Ming held up his hand. "Please. Hear us out. Darby?"

Darby pulled the cover away with a flourish, revealing an exact likeness of the crate beside him. "This is a scale model of Cabbel's remaining crate, and inside," the lid came away to reveal a miniature Foo dog. Darby lifted it out and handed the model of the crate to Ming.

"We have been puzzling over how not only the statue could be removed from the hold, but also the crate," Ming said." Please watch closely." He pressed on the bottom of the model, and the platform rotated to reveal a hollow underneath. A second manipulation reduced the dais to two-thirds of its width. Ming pressed in the four sides in sequence, and they folded neatly into the base. Pendleton's jaw sagged. Harcourt stared in disbelief. Cabbel turned pale.

"We were told that the dais of each crate was supported by lengthwise timbers, and we took Mister Cabbel at his word. When Pettigrew disassembled the remaining crate, he did not dismantle the dais because the half-ton statue was resting on it. But I submit to you that there are no timbers inside that dais. It is hollow, supported by steel rods. Open it and you will find that the missing crate never left the ship."

"That's ridiculous," Cabbel snorted.

"As for the oil stain on the deck, Detective," Hong said, "I would suggest that the oil was not used on the pulleys but rather to lubricate wooden parts of the collapsible crate that had swollen from moisture during the voyage so that they would operate silently."

"Even if the crate never left the ship," Pendleton said, "there's still a thousand-pound statue. Where did it go?"

"Through the porthole."

Pendleton stared.

"This is absurd." Cabbel started for the ladder, but Pettigrew caught him by the arm.

"No, you don't."

Cabbel wriggled in the first mate's grip. "Let go of me, you ape."

Pettigrew looked to Bingham, who shook his head.

"Is it?" said Hong. "Is it absurd, Cabbel?" He beckoned with a finger. "Darby."

"The missing statue wasn't bronze," Darby said, holding at chest level with both hands, "but it was a masterpiece of Chinese craftsmanship. The second statue was made of rubber and coated with metallic paint."

"I agree with Cabbel," Pendleton said. "This is ridiculous. Both statues weighed roughly the same."

"That's because," Darby went on, "The bronze was hollow cast, and the rubber statue was filled with water." He squeezed the miniature Foo dog, and a stream of water squirted out of its mouth, spattering Pendleton's face.

Ming went on. "The Hong Kong Customs agent, either careless or dishonest, passed both statues without a thorough examination. As for Beckley, he had no part in the scheme. Walsh hid that money in Beckley's duffel bag while all the crewmen were searching the hold after Cabbel raised a hue and cry about the theft."

Hong picked up the tale. "The night before the Empress docked, you, Cabbel, or your man Walsh, snuck into the hold, siphoned the water from the statue with a hose hidden inside the dais and pushed the empty shell through the porthole. You then collapsed the crate, and hid it in the hollow base of the other one."

"Three hundred thousand dollars in insurance money, Cabbel," Ming said. "Is that enough to stave off bankruptcy, or is it just more running money for the day you flee your creditors?"

Cabbel turned to Walsh. "You said the plan was foolproof."

"Shut up, you fool."

Harcourt took a step toward the pair, and Walsh pulled the revolver from his coat. "You can have him if you want, but nobody's sending me to jail. I'll kill you all if I have to." He aimed the pistol at Ming and Hong. "You first."

In a blur of motion, Raphael sprang from the beams above. He grabbed Walsh's gun hand from behind, and as Walsh tried to twist away, he began firing wildly, bullets thudding into the ship's timbers. Raphael plunged a short-bladed dagger into Walsh's spine, and he collapsed like a string-cut marionette to the deck. His mouth worked, but no words came out. Raphael wiped the blade of his knife on Walsh's coat and said to Harcourt, who stood frozen in place, "Take your time, sir. He will go nowhere."

• • •

"Cigars and brandy. That's a fine way to celebrate," Darby said, "and I mean that sincerely." In his lap lay the early edition of the *Chronicle* with the headline: TIMBER BARON FOUND GUILTY OF FRAUD.

"Well-deserved, I should think," Ming said.

"That was generous of you to allow Harcourt the credit for solving the case."

"It would serve no useful purpose to embarrass him and the Department," Hong said.

"Although it would have been eminently satisfying," Ming added. He turned to his brother. "We have one last chore, Brother. We must sign the letter to Mister Pendleton."

Hong nodded. "Pendleton can hardly refuse a fifteen percent fee for loss recovery, although nothing was truly lost, since it was never on the Empress from the outset."

"And we've saved ourselves a tidy sum, had the courts found against us. What should we do with the insurance fee?

"I understand that Cabbel's entire art collection will be auctioned to pay his creditors. I think we should attend and purchase a memento of the occasion, say, a bronze temple dog to stand at our gate."

"Won't she be lonely on her own?"

"Who knows, brother. Someday we may come across a suitable mate."

"Yeah," Darby said, raising his snifter in salute. "If nobody kills you first."

THE END

SAM DUNNE - Aging singer-songwriter Dunne cobbles a living from part-time teaching and working as a solo performer in bars and bistros after being kicked out of the rock group Gin Sing fifteen years before, just before the band hit it big. When Gin Sing's lead singer is murdered, Sam finds himself a suspect and uses every resource on both sides of the law to clear himself and set matters straight. As the series progresses, Sam finds himself in the middle of a murder on the set of an indie horror film, and tracks down hidden loot from a fifty-year-old six-figure bank job with the help of his girl friend Carlotta and his pal, heavy metal guitarist *cum* master burglar, Razor. In "Rescue Mission," the situation reverses, and Sam finds that repaying a debt can be deadly.

SAM DUNNE: RESCUE MISSION

The night Razor and Duchess broke up, I had a front row seat. Not exactly a seat, because the tables were all filled at Bendik's and Carlotta and I were standing holding our beers, but you get the drift. Sawtooth was onstage, ripping holes in the atmosphere with their raw music. I was five feet away from Razor and Duchess by the bar. Duchess looked pretty good that night. She was wearing black leather jeans and a red lace up bustier that made her look hot and dangerous at the same time, what the ancient Greeks called a *kalòn kakòn* – a deadly seductress, a beautiful evil.

Sawtooth was loud enough that I could hear every third word of their argument, then their voices got louder and it was every second word, then I distinctly heard Duchess scream, "You son of a bitch," and she punched Razor in the mouth.

He didn't go down, but she knocked him back a step. If it had been me, I might have punched her back, but Razor kept his cool. A fight would bring Bendik's unforgiving bouncers and their Louisville Sluggers. I couldn't hear his voice, but I saw him mouth the words, "We're done," with a finality that nobody could mistake. He turned and walked away, and I could see the look on her face. Razor's word was as final as a guillotine. Duchess had screwed up big time, and the realization hit her harder than his fist ever could.

She ran after him, but the crowd was shoulder to shoulder, and he hit the front door and was gone before she could catch up. He pulled out of the parking lot in his van with total deliberation, no revving the engine or squealing tires as he drove away. Duchess ran screaming down the street after him until she ran out of breath and fell to her knees on the pavement, sobbing.

A little background: my friend Razor is the lead guitar player for the metal soul band Blood Lightning; R&B with a heavy metal edge. Duchess is — was the lead singer. Neither of them was very big on commitment until they became an item a year or so ago, and have been together ever since, that is until she punched him in the mouth in front of three hundred people.

I hated to see that happen, because the chemistry between the two of them on stage and off was raw sex magic. Blood Lightning was a favorite regular at Bendik's, Hanniston's "bad guy" bar, and everybody who saw the fight knew them both.

Razor's complicated; Hanniston knows him as that stringy guy with the lank hair who plays heavy metal guitar. I also know him as one of the most accomplished burglars breathing. He can open the lock on your front door without the key as fast as you can with it.

He and I go back to the years of my youth. He's had my back and I've had his plenty of times, and no matter what happened between him and his woman, I'm on his side. Full disclosure: Duchess and I spent some time together a few years back, just long enough for her to decide I wasn't enough for her. I don't hold a grudge against her for that; she treated romance like an amusement park in those days, and I have to say she gave me one hell of a good ride while it lasted. But though I don't usually take sides in anybody's love life, where Razor's concerned, Duchess comes in second.

When Carlotta and I came out of Bendik's, Duchess was leaning, palms against the wall outside like she was being patted down by a cop, her forehead against the bricks. She was done crying and looked as if she were in shock. Her eye shadow and mascara had run and smeared, giving her face the look you see on the spook house zombies on the boardwalk at Wildwood.

I guess I shouldn't be too surprised that things happened that way. Their relationship was a hard play between the all-out performances with the band, and the party hard lifestyle behind the scenes. I'd seen it boil over a couple of times but never get physical. That night, Duchess crossed a major line.

Carlotta went over to her and put a hand on her shoulder. "Hey, you all right?"

Her head whipped around, swinging the thick braid of black hair that hung to her waist. "Back off," she snarled. "I don't need your help or anybody's."

Carlotta stepped back, hands palm forward like somebody pulled a gun on her. "Okay, Duchess, whatever you say."

As we walked to my van in the parking lot, Carlotta said, "Is it fair to say that she's her own worst enemy?"

I nodded. "She operates on impulse more often than not. It's too bad. Blood Lightning won't be the same without her."

"You really think he'll kick her out?"

"You don't know Razor like I do. She embarrassed him in front of his friends and a big chunk of the band's following. He won't tolerate that. At least she didn't do it on stage."

"The band. That's what you see as important?" She snorted. "Mister Sensitivity."

"There are plenty of people out there, but not nearly as many good bands."

"What do you think they were arguing about?"

"Could be anything from signing a recording contract to what time of day it was. Duchess is Duchess, and Razor is Razor. I've never known him to say no to her very much, but Razor's no stays no."

"So, it's as much his fault as hers."

"You know my take on it. Nobody owns fifty-one percent of the stock in any relationship."

As we drove away, Duchess was still in front of Bendik's, but now she was pacing back and forth on the cracked sidewalk. Someone had gotten her a bottle of beer, and she was chugging it between puffs on a cigarette. I pitied any cop who tried to bust her on the open container law.

As we drove back to the apartment, Carlotta said, "Sam, if I punched you in the mouth, would you hit me back?"

I drove on. There are some questions that are losers no matter how you answer them.

• • •

A word about myself: I'm Sam Dunne, lead guitarist for the now defunct Gin Sing, saloon balladeer, and embodiment of that old Jethro Tull album "Too Old to Rock 'n' Roll too Young to Die!" At 48, I have plenty of miles on my odometer, but plenty more to go. I've tried to age gracefully, segueing from loud bands in big arenas to quieter solo fare in smaller venues, and I manage to cobble a living between that and teaching an occasional English Comp course as an adjunct at the local community college.

What I'm best known for, however, is killing my former Gin Sing band mate Danny Barton before he could kill me. I've killed three people total in my life; two were self defense, and the third deserved it. But that's a story for another day.

My girl friend Carlotta and I live in a second-floor apartment on Hanniston, Pennsylvania's south side. She calls herself a "professional waitress," and has for thirty years or so. She loves her work, loves the customers, and loves her life. Who am I to argue that she could do better? We both believe that we are two of the luckiest people on the planet to have found each other.

Razor and Duchess maybe weren't so lucky. I won't say they fought like cats in a sack, but there was always tension between the two of them. If there are Alpha males, then there are also Alpha females, and Duchess would definitely qualify.

In the weeks that followed the big breakup, I didn't see much of Razor; coffee once or twice at Dora's, the diner where Carlotta works, and once at Bendik's where he stood at the bar with a beer watching the band and watching the crowd. He never mentioned Duchess, and I didn't ask. He'd say what he had to say when he was ready to say it.

In the meantime, he hired Glory Jones, a blues singer from Philly, to replace Duchess in Blood Lightning. Glory was a black woman built like a tree stump with a voice that could burn a hole in steel plate. I'd heard her before. She was a terrific singer, but she didn't have the stage persona that Duchess radiated. I wasn't sure how she was going to work out.

I found out when I got a text from Razor inviting me to Bendik's to watch the show. Carlotta and I were on the sidelines when the band walked onto the stage. The place was packed, and the crowd was eager to find out how Blood Lightning would fly without Duchess. The players took their places, the lights went down, and a blazing riff shot out of the speakers, ending on a low feedback vibrato. Razor strutted onto the stage in a tight black T-shirt and jeans I couldn't fit into when I was fourteen. He raised his Les Paul over his head to a cheer from the crowd. The drummer clicked his sticks and rolled in to the intro to "Knock on Wood." Razor extended an arm behind him and shouted "Glory Jones" into his microphone, and Glory came out to another ovation.

There's something unique about the mix of horns and heavy guitar that drives Blood Lightning and makes the crowd sweat and sway. Add that to the primal drums and bass of the rhythm section, and you have the first stage of a riot.

Glory rolled through the song as naturally as breathing. Razor punctuated Glory's vocal with the traditional Steve Cropper riffs in homage to the original, but when the horn break in the middle hit, his fingers flew through a blazing solo that scorched my eardrums. The crowd screamed and swayed side to side with the music. The song ended, and the drummer did three flams leading into "Ball and Chain."

"She's good," Carlotta said into my ear.

"Yeah, and the crowd likes her. That's a major item."

Halfway through the song, as Razor started his solo, the people on the dance floor parted like the Red Sea, and Duchess in a low-cut red satin gown strolled through to the front of the stage on the arm of Jojo DiCicco, one of Hanniston's more flamboyant criminals. Two of his bodyguards flanked them, and the crowd stayed back. She made sure Razor was watching as she put her arms around DiCicco's neck and rubbed her body against his like a sinuous cat. Then she grabbed a handful of Jojo's hair and pulled his face to hers, giving him a long sultry kiss. From where we were standing, I saw her eyes were open, staring into Razor's the whole time.

Razor didn't give in to the impulse to jump from the stage and tear out the gangster's throat for a couple of good reasons. First, although he could have succeeded, Jojo's bodyguards would have opened fire indiscriminately and probably killed a half dozen bystanders. Second, he knew that I wouldn't just stand still and watch, and I'd probably get killed too. Third, and likely the most important, Razor worked for Jojo's associates from time to time, and the Bardini family had no tolerance for internecine conflict, especially over women.

To his credit, Razor never missed a beat. He stared her down, aimed the head of his guitar at her chest and smoked through a solo popping staccato notes like machine gun fire. His solo was as hot as any he played that night, testimony to the autopilot function we all cultivate over years of guitar playing.

When the kiss ended, she turned away from Jojo and spat on the floor. They walked out, his arm at her waist and his hand on her satin ass, and the crowd closed behind them. Razor's trademark sneer was there, but it didn't match the look in his eyes as he watched Duchess walk away with DiCicco.

• • •

"That was a rotten thing to do," Carlotta said as we got in the van.

"I guess that's that scorned woman syndrome I've heard so much about. She couldn't have timed her grand entrance better, and in front of Blood Lightning's crowd to boot."

"Just like punching him in the mouth. Who's the guy she was with?"

"Joey DiCicco, everybody calls him Jojo. He's one of Hanniston's most successful hoods; mostly gambling but also extortion, and the other major sins."

"I guess he's good looking in a sleazy kind of way. After all, Razor looks like the bad end of a hangover most of the time."

"Ten years from now, Razor will look like those scrawny geezers in ACDC, but even then if the roles were reversed, Razor wouldn't need two bodyguards. The trouble with guys like DiCicco is they think like mobsters. Money and muscle give them a blank check to behave however they want. To them, women are property. Duchess is used to having her way where men are concerned. When the day comes she wants out, she may not be able to walk away from Jojo so easily."

"Maybe she won't want out," Carlotta said.

And that, I thought, might be the worst of all worlds.

• • •

Life went on. Blood Lightning played all its regular spots, and Duchess never repeated her performance. There was no need; the point was made. As the months went by, I'd hear that someone had seen Duchess with Jojo at this restaurant or that club or in a box at Penn National Racetrack having a grand old time then people lost interest and the gossip faded.

A few months more and I got an invitation in the mail for the opening of a new club uptown. The place was called Jojo's and it didn't take much imagination to figure out whose place it was. I showed it to Carlotta and she read, "'Entertainment featuring Big Band song stylist Anita Holgren.' Do you know her?"

"Yeah. That's Duchess's birth name."

Maybe Jojo didn't know I was friends with Razor, but Duchess did. I wondered whether they sent him an invitation too.

"Should we go?" Carlotta asked.

"Yeah, we'll go. I'm curious to see this place."

Jojo's was a remodeled restaurant, The Greenmont on 14th Street. It was a posh place in an earlier era, and DiCicco spent the bucks to make it look like the old days. His people did a good job of maintaining the black and white Art Deco style of the 40s night clubs, from the *maitre 'd* station to the bandstand where a tuxedoed twelve-piece orchestra was playing big band music. I flashed our invitation to the tux at the door, and Carlotta and I were ushered to a table on the dance floor.

She looked great, as always. Her thick black curls framed her face and contrasted the plain lavender sheath she wore. I decided a suit was in order but didn't bother with a necktie.

The orchestra was just finishing "Take the A-Train" as we sat down. "This place definitely has the feel of the forties," Carlotta said, taking it all in.

Beside the bandstand, I spotted DiCicco at what was apparently his personal table. He was laughing, making broad gestures, and playing the role of the genial host to three well-dressed couples I didn't recognize.

"Maybe you can put in for a job," I joked. "It's a notch up from Dora's."

"I doubt it. Look around. The servers are all guys. The only woman I saw here is the hat check girl."

One of the waiters came over to take our drink orders and asked if we wanted menus. We'd had supper a few hours before, but I said yes out of curiosity. The orchestra kicked into "One O' Clock Jump," and before the song was done, he was back.

I had a Tanqueray and tonic, and Carlotta ordered a Stinger. The drinks were good, but the prices weren't. I scanned the menu and figured that we could eat for a week at Dora's for what one meal at Jojo's would set us back. I was handing the menus back to our waiter when DiCicco strolled over with Duchess on his arm. He pulled out a chair for her and they sat down uninvited. One of his bodyguards, a slab of meat I knew only as Harry stood at a discreet distance behind them.

"Hello, Sam," he said and nodded to Carlotta. "How do you like the place?"

"Classy, Jojo. A real time machine." I looked over to Duchess, who tilted her head my way. She was wearing a floor-length shantung evening gown done in emerald green. Her hair was piled on her head in generous waves and held in place with one of those gold combs you see in pictures of flamenco dancers. She looked me over with half-closed eyes. "Aren't you going to say hello?"

"Hello, Duchess, or should I call you Anita?"

She took a long drag on her cigarette and let out a smoky laugh. "Either will do. I'm not embarrassed over my Blood Lightning days. The past is all part of the trip that got me here." The sarcastic edge that could flay your hide off was gone from her voice. "I think of it as paying dues."

"That's all behind us now, isn't it?" Joey said, putting an arm around her shoulders. They looked into each other's eyes and smiled. I wanted to puke.

Jojo flicked his wrist out of his cuff and eyed a gold Rolex. "Almost show time, babe." Then to us. "Just wanted to say hello and thank you for coming. He eyed the waiter holding the menus. "Not eating?"

I shrugged. "We ate earlier."

"What time?"

The question surprised me, and I answered without thinking. "Uh, five-thirty."

"That was hours ago. Order whatever you like. It's on me. I insist."

"Okay, we will. Thanks." I didn't want any charity from Joey, but I didn't want to start an argument with him in his own place either. There was a reason all the servers were men.

He told the waiter to bring whatever we wanted and put it on his tab. "Eat up. Enjoy yourselves. Now, if you'll excuse me, I have to get the lady back stage."

"Hope you like the show," Duchess said to me, looking past Carlotta as if she were one of the potted plants.

We both ordered prime rib, mine medium, hers rare, and chef's salad. The waiter scurried off, and Carlotta said, "Glad you didn't turn down a free meal."

"I was trying. Remember the old blues song 'The Ballad of Louie Alexander?' It says that a gift from the Devil is a debt in the end."

"What could he possibly want to collect from you?"

"I don't want to find out."

The prime rib was first rate. One more number from the orchestra, and the lights went down on the bandstand, leaving the leader, a bald guy with thick glasses and an alto sax on a chain around his neck in a spotlight at the center stage microphone. "Now, ladies and gentlemen, someone we've all been waiting to see and especially to hear, the wonderful Anita Holgren."

He stepped out of the spot and she stepped into it as the leader cued the band for the intro to "They Can't Take That Away From Me." I'm not sure what I expected to come out of Duchess's mouth after years of hearing her sing screaming R&B, but it wasn't what I heard. Her whiskey-and-cigarettes voice rolled out a sensuous, mellow version of the old standard that reached right into my ear and took over. I felt the same enthusiasm I did when Linda Ronstadt switched from Top 40 to a three-disk set of standards with Nelson Riddle or Annie Lennox cut her big-band CD. The voice was enough, but Duchess knew how to sell a song to a crowd. Her delivery was spot on and the audience loved it.

Duchess was as good as a torch singer as she was a rhythm and blues diva. Her breathy delivery of "How Long has this been Going On" backed by a terrific arrangement for the band gave me chills. The applause wasn't the raucous hooting of the Bendik's crowd, but it was no less enthusiastic. I was impressed, and so was Carlotta. "She should have gone this route a long time ago."

"Maybe so, but the time just wasn't right for it."

"But it is now." I turned to see Jojo standing behind us. "You must admit, she is great."

"She always was," I said, letting DiCicco know that in my opinion, she didn't need him to shine. Jojo let the remark slide by. "How was your meal?"

"Delicious," Carlotta said.

"I'm glad. Tell all your friends." I knew he wasn't talking about the prime rib, and that he had one specific friend in mind. He walked away from the table, and I reached for my wallet. I peeled off three twenties, laid them on the table, and set my water glass on them.

"What are you doing?" Carlotta asked.

"Making a statement. I'm letting Jojo know I do my own." I stood up. "Time to go home."

As we drove to the apartment, Carlotta said, "Joey DiCicco went to a lot of trouble and expense to create that set up for her, didn't he?"

"The renovations to the Greenmont cost a bundle, that's for sure. It's typical of a hood like Jojo to name the place after himself. I think keeping

"Joey DiCicco went to a lot of trouble and expense to create
that set up for her, didn't he?"

the old recognized name would have been an extra touch of class, but like I said before, DiCicco behaves like he thinks gangsters ought to behave. A big splash, a grand gesture; Donald Trump on a smaller scale. Another thing, those band arrangements were tailored for Duchess. That doesn't come cheap, either."

"She looks like she's enjoying it. I was surprised after all the flash of Blood Lightning that she shifted gears so easily to a quiet act."

"Me too." Carlotta didn't mention it, but I knew she noticed because she notices everything. Maybe Duchess swapped the trademark fishnet gloves that reached her bicep for opaque ones because they went better with her gown, or maybe she had something to hide under them. Billie Holiday, call your office.

• • •

I wouldn't have gone to Jojo's again if two things hadn't happened; if I hadn't seen Razor on the street a few months later, and if I hadn't run into Cotton Breakiron the day before at Dora's. Cotton's one of the best tenor sax players I've ever heard and fronts a primo jazz trio. I was having breakfast when the Great Black Hope dropped into the booth across from me.

"Hey, Cotton, how's the biz?"

He flashed his three-foot smile and said, "What can I say? I'm a saxy beast." He reached for a piece my toast and I fended him off with my fork. Carlotta came over with the coffee pot and gave Cotton a kiss on the cheek. "The delightful Miss Carlotta," he said. "Why do you hang with this loser when there are men like me around?"

"Pity, I suppose." She pulled out her pad and took Cotton's order. When she left, he said, "So, still gigging at Mike and Kelli's?"

"Every Thursday. How about you? Still doing the Regent?"

"The lounge is closed for remodeling. I've been filling in with the big band at Jojo's."

"How's that doing?"

"Good crowds every night. I got to say, though, Duchess doesn't look so hot."

"I thought she was thriving over there."

"Her voice is still good, but in my professional estimation, she's drowning. I been around long enough to know hooked when I see it."

"DiCicco's giving her drugs?"

"Or she's finding them on her own. I tried to get her aside to talk a few nights ago, and before I got past 'How ya doin'?' two of DiCicco's big boys come up on either side of me and told her, 'Jojo wants you.' That ended the conversation."

"She's an adult. She'll make her own choices."

"Maybe it's none of my business, but I think these days they're being made for her."

• • •

A day later, I saw Razor at Johnny Malone's music store on Seventh Avenue. Malone's is a retail dinosaur, a music store that doesn't belong to a chain, doesn't sell online, and doesn't need to order anything for a customer; it's all in the inventory. As a result, he does regular business with name bands from every style of music. I needed strings for my Martin, and I stopped on the sidewalk to admire a vintage Gibson L-4 in the display window, strategically placed to keep it out of the afternoon sun. I saw Razor's reflection over the guitar like a double exposure as he crossed the street and came up beside me on the sidewalk. "Hey, Sam."

Razor looked leaner than the last time I saw him, if that's possible. He hadn't shaved for three or four days, and the rings under his eyes said the Sandman was out of town. His blonde hair hung limp from a Phillies ball cap and curled up at his shoulders. An unlit cigarette hung from the corner of his mouth as if he'd been about to light up then got distracted and forgot about it.

"And I thought you couldn't look any worse," I said to his reflection.

He shrugged and pretended to study a black B.C. Rich Warlock beside the L-5. Finally, he said, "I never thought a woman could get to me, but what's the title of the Mike Bloomfield song? 'Fooled Around and Fell in Love.'"

"There's a word I thought I'd never hear you say." he shrugged again. "Have you seen Duchess? Talked to her?"

"She's turned into Dracula's daughter. Nobody sees her in the daytime. When she isn't onstage at Jojo's club, she's on his arm in one place or another. She doesn't answer her cell phone, and I'm sick of hearing that canned voice tell me her mailbox is full. I guess that's karma. I acted the same way to her when we first split up."

"None of her friends have anything to tell you?"

He shook his head. "Nope. Nobody's heard a word. It's as if she just turned into somebody else."

I thought better of telling him about Cotton's take on her situation. Then he said something that made me glad that I didn't.

"I want to kill Joey." Razor's not one for hyperbole, so I gave a neutral answer.

"I understand."

"It wouldn't get me anywhere but dead. Jojo's Tito Bardini's nephew. It'd be a pretty even match between us, but if I won, they'd find my head nailed to my guitar. I can't blame Joey anyway. It's her choice, him or me."

"Maybe she'll get tired of him."

"Maybe he'll get tired of her, you mean. Women don't 'get tired' of guys like Joey."

"She'll come around."

"Maybe, if he lets her. All I can say is, if he does her any harm, I'll see he pays for it."

"Think hard about that, man. You're talking things you can't undo."

He finally lit his cigarette, nodded, and walked away without another word. It was then I decided I needed another look at Jojo's and at Duchess before I started something that could only end badly.

• • •

"I thought you didn't want to go back to Jojo's," Carlotta said as we drove across town.

"I don't, but what Cotton said about Duchess has me worried."

"I thought you didn't get involved in other people's business."

"Normally I don't, but if Cotton's right and Jojo's got Duchess hooked on smack, it could be the end of her. It's not her I'm worried about so much as what Razor might do." That wasn't entirely true, but if Carlotta picked up on it, she didn't say so.

When we walked up the sidewalk to the front door of the club, I noticed that the shrubs needed trimming. Inside the door, one of the floor tiles was missing a corner as if something heavy had fallen on it and broken it off. A burned-out light bulb here and there and other little details gave the impression that Jojo was already losing interest in his new toy, and it had become just one more venue to launder money.

We were ushered to a table at the dance floor and the white-jacketed waiter who took our drink order wasn't the typical college student you usually find as a server. He was beefy and had eyes like a lynx. Most people would have missed the bulge in his armpit, but I didn't. I passed on the

menus this time, figuring that Joey already had more of my money than
he needed.

The band sounded great. Cotton spotted us through the glare of the
spotlight and nodded a greeting. They played "Body and Soul," and when
it was his turn, he stood up to deliver a solo that was as throaty and
passionate as Duchess's voice. We clapped at the end of it, like the first
patter of a rain storm, then the rest of the crowd joined in twos and threes
until the whole room applauded. Cotton smiled, blew a kiss, and bowed as
if he'd just walked across Niagara Falls on a tightrope.

Two songs later, Duchess came onstage to polite applause from the
patrons. The band did an elaborate jump tempo intro and she stepped up
to the mic. She was wearing the red satin dress she wore at Bendik's, and
again the long gloves. Her hair was swept across her forehead from left to
right, shading her eyes, and pulled back from her ears to show off a pair of
diamond earrings that sparkled like stars in the spotlight.

If I had to choose one word to sum up her look, it would be tired. Not her
face — good makeup covers a multitude of sins — but her body language.
The set of her shoulders was lower, her head tilted a little forward so that
when she sang, she had to raise her mouth to the microphone. She did a
good version of the Sinatra classic "Angel Eyes," but it wasn't the effortless
delivery she gave the time before. She had to work to sell the song. She
followed up with "Can't we be Friends" then a soulful rendering of "As
Time Goes By."

Some people got up to dance, and I took Carlotta's hand. "Shall we?"
She nodded, and we went onto the dance floor. Dancing isn't my strong
suit, the result of spending thirty-odd years of making the music instead
of moving to it, but C managed to steer me around the floor without too
much damage to her toes. What I wanted was a closer look at Duchess and
for her to see us and know we were there in the hope she'd come to the
table.

She happened to look our way as we danced close to the bandstand, and
her eyes widened, but she made no sign of recognition. The song ended,
and we sat down. I ordered us another round of drinks, and waited for the
set to end. Four more songs and the bandleader started clapping and said,
"Anita Holgren, ladies and gentlemen. Let's hear it for her." That made me
sad, remembering the days when people didn't have to be told to applaud.
She left the stage, and the band moved back into instrumental mode.

Five minutes later, she came out and went from table to table, shmoozing
the crowd. Jojo wasn't with her, but one of his gun thugs followed at her

heels like a tuxedoed pit bull. When she got to our table, she gave me a polite hello and introduced her chaperone as Milt. I remembered him from his younger days as the bouncer at Rigo's. Then she chatted up Carlotta as if she were her lost sister. I thought that was odd, considering that she'd all but ignored C last time. It gave me a chance to study her face, especially her eyes. The pupils were tiny, even in the subdued light.

"Isn't Joey here tonight?" Carlotta asked.

Duchess turned her head toward Milt, as if seeking permission then said, "He's out of town on business." Unconvinced and unconvincing. "I'd better get back stage," she said and leaned in to give Carlotta a hug. I saw it, but the bodyguard didn't. He was too busy watching me. Duchess whispered something in Carlotta's ear, and C's smile froze on her face. Duchess nodded to me and said, "Please come again, Sam," and she turned to walk away. Milt gave me a cold once over and followed her across the dance floor.

"What did she say?"

"Wait 'til we're outside."

"Drink up." I downed the last of my T&T and we walked out of Jojo's with a wave to Cotton.

As I started the van, C said, "I didn't want the wrong people to hear me, Sam. She said, 'Please help me. Get me away from this.'"

The message wasn't really meant for Carlotta or even for me. But I knew what it would mean once I delivered it.

· · ·

I called Cotton the next day at noon and woke him. The phone rang nine times before he answered. I imagined him hunting for it in the perpetual mess and clutter that made his apartment look as if cops with a cruel sense of humor just executed a search warrant. "Did I win the Powerball?" he mumbled.

"Sorry, no dice."

He groaned. "Then why'd you wake me up?"

"I need your help."

"Aw, man, the last time I helped you I damn near got my lip cut off by Tiny Settles."

"It's a way of life. Meet me at Dora's?"

I heard the rattle and clank of him fumbling for his wristwatch on the night stand. "It's only noon?" Cotton sighed. "I'll be there at one."

My phone beeped and I knew he'd hung up. I waited five minutes and thumbed redial. Cotton's phone rang a while before he answered, as sleepy as before. "What."

"Just making sure you're perpendicular."

"If I go to hell, you'll be right beside me, won't you?"

"If? Come on. Cotton. Out of bed." He mumbled something I couldn't make out and hung up again.

• • •

At one o'clock, Dora's lunch crowd had thinned, and I waited on a stool at the counter drinking coffee 'til the booth at the back was empty. I needed to talk without any curious ears around. Cotton was late, but that was no surprise. When he showed up at Dora's, you'd never have known I dragged him out of a deep sleep. He was wearing a tan suit with a dark brown silk shirt open at the collar, and a pair of cordovan loafers with no socks. He sported a fresh shave, including his scalp, and I understood why he was late. I often wondered whether he rented a separate storage space so his clothes didn't end up looking like his apartment.

"Doing an ad for *GQ* today?"

"Always on stage, Sam. That's a lesson you never learned."

I looked down at my jeans and flannel shirt. "You know what they say about old dogs."

"They still bite but with less teeth."

"Fewer."

Cotton snorted and replaced his shuck and jive voice with articulation worthy of George Will. "I employ the grammar of my public," then back to basic street. "You didn't wake me up for no English lesson, Sam, so what's doing?"

Betty, one of Carlotta's co-workers came with the coffee pot and her order pad. Cotton ordered a mushroom omelet with cottage fries, and I got Dora's special, the hot roast beef sandwich with mashed potatoes and gravy.

"So, tell me what you need before the food gets here. My ears shut off when I'm chewing."

"Duchess."

"Oh, shit." He rolled his eyes. "What about her?"

"I think you're right; DiCicco's got her on H and holding her almost a prisoner. We saw her last night. She wants out."

Cotton stared at his coffee and nodded. "I knew you'd get us both killed someday. I just didn't think it would be this week."

"Just tell me about the club and Duchess coming and going."

"You've been in it. The basic layout looks like this." He pulled a ball point pen from his jacket and sketched the main floor of Jojo's on a napkin. "No surprises there. But downstairs —" He turned the napkin over and started another sketch. "A stairwell goes from behind the kitchen down to the dressing rooms and a storage area in the basement. There's a door here — " he drew an angled line and put a star beside it. "This opens to steps to the alley in the back. That's where the band and the kitchen staff come in. It's locked all the time, and there's a whale named Ernie in a chair who lets people in and out. He's there when I show up, and he's still there when I leave."

"Always the same guy?"

"Most of the time. He'd make at least two of you and three of me."

"Heeled?"

"I saw him once with his jacket off. Had a big automatic in a shoulder holster. Probably carries it all the time, plus a shotgun propped by his chair."

"What about DiCicco's waiters? I counted eight."

"That sounds about right."

"They look like muscle."

Cotton nodded. "I'd say so. He doesn't have a bouncer. Guess he doesn't need one with those boys around."

"And Duchess?"

"She comes in about an hour before show time, sometimes with Joey, sometimes with one of his men. Never by herself. I see them coming down the stairs from the kitchen, so I'm guessing she comes through the front door, not the alley. When she goes into her dressing room, Joey's man is right outside the door all the time."

Our food arrived and we didn't talk for a while. I could see that trying to snatch Duchess from the club was a suicide mission.

"When they leave the club, where do they go?"

"I was on my way out, walking past her dressing room one time when I heard the bodyguard say, 'I'm taking her to the Mansion.' I guess he meant DiCicco's house on Penn's Hill."

DiCicco's mansion was a monstrous pile of bricks built in the early twenties by a bootlegger named Barney Schiff. It was notorious for the piping and tanks hidden in the walls and under the floors, and the jumbo boiler that was really a whiskey still. Barney was machine gunned to death in his bed over turf issues in 1928, and the house changed hands several times, but nobody ever went so far as to rip out the illegal plumbing. I guess Jojo thought it was some kind of legacy, and he took everybody who came to the place on a grand tour.

"I was in it one time," Cotton said, "when DiCicco threw a party and had the trio play for it. I only saw the main room on the ground floor, nothing else, but the place is big and the furniture looked expensive. That's all I can tell you."

"That's plenty. Thanks, Cotton."

"And, Sam, do me a favor."

"What's that?"

"Whatever you're going to do, tell me a day or two ahead of time so I can be in Atlanta or Chicago or someplace when it all goes down."

• • •

Bob Seger sang about turning the page on the radio. Razor stared through the windshield of his van, watching the lights zoom by on the Interstate below. I told him what I suspected and I told him what I knew. Razor stayed away from drugs, and he was outraged at Duchess's plight. He smoked through one Lucky and half of another before he said anything. "You know why I haven't done anything to Jojo up to now?"

I shook my head then realized he wasn't looking at me. "No, why?"

"Because it would be too obvious. Somebody whacks DiCicco the day after Duchess skips off with him, your pal Kearny down at Homicide would have cuffs on me in five minutes and look no further. Case closed. It's been seven months now, and every day I've waited makes me a little less of a suspect. Things have cooled off. Maybe now is the time."

The pale green of the dashboard lights made Razor's expression scary, the way the guy telling the campfire ghost story with a flashlight under his chin looks. The cold rage in his voice made him scarier.

"Whatever you decide, I'm with you, man. Whatever it takes."

"I can't ask you to do that. People are probably gonna get killed; maybe me, maybe you."

"Doesn't matter. You helped me rescue Carlotta. I'll help you rescue Duchess."

"From what you've told me and what Cotton told you, the odds are we can't snatch her from DiCicco's club. That leaves his mansion. We're outgunned, so kicking the door down and running in with a Mac 10 in each hand probably wouldn't be the best idea. We need a plan to get Duchess out that won't get us killed or land us in the State Pen."

"Speaking of plans, do you know anybody down at City Zoning would let you look at the blueprints for DiCicco's mansion?"

"No need. It's all up here." He tapped his forehead.

"Huh?"

"I've been there."

"When?"

"Years ago, before Joey bought the place, the former owner and his wife had a nasty divorce. He locked her jewels in his safe and said he didn't know where they were. I got them back and he never knew it because two days after I did the job, he keeled over from a stroke. Good thing I got the jewels when I did. By the time his will was settled, she may never have gotten them back."

"Timing is everything."

"It is. Anyway, I know something about the Schiff Mansion that maybe even DiCicco doesn't know. There's a passage from the coal cellar into the old storm sewer system Schiff used to sneak out his hooch. That's how I got in to boost the jewels, and I'm betting it's still there."

"You think so?"

"One way to find out." He started the engine and we rolled toward town.

• • •

A quarter mile or so away from Penn's Hill, Razor pulled into an alley and shut off the engine. "This is where Barney Schiff loaded his bootleg whiskey onto the trucks." I looked around and saw only an abandoned warehouse on one side and a crumbling foundation supporting part of a building on the other. Razor reached behind the seat and brought out a six-cell maglite and a Glock in a clip-on holster. "Follow me."

We stepped over a cable with a no trespassing sign and into the foundation. Waist high weeds and a few small trees had grown up through cracks in the concrete. In a back corner of the ground floor, a door hung from one hinge. Razor pulled it open gently so it wouldn't come the rest of the way off. He shined the beam of the flashlight down a flight of rotting stairs, the upper treads burned and blackened.

"Last time I was here, the building was empty but intact. The stairs were safe. Goddamned kids set fire to the place last year. We'd better go one at a time." He eased onto the top step and carefully picked his way down, feet on the outside of the treads. The stairs groaned a little, but held.

My turn. I was a good thirty pounds heavier than Razor, and if one of the steps was going to let go, it would be under my weight. I groped for a handrail and realized it was long gone. I breathed a lot easier when I reached the bottom. At a far wall behind some rubble, I saw a two-foot-by-four steel plate behind some rubble. It was orange with rust, and in the flashlight's beam, I could barely make out the flush screw heads that held it in place. The panel was tack welded to the metal frame.

"This panel is a maintenance access to the old sewer system."

"How will you get those screws out? They look rusted up solid."

"Secrets of the pyramid, Sam." He swept the flashlight up the wall along the panel, counting the terra cotta blocks. He pushed at one to the left of the rusted steel and nothing happened. He pushed again and I heard a metallic click. The panel, frame and all, popped out an inch.

Nothing Razor does should ever surprise me, but this caught me totally off guard. "Whoa. How did you know about that?"

"An old mug named Elmer Headley. I did him a favor once, and he repaid me by telling me about the tunnel."

I didn't ask what kind of favor Razor had done for Elmer. I probably didn't want to know.

Razor nimbly scrambled over the rubble and tugged at the plate. It groaned as it swung outward, opening into a tunnel. I followed him a little less nimbly.

When I think of city sewers, I think of big pipes. In the old days they were built more like passageways, arched brickwork. I'm sure they were bigger in New York and Chicago, but Hanniston's was an inch or two shy of five feet tall. The floor sloped very gradually downward to facilitate drainage. Overhead, I saw empty light sockets strung together with old style parallel wiring that disappeared into the darkness like train tracks, harkening back to the days when the system was regularly maintained. I heard dripping down the tunnel. Stagnant water lay on the floor, and I could feel it creeping cold into my shoes. I was glad it wasn't raining outside.

Razor and I had to hunch down to walk through the tunnel, and I imagined Barney Schiff's minions rolling kegs of whiskey to the waiting trucks while gun thugs stood by holding shotguns at their hips. Razor shined the maglite on the water to reflect the beam as far as it would reach. I was about to say something when I heard him counting paces under his breath and I shut up so I wouldn't distract him. Every so often we'd pass under a grating chute and I'd see a feeble ray from a streetlamp or hear the rumble of tires from a passing car. Otherwise, the tunnel was a self-contained universe.

"This panel is a maintenance access to the old sewer system."

Ahead in the dark, I heard the squeak and scuttle of rats, or whatever lived down there. Ten minutes in, we passed a crossroad type juncture that sent other shafts at ninety-degree angles. The brickwork was domed here and I was glad to straighten up. My neck and shoulders ached. "How much farther?"

"Are we there yet? Are we there yet?" Razor snickered. "Keep your pants on, Dunne. We're almost there. Be quiet."

A few more minutes, and Razor stopped. He shined the beam of his light up and down the bricks to his left and stopped at one about waist level. He opened his pocket knife and slid the blade into an almost invisible gap between the bricks and worked it back and forth. "Open Sesame," he whispered. I heard a dull clank and a section of brickwork large enough to step into swung into the tunnel. We climbed through it and I found myself in an oversized storage closet full of dusty tools and other junk.

Razor put an ear to the door then spent the next minute delicately turning the knob. The door opened into the mansion's cellar. The boiler for the heating system took up one corner, and I pictured it working away, rendering sour mash into high-test alcohol. Old furniture and boxes littered the floor in odd places, and a set of plank steps led to the first floor. A recently built wine rack stood against one wall, bristling with bottles. My hand automatically dropped to the pistol clipped to my belt. Razor stood perfectly still, listening to every noise and divining what it meant.

I could hear heavy footsteps on the floorboards overhead, the muffled sound of a television set, laughter, and for a minute the drone of a blender as someone mixed a drink. Razor motioned me back into the closet. In a moment we were walking back the way we came down the sewer.

When we passed the junction, I said, "I thought for a minute that you were going to try to snatch Duchess tonight."

"Too much traffic upstairs. Tonight was for recon anyway. We'll go back when Jojo and most of his people are occupied elsewhere."

"How will you know?"

"I'll know because I'll make it happen."

I figured the less I knew, the better, but I just had to ask. "What was the argument that night between you and Duchess all about anyway?"

"At this point, does it really matter?"

I had to agree that it didn't.

• • •

Carlotta was asleep when I got back to the apartment. It was already three, and she started her shift at five-thirty. I undressed and climbed into bed. She rolled over and cuddled up to me, never quite waking. I lay beside her and stared at the ceiling wondering how it would all turn out until I drifted into an uneasy sleep.

I opened one eye in time to see her through the bathroom door toweling off her hair from the shower, her body glowing in the bulbs over the medicine cabinet mirror. I wanted to reach for her, hold her, and stop time in that moment, a sweet, quiet time before she left for her obligations and I had to leave for mine. She turned on the hair dryer and the whine reminded me of the blender in DiCicco's mansion. The moment was gone.

• • •

I didn't hear from Razor for three days, and it grated on my nerves. Shakespeare had it right when Macbeth said, "it would be best to get it over with quickly." But I knew Razor had stayed out of jail all these years because he thought things through and never took a step that didn't mesh with a larger plan.

On the fourth day, my cell phone rang. I didn't recognize the number, but that was because Razor used burners a lot, and I rarely called him at the same number more than two or three times. I answered and took a long breath before I said hello.

"Mailbox." The line went dead.

Downstairs, I opened the apartment mailbox and a single sheet of paper tumbled out. It read: Bendik's lot three a.m. Dress for the occasion." That meant dark clothes, quiet shoes and a holster. Upstairs, I burned the note in the wastebasket.

Now came the worst part, deciding how to tell Carlotta or whether to tell her at all until after it was done. It was a Thursday, and I had my regular gig at Mike and Kelli's from seven to ten. If things went bad and the cops looked my way, my life had to seem business as usual, so I couldn't cancel. I knew that once things got rolling, I'd be okay. It was the five hours dead time between ten and three that were the killer.

I'd been edgy for the past few days. Carlotta didn't say anything about it, but I was sure she knew something was up. When she came home from her shift at Dora's, I gave her the news.

"I'm going with Razor tonight. We're going to take Duchess out of DiCicco's place."

Carlotta surprised me. She nodded and calmly said, "And then what?"

I stared at her. "Then Razor gets her out of town, out of Jojo's reach 'til she's clean again."

"What if she doesn't want Razor back?"

"At least she'll be free to make the choice."

"And what about you two? You think somebody like Joey DiCicco will just shrug and say, 'Oh well, it was fun while it lasted?' He'll come after both of you, and her, out of that same macho attitude that got Razor and Duchess into this mess in the first place."

"Maybe. But I can't let Razor go at it alone. I owe him. *We* owe him."

She nodded again. "I'm not forgetting he helped rescue me when I was kidnapped. I just don't want both of you killed on some *kamikaze* mission. What's the plan?"

I told her about the sewer line and the access to the mansion's cellar. "We sneak into the place in the middle of the night, grab Duchess, and take her out through the tunnel.

"That's it?" C shook her head.

"There's more to it, but Razor hasn't filled me in yet."

"Just the two of you." A statement, not a question. "And how many people will DiCicco have with him?"

"A half dozen maybe, but Razor says there'll be a diversion to get most of them out of the house."

"Two of you isn't enough. I'll drive."

"No. You can't. It's too dangerous."

"If it isn't too dangerous for you, it's not for me either. You and he plan to break into a gangster's house, kidnap his drugged-up girlfriend, and drag her through a quarter mile of sewer. Then you'll pop out like rabbits from a hole and drive away? You'd better have the engine running when you get out of the tunnel. And if the police or anybody else see me driving a van, I'm just a humble waitress driving to work."

She was right, of course, but I couldn't let her put herself at risk. "I can't let you do this."

"Who said anything about 'letting' me do anything? You're not the only one who owes Razor."

"Okay," I said, putting my hands on her shoulders. "You come with me, but if Razor says no, you go home. Deal?"

"Deal. What do you want for supper?"

• • •

At six-thirty, I set up in my corner at Mike and Kelli's. I play there every week for next to nothing and the best Reuben sandwich in Hanniston. I've been there every Thursday for a couple of years, since they took over the bar and grille. It's six tables and a dozen seats at the bar. They're good friends, and I'm doing my part to see that they ultimately succeed.

Business wisdom used to say that a small business owner should have seven years' worth of operating cash on hand before opening the doors and never touch the income. The most recent figure I've heard is ten to twelve. Who has that kind of money? So, I entertain the troops every Thursday and try to ramp up their income a little.

Mike waved from behind the bar as I set my stool under the cardboard star with my name on it that Kelli hung from the ceiling the first month I played there. Carlotta walked in behind me carrying my guitar and the tool bag that held my microphone, my cables and other tools of the trade. In five minutes, I was set up and ready to play. In past years, I've worked with bands that carried two truckloads of sound equipment, took two hours to set up and an hour to tear down. I decided years ago that the simple life of the solo player is a lot better.

C parked herself on a stool at the end of the bar. I suggested that she might want to get some sleep before the night's adventures, but she passed on it. I think she was afraid I'd sneak off without her. She ordered a draft for herself and brought me a glass of ginger ale on ice. She kissed my cheek and whispered, "Play 'Misty' for me." I got the joke, but didn't laugh as hard as I might have. Like John Mayer's song put it, I felt as if we were slow dancing in a burning room.

The crowd came in early and stayed late, making plenty of requests. I played an extra half hour because the bar was still doing a brisk business. Kelli gave me a thumbs up, and Mike was all smiles. I closed with one of my own songs, "Lady, Will You Stay?" and turned on my stool toward Carlotta. That song marked the start of our relationship a few years before, and I saved it for the nights when she came to a job with me.

C smiled at me, and I knew I could count on her. I was glad she volunteered. She was street tough and not afraid of much, but I knew that worry over her would be a distraction if I let it. Help was always good, but I was hoping that Razor would turn thumbs down on it.

When we got back to the apartment, we made love, hot, heavy, no frills, with the thought that it might be the last time, but I suppose, life being what it is, that's true every time. We lay silent side by side, both wanting to sleep but both too wired for it. At a little after two, I got up and put on coffee. We sat at the kitchen table and I got the same thought I'd had earlier. Would this be the last time we sat at this table? I shook my head and did my best to push thoughts like that out of my mind.

"Come on, Sam," Carlotta said. "Let's get dressed. We don't want to be late." I wore my sneak clothes, and she wore her pink rayon uniform. Like she said, just a waitress going to work the breakfast shift.

C drove my minivan to the East End. There was almost no traffic on the street, and we got the eye from a pair of uniforms in a prowl car that pulled up beside us at a traffic light. Carlotta may have been right; the cops saw her driving and pulled away without another look. I guess they didn't consider that in this world of equality, she might have been abducting me.

Bendik's lot was still near full although the bar technically closed at two. The Liquor Control Board didn't bother Bendik's much for the same reason the cops didn't. The longer the crowd of bikers, thugs, and generally bad actors stayed there, the longer they weren't out on the streets causing trouble. I spotted Razor's van in the third row of the gravel lot. The orange glow of a cigarette let me know he was in it and waiting.

Carlotta and I walked up to the driver's window and he rolled it down. He eyed her and didn't say anything.

"Carlotta wants to help. She can drive."

Razor still didn't say anything. He looked her in the eye and something silent passed between them. He nodded his head and said, "Okay." He wore a black long-sleeved t-shirt, dark work pants and steel toed crepe soled shoes. "We'll take your van. I'll have to hide mine. Follow me."

Razor drove a few blocks to a storage facility and opened one of the bays. He pulled his van in and as he climbed out, he reached behind the driver's seat for a canvas mason's satchel. He pulled the door down, padlocked it, and climbed in behind me.

"I've kept a watch on DiCicco's house the last three days," Razor said as Carlotta drove toward Penn's Hill. "Like most people with no imagination, he runs the same game plan every night. Home from the club at three with Duchess. He usually has two of his goons come with them while two are at the house. They don't exactly rotate, but sometimes the faces change. The fat old Mama Mia who cooks and cleans for them is gone by eight. Duchess has her own room on the second floor at the back of the house."

"How do you know that?"

"Because I've been in the place twice since we talked." I knew he was good, but not that good — like I said about Razor and surprises. "By the way, Sam, you were right about the drugs. I stood in a closet and watched

Milt shoot her up. I wanted to kill him on the spot, but I knew I couldn't get her away if I did."

"So how is tonight different?"

"Tonight at four thirty, a fire is going to start in the basement of Jojo's club. A little burner on a timer in a Coke can is going to go off like a flame thrower out the hole in the top. I figure DiCicco will come running. That's when we grab Duchess."

"I'm afraid to ask how you got the burner in the club."

"A mutual friend delivered it this evening." I imagined Cotton, cold sweat running down his spine, bending down to tie his shoe lace and setting the can on the floor beside something flammable.

"And if DiCicco doesn't take the bait and stays home?"

"Then things will be a little more complicated."

"Assuming we spring her, how will you keep Joey from killing you after the fact?

"The second time I went in the house, I opened the safe and took six keys of uncut China White. I don't know to the last dime what it's worth on the street, but I'm guessing it runs into seven figures."

"Holy shit. He doesn't know it's gone?"

"I haven't heard, but it's not something he'd brag about all over town. I figure he's afraid the people over his head will hold him accountable no matter who took it. He'll try to find it first."

"That's a hell of a bargaining chip."

"A couple of million, maybe three."

My head spun. The whole situation had ratcheted up a few notches. Carlotta just drove and didn't comment. Either she didn't realize what was at stake here, or she had more nerve and resolve than I did. I was betting on the latter.

"Put these on before you handle the hardware." He handed me a pair of baby blue industrial nitrile gloves. I pulled them on, and he said, "What's the number of Carlotta's cell phone?" I told him and he punched it in. A few seconds later I heard the muffled ring tone from her purse. "Now we can get in touch with each other. Shut off the ringers and leave them on vibe."

Razor reached into his tool satchel and pulled out a hammerless Smith and Wesson in a clip-on holster. "Leave your automatic with Carlotta. If we have to shoot at anybody, I don't want it to be with a registered gun. This is a phantom." He got an identical pistol from the satchel and clipped it to his belt. "I hope we don't have to shoot, but if we do, I don't want shell casings flying around that we don't have time to pick up." He handed me my own maglite.

"One more item." He handed me what looked like black silk jockey shorts; it was a full head mask with holes for the eyes and mouth. He pulled his over his head and slung a small black pouch like a camera case over his shoulder.

"What's in the bag?"

"A can of Coke."

Carlotta dropped us off at the entrance to the tunnels, planning to drive away and wait in the parking lot of a nearby apartment complex. From there, on our signal, she could be at the pickup point in less than five minutes. "I'll text you every so often to see whether you're getting a signal from underground. I'm betting it's not gonna be five bars. You text me back that you got it. If you don't text me back, I'll have a pretty good idea of our communication range."

"I guess I don't have to tell you to be careful," Carlotta said. "You wouldn't listen anyway."

I leaned into the driver's window and kissed her, once lightly then once hard and passionate. She put the van in gear and was gone.

It had rained earlier in the day, and ankle-deep water trickled over the bricks. A hundred yards in, Razor pulled out his phone. "One bar. Not good." He thumbed a text and waited. In a few seconds, his phone buzzed from the reply.

At the tunnel juncture, he tried again and got no answer. "That's it. We're on our own from here."

It seemed we got to the entrance to DiCicco's mansion in no time. Maybe a trip seems longer when you don't know what's ahead and you're watching every detail as you go. Anyway, when I looked at my watch, it read 4:13. "We'll wait a while before we go in," Razor said. He sat on his haunches and lit a cigarette. We shut off the lights to save the batteries and in a minute, I heard the rats again.

At 4:25 by my watch, Razor stood up and opened the entry to the Mansion's basement. No sound from the hinges. I smelled WD-40. We crept into the cellar and crouched behind a mound of boxes. Razor shielded his watch with his hand and stared at the illuminated dial. 4:30 passed by without any disturbance but three minutes later, I heard the ring of a phone upstairs, shouting, and the clumping of several pairs of feet. Doors slammed, a car started and roared away, tires squealing. Then it got quiet again.

Razor cocked his head to the side, listening. We heard footsteps overhead and he held up one finger. From the front of the house, we heard a door slam. Razor held up a second finger. Muffled noise from the second floor. Three fingers. Feet on the grand staircase. Four.

He nodded then pointed to the steps leading to the kitchen. The stairs were old but built for weight, thick slabs of pine. They didn't creak or groan the whole way up.

At the top, Razor opened the door a crack and peered out. He jerked his head at me and I followed him. We were at the back of the house in what looked like a pantry, shelves well stocked with food and booze. A door beside us led to the back yard. It had a deadbolt high up and the key dangled from the lock. Razor turned it to unlock the door and slipped the key into his pocket, leaving an emergency out, just in case.

I followed him up a narrow flight of servant's stairs to the second floor. Razor craned his neck around the corner and reached overhead to unscrew a light bulb from a wall sconce.

He gave me a hand signal to stay put then pointed two fingers to his eyes and at the hallway in one direction and the back stairwell in the other. That done, he slithered down the hallway, back to the wall, the carpet muffling his steps.

I shifted so that I had a line of sight and could fire both ways. My grip tightened on the revolver, and sweat trickled down my spine.

Razor came to a door near the end of the hallway and crouched. Above the doorknob with its antique key plate, a modern deadbolt had been added. He slipped his lock picks from his pocket and went to work as I heard a voice drift up the stairwell.

"Everything's locked up downstairs."

Another voice replied, "Milt's on the balcony watching the street."

"What do you think? Somebody set the club on fire?"

"Something's going down we don't know about. Joey's been chewin' the rug for the last two days and he ran out of here like his dick was on fire. And it don't take four of us to babysit the junkie. What the hell. I'm going out to check the garage. You watch the front."

At that moment, Razor popped the lock on the door and it swung inward. He slipped inside leaving me alone in the hallway. Where was the fourth man? A toilet flushed down the hall, and I knew the answer. I tiptoed toward the only door in that direction that was closed and stood against the wall, gun in hand. The knob turned, and when the guy inside stepped into the doorway, I was already swinging when I whispered, "Hey!"

and he turned his head my way. I clocked him in the forehead with the .38. He was my size, but I had to grab him by the shirt and hit him again before his eyes rolled back in his head. I eased him onto the floor and shut the bathroom door behind me.

He had a Glock nine in a shoulder rig. I dropped the clip and threw it down the laundry chute then ejected the round from the chamber. It rolled across the black and white tiles and under the ball and claw bathtub. No time to look for it now, I thought. I stuffed a washrag in his mouth and used his belt to strap him to the base of the pedestal sink.

In the hallway, I saw Razor walking Duchess out of the bedroom. She was dressed in shiny workout sweats, her makeup from the club pillow-smeared, and her hair undone. She moved with that wading through Jello sluggishness of someone who just woke up with a hangover. I wasn't even sure she knew where she was, let alone who.

Razor gripped her shoulders and steered her toward the back stairs. "Wait," she mumbled reaching for her earlobe. "My earrings."

"I'll buy you new ones," Razor hissed. "Now shut up and walk."

"Mickey?" A voice from around the corner. I recognized its rasp as Milt, her handler from the club. "Where the hell are you?"

Razor whispered in Duchess's ear, "Go get your earrings." He shoved her, and she stumbled into the hallway, falling on one knee.

"What the hell are you doing out here?" Milt yanked her to her feet by one arm, and she turned her head to look in our direction. Milt caught the cue, but too late. He turned his head and found himself staring down the barrel of Razor's revolver.

"Not a word," he whispered, taking the pistol from Milt's holster. He shoved him toward the bedroom door. "Move."

Halfway to the room, a gun boomed and Razor went down clutching his calf. Mickey had wakened and found the bullet under the tub and crawled into the hallway. Milt dropped onto Razor and started wrestling for his .38. Without even thinking, I pulled the trigger and caught Milt in the shoulder. I heard shouting from downstairs. We lucked out. They stormed up the main staircase, leaving the back stairs open.

I hauled Razor to his feet, grabbed Duchess by the arm, and dragged them to the stairwell. Razor was managing pretty well, so I went first, half carrying Duchess behind me. We weren't exactly quiet, and it didn't take Joey's men long to figure out which way we went. We had to clear the stairwell fast, or it would be like shooting rats in a drain pipe.

At the top of the stairs, a silhouette appeared, and Razor popped off a shot. The thug at the top ducked back. "Go," Razor said, firing again.

I lifted Duchess off her feet and carried her across the pantry to the cellar door. Shots went back and forth, and as I got the door open, Razor came limping out of the stairwell. We got through the cellar door and Razor slammed it behind him. There was a slider bolt on the cellar side, and Razor threw it as DiCicco's men were turning the knob.

The thugs threw themselves against the heavy door, but it held. I was at the bottom of the steps when I heard gunfire and saw splinters flying from bullet holes through the door. Razor took the Coke can from his bag and tugged at a cord hanging from its mouth. He aimed the can under the door and a fan of white fire flared from the hole in the lid. I heard screams from the other side. The shooting stopped.

Razor practically tumbled down the steps and into the closet. He opened the wall and in a minute, we were in the sewer. I pushed the brickwork shut, and we were out.

I took off my mask and tied it around Razor's calf to slow the bleeding, but when we started walking, I could hear the blood squishing in his shoe. I offered him a shoulder, but he waved me away. "Help Duchess."

It was slow going to the juncture, and when I got there, we stopped long enough for me to text one word to Carlotta: pickup. No answer. From the drains overhead, I heard the rumble of a garbage truck and no sirens. Duchess was a zombie, and keeping her on her feet on the wet bricks was a chore. If I could have stood up straight, I would've carried her over my shoulder, but the tunnel was too low. We walked another hundred paces and I tried texting C again. I watched the phone for a few seconds and the screen lit up with her message: OK.

"Come on," I said. "Carlotta's on the way."

For another ten minutes, we slogged and splashed our way 'til we reached the exit panel. Razor worked the catch and I climbed through the hole then reached in and helped Duchess through. I was glad to see the stars. Razor hoisted his injured leg over with both hands and when he got through the hole, he fell face down in the weeds.

I put my shoulder against the heavy steel plate, it swung shut, and the locking mechanism clicked. I looked around and saw the shadowy bulk of my van parked outside the foundation. I blinked my light at Carlotta and she started the engine. I took Duchess first, leading her by the hand with an arm around her waist. Carlotta helped me get her into the cargo space in the back. Then I went back for Razor. I took him in a fireman's carry and laid him between the front and middle seats. I rode shotgun with my seat cranked back 'til I was almost flat, my revolver clenched in my fist in case of trouble.

Carlotta fish hooked the van around and drove away from the tunnel entrance. "Watch your speed," I said, when she pulled onto the street. "Not too fast, not too slow. Don't attract attention." As the words left my mouth, colored lights lit up the ceiling of the van and flashed away as a patrol car shot past in the other direction.

"The way he's driving, I don't think he even noticed I was on the road."

Razor had booked two rooms at the Quakertown Motor Court twenty miles out of Hanniston. It was close enough and far enough away at the same time. By the time we got to the motel, he was unconscious. Nobody was awake or around to notice when we pulled up to the room and I stood Razor on his feet and drunk-walked him to the door. Carlotta helped Duchess out of the car and into the room.

I waited until the door was shut and the drapes were closed before I turned on the light. I put Razor on one side of the bed and C put Duchess on the other.

The room was cleaner than most one-off motels I've been in, but the room still smelled of Lysol and the carpet stuck to my shoes every time I stood still for more than two seconds. I pulled off Razor's shoe and found the sock inside it soaked with blood. He opened his eyes. "How bad?"

I flicked my knife open and slit his trouser leg to the knee. "You probably won't roller blade for a month or two. There's a hole in and a hole out. No slug to pry loose."

He took his phone and punched in a number then handed it to me. It rang six or seven times then a gruff voice answered. "Where."

"What?"

"Where are you, asshole?"

"Uh, Quakertown Motor Court, room fourteen. It's on —"

"I know where it is." Click.

I told Carlotta to go to work so that things looked as normal as they could. She'd come back to pick me up after her shift. Also, I didn't want her hanging around in case DiCicco and his people somehow found us. She left, and after a nail biting forty minutes, someone knocked on the door.

"Yeah?" I said.

"You called me."

I opened the door and saw a scarecrow of a man in jeans, a denim jacket, and a tattered straw cowboy hat. His eyes were bloodshot and his wispy salt and pepper beard hung halfway to his belt buckle. An Army drab knapsack was ready to fall off his bony shoulder. He came in and looked to the bed. "Which one?"

"Him." I pointed to Razor, and the cowboy unsnapped his bag and went to work. He gave Razor a shot and cleaned and bandaged the wound. I was amazed that he managed to keep his ratty beard clear of his work. Razor was half awake for the whole show and gritted his teeth without so much as a moan.

The cowboy rattled a bottle of pills. "Streptomycin. Take these twice a day 'til they're gone."

"Got any morphine?"

"For what? I already gave you a pain shot."

"Not for me, for her."

The doctor eyed Duchess. He pulled up her sleeve and eyed the tracks. "Right." He rummaged in the bag and pulled out another pill bottle. "Hydrocodones. Go slow on them, they're five hundred mils."

Razor pulled a roll of bills from his pocket and peeled off what looked like four hundreds. "We good?"

The cowboy folded the cash without even counting it. "Good enough." He shouldered his knapsack and left me with the invalids. Razor segued in and out of consciousness 'til dawn, and Duchess didn't move. I sat in a chair with my pistol pointed at the door until sunlight showed under the hem of the drapes.

• • •

Razor woke first. He tried to sit up on his own, but his damaged leg made that difficult. I pulled him into a sitting position, his feet dangling over the foot of the bed. He sat a while with his head in his hands, elbows on his knees.

"I'm not going to ask how you are."

"I need coffee. Gotta get sensible." He shook his head side to side slowly, as if something fragile would break if he moved too fast. He reached with his left hand and touched Duchess's thigh then smiled. "We got her out."

I nodded. "Yeah, we did." The room had one of those one-cup courtesy coffee brewers, so I filled it with water and emptied the envelope of instant coffee into the cup. Although it probably tasted like battery acid, Razor drank it down. While he did, I thought about the cliché of holding a tiger by the tail and decided between Duchess and the dope Razor had one in each hand.

Carlotta came back around eleven. We got Duchess on her feet and Carlotta took her into the bathroom to clean her up. Razor was sitting at the little table beside the window tracing the cigarette burns on its edge with his finger.

"So, who was that guy who came in last night?"

"Bronco. No other name, just a phone number that changes every two or three days. He was an Army Medic in Viet Nam. Has a degree in gunshots and stab wounds."

"I guess you've done business with him before."

Razor nodded. "He's a handy resource."

"With an exclusive clientele."

Razor was surprisingly lucid considering he took one of Duchess's pills to kill the pain in his leg. My only experience with hydrocodone was when my dentist gave me a dozen or so once when I broke a tooth. I took one and it knocked me cold for twelve hours. I flushed the rest of the bottle down the john and lived with the agony.

"What now?" I asked.

"Priority one is to get Duchess off the smack. Later today, I'll take her over the border to some people I know in Maryland who'll help her. Then I'll deal with Jojo."

"Deal with him how?"

"I have a few options. I'm still thinking them through. Right now, I have to make my life look normal for a couple of days."

"That'll be a stretch. You know you're on the top of DiCicco's list. What will keep him from whacking you at the first opportunity?"

"He still doesn't know who's got his China White or where it is. Between losing Duchess and losing six keys of heroin, I think she'll come second on his to-do list."

"Yeah, but what'll he do when he gets the dope back?"

"Who says he gets it back?"

I have to say that question worried me as much as sneaking into Joey's mansion.

• • •

The fire at Jojo's happened too late for the morning papers but it was on the local TV news all day. The damage was minor, but the smoke and cleanup would keep the doors shut for a week. Any rookie cop could see the earmarks of arson, but the official report blamed old wiring in the building after some strings were pulled and payoffs made. That meant that Joey planned on dealing with the incident on his own terms with no police invited. Some speculation floated about underworld rivalry, maybe Tiny Settles' people having a hand in the fire as payback for one thing or another, but it died out in a day or two, and life in Hanniston went on pretty much unchanged.

There was no word on the street or elsewhere about Duchess or about six missing keys of heroin. If it wasn't part of Razor's plan, it was serendipity that the fire closed the club and no one would miss her on stage. Either way, it meant Jojo didn't have to make any excuses.

Every day that passed I breathed a little easier. The weekend came and went. Blood Lightning did their show Saturday at Bendik's without incident, and somehow Razor managed to strut around the stage all night as if he didn't have a throbbing wound in his calf. I went to watch his back. I wanted to leave C at home, but she pointed out that me by myself would look odd. I had to agree. I didn't see any of Joey's crew in the crowd, and believe me, they would have stood out like bishops in a whorehouse. That didn't mean he didn't have other eyes in the crowd of bikers, babes, and bad guys.

At the end of the night, Razor caught my eye during the last song and gave me a wink. So far, so good, but I knew it couldn't last.

• • •

I was having breakfast at Dora's when Cotton dropped into the booth.

"What up, Sam?" He was grinning, but his eyes gave away his worry.

"Nothing much. I hear Jojo's is closed for a while, so where you working?"

"I have temporarily joined the undistinguished ranks of the unemployed." Carlotta came over and set down a cup and saucer. "Just coffee, hon." She filled his cup, and Cotton stirred in a spoon of sugar for a lot longer than it took to dissolve, staring into the cup.

"What?" I said.

"Waiting for the shoe." He looked across the table and his grin flat lined. "I expected fire and thunder by now, and to coin a cliché, the silence is deafening."

"Maybe the shoe won't drop." I speared a bite of sausage with a fork. "This is no hipshot rodeo. The choreography is first-rate." Then I said under my breath, "Always on stage, Cotton. Laugh."

He caught the hint and laughed out loud as if I'd just told him the dirtiest joke on the planet. People turned their heads to look, and Cotton said to me, "Wicked, Sam, just plain wicked." He turned and said to the diner at large, "This man," he pointed at me, "gonna burn in the fires of Perdition."

I gave him a lopsided grin. "No sweat allowed, brother."

He finished his coffee and left without much more conversation. I was glad he did, because his worry was contagious, and in a minute or two, I'd've been sweating myself.

• • •

My cell phone rang that afternoon, and I saw a number I didn't recognize. It was Razor on a new burner. "Sam? You busy?"

"Not really. What's up?"

"Take a ride with me. I have a delivery to make and I want to be sure it gets there."

I took a long breath then thought, in for a penny. . . . "When and where?"

"I'll pick you up in half an hour." The phone went dead.

Razor pulled up to my building in his van in exactly thirty minutes. On the floor in front of my seat, there were two items, a canvas tool bag and a sawed-off pump shotgun.

"Keep it in reach. I don't expect any trouble, but you never know what might happen."

"Contingency planning."

"Yep."

"Where are we going?"

"Benno's."

That made my ass clench. Benno's, the Italian restaurant across town was the unofficial headquarters of Tito Bardini, the *capo di capo* of Hanniston, Joey DiCicco's uncle. "You're taking the dope to the old man?"

Razor nodded. "Who better? He'll keep a leash on Jojo."

"What did you tell him?"

"I sent word that I was asked to return property that belonged to him, and he agreed to see me. Don't worry, you're just walking me safely to the door. I'll go in alone."

• • •

We pulled up in front of Benno's. Two mean looking bruisers flanked the door. "Keep the pump under your jacket and just stand outside the van. No quick moves."

"They won't see me as a threat?"

"No, just a necessary caution."

Razor took the bag, and I took the shotgun. I stepped onto the sidewalk and stood as still as a cigar store Indian. The hoods stiffened and put their hands into their jackets. Razor walked around the front of the van and said, "I'm expected." He handed the bag to one of the men, who opened it, and looked inside. His eyes widened, and he handed it back. The other thug opened the door and held it for Razor. The one who looked in the bag pointed at me and said, "Him too." Razor turned his head to me and nodded, and suddenly I was invited to the party.

In the vestibule, I surrendered the pump and Tito's men patted us down. I'd trusted Razor with my life more than once, and I knew he'd play it right. He knew the protocols and what to say. I planned to just keep my mouth shut, pray silently, and remember my advice to Cotton: no sweat allowed.

We crossed the dining room where the wait staff was setting tables for the supper crowd. They either looked around us or through us as if we were ghosts drifting through the place. Maybe before the afternoon was over we would be. Up a flight of stairs and we were led to a closed door. Three knocks and it swung inward.

We found ourselves standing in front of a desk, and behind it sat Tito Bardini. The old man was short, and thick, a barrel chest and shoulders that strained his suit. A fringe of white hair ringed his head just above his ears, and a pair of thick horn-rimmed glasses perched on his bulbous nose. The eyes behind them were cold and calculating. His hairy hands lay flat on the desktop.

The door closed behind us, and Bardini said, "You are the one called Razor." His voice had a guttural timbre to it, half a growl. "I have heard of you. Your reputation is solid. And your friend is?"

"He is —"

Bardini put up a hand. "He can speak for himself."

"I'm Sam Dunne, Mister Bardini."

He eyed me up and down, weighing and appraising. "You capped Danny Barton."

I nodded. "Yes, sir, I did."

He took off his glasses and locked eyes with me. I could feel his stare boring through the back of my skull. He grunted and broke contact, and I felt as if a fist around my neck just let go. He nodded to one of his men who stepped out of the room. When he returned, my heart jumped. Jojo was with him. He walked around the desk and stood beside Tito's chair. He glared at Razor, but Razor ignored him, keeping his eyes on the old man.

Bardini said, "You have something that belongs to me?"

"Yes, sir." Razor nodded. "I was asked to return this to you with the apologies of those who found it." Razor opened the bag and one by one set the bricks of heroin on the desk. I watched Joey's eyes widen a little more with each one.

I would never want to play poker with Tito Bardini. If he was surprised, his face didn't show it. If he was angry, his face didn't show it. Bardini said to one of the bodyguards, "Open one."

The thug took a knife from his pocket, flicked it open and slit a corner of one of the bricks. He wet his index finger and took a sample, touched it to his tongue and said, "Pure H."

"And where was this 'found'?"

"In Joey DiCicco's mansion, sir," Razor said, as if Jojo wasn't in the room.

Bardini turned slowly in his chair and stared at Jojo, whose eyes betrayed his panic. "Is this true, Joseph?"

"Uncle, you don't believe this cheap punk, this burglar."

Bardini's hand slammed down on his desk like a gunshot. Something strange happened to his eyes. It was like watching a horror flick when the demon possessed villain reveals himself. "You think this man brought me a couple of hundred Gs worth of horse as a *joke*?" Tito's words came down like a cleaver. "It isn't our dope, so it must be yours."

The light snapped on in my head. Razor knew all along that Joey D was running his own show on the side, a distinct no-no in the Bardini organization.

He turned to Razor. "I apologize for my nephew's outburst. He does not speak for me. You have done me a favor; how can I repay you?"

"Nothing for myself, Mister Bardini," Razor paused, "but there is a woman, Anita Holgren, the featured singer at Jojo's; she would like to be freed of her obligations to the club and to Joey without fear of retribution."

"But he—he!" Jojo cried, pointing his finger.

"Consider it done. You have my word." He turned and gave Joey a look that would stop my watch then turned back to us. "In a way, you have done me two favors. The same guarantee goes for you, both of you."

"Thank you, Mister Bardini," Razor said. I murmured my thanks as well.

Just the faintest hint of a smile turned up the corner of his mouth. "It does an old man's heart good to see that chivalry isn't dead." He swiveled his chair away from us, and the meeting was over.

Downstairs, I was handed back the shotgun in one hand and the shells in the other. Without a word, Razor and I climbed into the van and rolled away. "Jesus," I said. "How did you know Jojo was running his own game?"

"I didn't. I just rolled the dice. If I was wrong, they would get their dope back, but Jojo would still be in a crack for losing it. We just hit it lucky. I'd like to hear what Tito Bardini is saying to Jojo right now."

I decided I'd rather not.

• • •

Jojo's never reopened. Joey DiCicco left town, and the word is he was relocated in Newark on what the Family calls a "last chance" basis. Glory Jones is still fronting Blood Lightning, but the last time they played Bendik's I saw Duchess sitting at a table with Razor's friends. Carlotta told me later that Joey D got Duchess hooked by telling her they were sharing something special, shooting up together, but after he'd dose her with smack, he'd pump his own vein with tap water. Joey made her his slave while he stayed clean. According to Razor, she came down hard, but fought through it, and now she's clean too. Razor and Duchess still aren't back together, but I figure that sooner or later, if there's any justice in the Universe, the wheel will turn and they'll be an item again.

As for me, I'm just happy I'm still breathing. Sometimes late at night I wonder whether old man Bardini knew what Jojo was up to all along. Maybe he turned a blind eye until he was forced to address it. Maybe he was just waiting for an excuse. Like Shakespeare says, "All's well that ends well," that is, if it ever really ends.

THE END

ABOUT OUR CREATORS

WRITER –

FRED ADAMS, JR. is a retired Penn State University English Professor who spends his days writing pulp fiction and his nights working as a singer-songwriter. His Sam Dunne novel *Dead Man's Melody* was nominated as Pulp Novel of the Year in 2017's Pulp Factory Awards, and his Smith Brothers novel *The Eye of Quang-Chi* was nominated for the same award in 2018. His titles include *Hitwolf* 1 and 2, *Six Gun Terrors* vols. 1, 2, and 3, and *C.O. Jones: Mobsters and Monsters, Skinners,* and *The Damned and the Doomed.* His original Sherlock Holmes anthology *The Affair of the Chronic Argonaut* was recently published by Pro Se Press. Forthcoming titles from Airship 27 include *C.O. Jones: Home Front, Six Gun Terrors 4: The Town Killers,* a Sam Dunne Mystery, *Blood is the New Black,* and *Holster Full of Death,* a Dead Sheriff novel. He lives in Mount Pleasant, Pennsylvania in "perpetual terror of boredom."

Visit Fred's website at http://drphreddee.com/author

INTERIOR & COVER ARTIST -

ROB DAVIS - began his professional art career doing illustrations for role-playing games in the late 1980s. Not long after he began lettering and inking, then penciling comics for a number of small black and white comics publishers—most notably for Eternity Comics, which eventually became Malibu Comics in the 1990's, on their book SCIMIDAR with writer R.A. Jones. Branching out to other black and white publishers and eventually working at both DC and Marvel Rob worked on likeness intensive comics like TV adaptations of QUANTUM LEAP and STAR TREK's many incarnations mostly on the DEEP SPACE NINE comics for Malibu. At Marvel he worked on the Saturday morning cartoon adaptation PIRATES OF DARK WATER. After the comics industry implosion in the late 1990's Rob picked up work on video games, advertising illustration and T-shirt design as well as some small press comics like ROBYN OF SHERWOOD for Caliber. Rob continues to do the odd self-published comic book as well as publisher and designer for his small-press production REDBUD

STUDIO COMICS. Rob is Art Director, Designer and Illustrator for the New Pulp production outfit AIRSHIP 27 partnered with writer/editor Ron Fortier. Rob is the recipient of the PULP FACTORY AWARD for "Best Interior Illustrations" in 2010, 2014, and 2016 for his work on SHERLOCK HOLMES: CONSULTING DETECTIVE and has been nominated for the same award every year since its inception. He works and lives in central Missouri with his wife and two children.

For examples of his work surf the internet to: robmdavis.com

BOOKS BY FRED ADAMS JR.

FRED ADAMS JR. PULP WRITER

SIX-GUN TERRORS Vol One
SIX-GUN TERRORS   Vol Two
SIX-GUN TERRORS Vol Three – The Slithering Terror

HITWOLF
HITWOLF 2 – The Pack

C.O. JONES
C.O. JONES – Skinners
C.O. JONES – The Damned and the Doomed

(SAM DUNNE MYSTERIES)
Dead Man's Melody

(THE SMITH BROTHERS SERIES)
The Eye of Quang Chi

DESERT GHOSTS